I Was Jane Austen's Best Friend

I Was Jane Austen's Best Friend

Cora Harrison

ILLUSTRATED BY SUSAN HELLARD

EMBER

Text copyright © 2010 by Cora Harrison
Cover art copyright © 2010 by Larry Rostant
Illustrations copyright © 2010 by Susan Hellard

Visit us on the Web! www.randomhouse.com/teens

Educators and librarians, for a variety of teaching tools, visit us at
www.randomhouse.com/teachers

The Library of Congress has cataloged the hardcover edition of this work as follows:
Harrison, Cora.
I was Jane Austen's best friend / Cora Harrison ; illustrated by Susan Hellard. — 1st U.S. ed.
p.   cm.
Summary: In a series of journal entries, Jenny Cooper describes her stay with cousin Jane Austen
in the 1790s, and her entrance into Jane's world of beautiful dresses, dances, secrets, gossip, and romance.
ISBN 978-0-385-73940-5 (hc : alk. paper) — ISBN 978-0-385-90787-3 (glb : alk. paper) —
ISBN 978-0-375-89753-5 (ebook) I. Austen, Jane, 1775–1817—Juvenile fiction.
[1. Austen, Jane, 1775–1817—Fiction. 2. Cousins—Fiction. 3. Friendship—Fiction. 4. Courtship—Fiction.
5. England—Social life and customs—18th century—Fiction. 6. Diaries—Fiction.]
I. Hellard, Susan, ill. II. Title.
PZ7.H2467Ian 2010
[Fic]—dc22
2010015309

ISBN 978-0-375-86212-0 (pbk.)

RL: 6.0

Printed in the United States of America

10 9 8 7 6 5 4 3 2 1

First Ember Edition 2011

For my daughter, Ruth Mason, a fan of the Jane Austen novels since her early teens

Tuesday, 12 January 1796

Dearest Jane,

Yesterday I was up in the attic and discovered a bundle of my old journals - I spent half the night reading this one. I'm sending it to you because I think you will enjoy it too.

I can't believe how much my life changed in that spring of 1791! It was like coming out of a dark room into bright sunlight. With you as a friend, I learned so much that year - about life, about love - and about how to have fun!

Do you remember our new sprigged muslin gowns for the ball at the Basingstoke Assembly Rooms? And getting ready for the ball? And how Eliza did our hair?

Well, it's all here in my journal so I hope you enjoy reading it. I'm looking forward to visiting you next month and then we can talk over old times.

Yours affectionately,

Jenny

PS I LOVED your book about Elizabeth Bennet and her sisters! I think your father is quite right; it should definitely be published, and when it is, I shall give myself such airs and will go around telling everyone that I was Jane Austen's best friend!

MY JOURNAL
Monday, 7 February 1791

Jane looks like she could die.

It's a terrible thing to write: *Jane looks like she could die* — but it's even worse to have the thought jumping into your mind every few minutes.

I'm just sitting here in this cold dormitory looking at Jane. The only light is the light that comes in from the street. It's enough though, as Jane's bed is next to the window. I can see her face. It is very red; it's been like that for the last few days. She's pushed off her nightcap and her dark curly hair is soaked in sweat. Her eyes are widely opened, but there is nothing of Jane in that gaze. She looks at me, but she doesn't know me, just carries on muttering through swollen, cracked lips. Her skin is burning hot when I touch her. She's burning with fever. Becky, the kitchen maid, had that fever last month, but she recovered after a few days.

But Jane is not recovering.

And I am frightened.

Mrs Cawley is the owner of the school. She's responsible for us all. Why doesn't she look after Jane?

But she doesn't want to talk about Jane and how ill she is. She wants to pretend the illness isn't happening.

She doesn't even come up to the dormitory.

She just sends Becky.

And Becky is frightened too. I saw it in her face tonight when she was trying to get Jane to swallow some of that medicine that the doctor left for her.

I know I must do something. It's no good just sitting here staring at Jane and writing a few sentences in my journal and then looking at her again. It's eleven o'clock of the evening. The house is quiet, of course, because Mrs Cawley makes everyone go to bed early in order to save on fires and on candles. All the girls in the dormitory are asleep except for me — Jane is still burning with fever and her breathing sounds like the watchman's rattle.

I'm scared. I've begged Mrs Cawley to send for Jane's mother and father. My Aunt Austen will know what to do; I remember my mother telling me how good her sister was at nursing — that she had shelves full of remedies in her pantry. I'm sure that Jane would improve if her mother were here. I don't trust that doctor who comes every day. His fingernails are dirty and he hardly comes near enough to Jane to know what is wrong with her. He just keeps leaving bottles of something that smells like tar water with a few bits of dried herbs floating in it.

Jane's mother must come. Jane's mother must come. Jane's mother must come.

So I have written to her. I managed to write the letter earlier today when we had silent study in our dormitories while the maids were cleaning the schoolroom. I even managed to steal some sealing wax from

Mrs Cawley's desk and use the candle to melt it without anyone's seeing. I turn the letter over and over in my hands. The neatly folded paper is beginning to look grubby, and the wax seal that keeps it fastened will break and fall off if I handle the sheet any more. Once again I read the address that I have written on the back of the sheet in my best handwriting:

Mrs G. Austen,
Steventon Parsonage,
Steventon,
Hampshire.

I tried to bribe Becky to take it to the post-inn for me, but she was too scared of Mrs Cawley to go. She had heard Mrs Cawley scream angrily at me when I mentioned writing to Jane's mother. There is only one thing to do . . .

I've just been over to the window for the third time since deciding on my plan. The streets are still full of light and noise. A young officer wearing a red coat, with a sword girded about his waist, has just passed. I think about Jane telling me that her brother wants to join the army. If only one of her family were here now! There are crowds out in the streets, but I know no one. I will have to do it. I could never forgive myself if Jane died here in this horrible dormitory in Southampton and her mother was not by her side during the last moments.

I owe Jane so much.

I don't know what would have happened to me in this terrible school if I didn't have Jane as a best friend.

The cold, the lack of food, the misery of it would have given me a wasting disease, I'm sure of it.

I'd have died or gone mad.

All sorts of pictures are going through my head:

Jane on the day we came here, making a joke of the terrible dormitory when I just felt like crying because my brother and his wife had sent me away. I can hear her voice declaring loudly that the place smelt of death and demanding to know where the vampire was and giggling about the enormous fungus in the corner of the room.

Jane mocking the teachers when they scolded and punished – '*You know, Jenny, Miss Nash is a woman of such elegance and beauty; except for the fact that she walks like a hen and has a face like a squashed potato . . .*'

Jane standing up for me when Lavinia made fun of my gown, pretending that Lavinia was a secret drinker . . .

Jane telling me stories of her family – her five brothers and her sister, Cassandra — to distract me from the hunger and the cold . . .

Jane coaxing the cook to fill a bottle with hot water to warm my bed when I had a bad cold . . .

Jane sneaking out of the kitchen door and running up the basement steps to buy a couple of hot pies from the pieman for the two of us . . .

Jane reading her stories of great romances aloud in the dormitory at night . . . about a girl whose face was her fortune . . .

Jane laughing at the expression on my face when we got just a tiny slice of bread and a cup of watery milk for our supper and telling me to think of it as a seven-course dinner for a cockroach.

What would I do without her?

Just in case I never come back again, I am going to tuck this journal under Jane's pillow as soon as the ink dries. If I am still missing by morning, at least people will know where I went.

And they will know why.

Southampton at Midnight

Down the stairs . . .

Every stair creaks . . .

Every minute I think that I hear my name screamed by Mrs Cawley.

'Miss Cooper!' she will shriek at me.

I stop and listen, but there is nothing to hear. My hands are damp and I am shaking. My bonnet strings come undone and the bonnet falls off my head and rolls down to the bottom of the stairs, only stopping when it reaches the front door. And it makes a sound that I feel could wake the house. I leave it on the floor as I struggle with the bolt. Eventually the bolt slides back with a rusty screech.

The cold damp air of the street rushes in. I pick up my bonnet by its blue ribbon, but I dare not stop to put it on. I close the door as carefully as I can and pray that no burglar tries the handle before I can get back, and then I am off running down the street, my bonnet swinging from one hand and my folded letter in the other.

Lights flash in my eyes: the watchman is ahead of me. I must not overtake him. He would want to know what I was doing out here on my own. I stop in a shadowed shop door and tie on my bonnet and then I go on, walking as fast as I can.

More lights now. Some runners with flaring torches,

and four men carrying a lady in a sedan chair – through its window I can just see her powdered hair piled very high and the low-cut frilled neck of her yellow gown. The sedan is painted in very fine colours of black and gold, but the poles in the men's hands are rough and look full of splinters. I shrink against a gateway with my back turned, and they pass me without breaking step. I can hear their trotting footsteps grow quieter and quieter.

And then a crowd of rough sailors laughing and shouting. Southampton is full of sailors. They're the ones that brought this fever; the kitchen maid told me that. The men are on the other side of the road so I slip quietly behind a tree and stand there very still, my head down so that my bonnet hides my face. I will just have to wait until they pass, and then I will turn left, go through two small lanes and then into Bargate.

The post-inn is in Bargate. The mail coach will set out at midnight; I know that. I will be in plenty of time. I peep out to see whether the sailors have gone as I can't hear their voices.

And then something dreadful happens. The sailors have not gone. They are all drinking from flagons. That's why they've stopped talking. Another sedan passes and the torch held by one of the chairmen at the back casts a light over my face, making me blink. There is a shout, a sort of a cheer from across the road.

'Look what I see!' shouts one.

'A little beauty,' shouts another. He sounds quite drunk.

'Come on, pretty girl. We'll give you a good time.' This sailor puts down his flagon and starts to cross the road. I shrink against the wall. My heart jumps and my mouth is dry. I open my mouth to shriek, but no sound comes out. I used to have nightmares like that sometimes, where I struggled to scream but could not. It's a cold night, but I feel sweat run down between my shoulder blades.

And then there is a clatter of hoofs. An open-topped barouche comes swiftly down the road, drawn by a pair of grey horses. Two young men are in it. I think by their uniforms that they are naval officers.

'Whoa,' shouts one of them, and the horses stop with a skidding of hoofs and a squeal. For a moment I think that I am completely lost, that they will drag me into the barouche like what happened to Clarissa in the novel Jane lent to me. I will be ruined.

But they are not looking at me.

They are shouting angrily, but not at me. They are scolding the sailors for drinking in the street, for disgracing their uniform, and they are telling them to get back on board their ship.

Suddenly my courage comes back. My gown is well looped up over my petticoat, and my petticoat is quite short; it barely reaches my ankles. I start to run as fast as I can. The angry shouts ring out as I continue up the High Street, but it is still the young naval officers shouting at the drunken sailors. No one has seen me.

And now I turn into the lane.

I had been afraid that it would be very dark, but there is an inn there, halfway up the lane, and the lights are on in every window. Even the door stands open and lets a pool of light come out on to the cobblestones. I tiptoe over their bumpy, uneven surface. I will be able to go quickly once I pass the inn, but I am scared of the rough voices that I hear from within.

There is a sudden silence from the inn. I'm afraid that someone has seen me and I step into a darkened doorway. I wish that my cloak were a dark colour, but it is a light blue, and my petticoat shows shockingly white below it. I reach inside and let my gown down to cover the petticoat, but the gown is also a pale blue; it will be easy to see against the darkness of the door.

Then there are a few notes from a fiddle and someone starts to sing – a horrible, rude song, but I don't care. The man sings so loudly and the noise as the others join in is so deafening that it means that no one could possibly hear the sound of my footsteps. I move on as quickly as I can go, but I don't run and I keep my face turned to the wall as I pass the inn.

Now I am at the top of the lane. There is a house there with a torch burning in the holder outside. All the windows are lit up. I can see an oil lamp burning in the parlour. The curtains are not closed so the light from the room spills out. I wait for a minute. My heart is still thumping hard. I tell myself that I am just waiting for it to slow down, but I know that I am too scared to go on. There is a young lady sitting at the piano. She turns her head and I can see that she is not much older than me. She looks about seventeen. She has lovely curling dark hair; some of it is piled up on top of her head, but other long curls hang down behind her neck and a few fringe her forehead. She is wearing a pale yellow gown and a string of pearls around her neck. Although the window is closed, I can hear the notes of the piano and the sound of a high, sweet voice singing a love song.

One more lane to go and then I will be in Bargate. In the distance I hear the watchman call out, 'Half past the hour of eleven o'clock and all is well.'

Only half past eleven o'clock. That's fine – still half an hour to go, and Bargate is not far now. I linger for a few minutes; somehow I feel safe there outside this well-lit house, but an elegant lady, her hair piled on top of her head and powdered in the old-fashioned way, comes to the window. Her hand is on the cord of the window blind and for a moment her eyes meet mine. Hers are full of curiosity and mine are probably filled with panic.

And so I turn away quickly and I go on. I go into the second lane. My eyes are getting used to the dim light and I don't need to touch the wall. I am clenching my fists so tightly that my nails are digging into the palms of my hands. I know all the reasons why I should not be out here alone at night-time. This town is rougher than Bristol, and Mama would never dream of walking after dark in Bristol.

But I also know that I must send this letter to Mrs Austen – Jane's life may depend on it – so I cannot give up.

Now the street is less crowded. I am trying to see the post-inn. It should be near. I passed it one day, but I cannot see it now. I am straining my eyes so much to see it that I almost don't notice that a man with a sword is coming towards me. He's looking all around him, and his hand is on the hilt. He hasn't seen me yet, but he will do in a minute. I stop. There is nowhere to hide.

The man lifts the sword and shouts, *'En garde!'* Then he screams something. For a moment I am frozen, just standing there, watching the light of the street torches flash on the steel of the naked blade. He draws back the sword and then makes a stabbing motion. The sword is very near to me. I can't move. My mouth is dry and my legs have no strength in them. I feel paralysed. The man shouts again. He is staring straight at me, but I know from the strange look in his eyes that he doesn't see me. He doesn't see a sixteen-year-old girl, small for her age; he is seeing some enemy. I don't know the meaning of the words that he yells, but I know that I must get away quickly. Now the man points his sword at the ground and examines the blade carefully. He is talking to himself in an angry, loud voice. He lifts the sword again and it flashes in the torchlight. Suddenly the strength comes back to my legs. I turn round very quickly and start to run in the opposite direction. The railings in front of the houses and the bright rectangles of window light blur in front of my eyes. My feet in their soft shoes patter on the cobblestones. My chest hurts. I can hardly draw a breath.

I turn back into the lane.

And I run straight into another man.

'What's the matter?' he says, and he sounds quite alarmed. 'Where are you off to, young lady?'

I stand very still. He has a tight hold on my arm and I don't struggle. I just wait, my heart racing. I think about resisting so that he has to let go of my arm, but my legs are still so weak that I am quite glad to be held. And then the dangerous-looking man with the sword passes us, going straight along the well-lit street of Bargate. His face is terribly scarred by a puckered line that runs down one cheek from eye to chin. He takes no notice of us; he is too busy looking over his shoulder and muttering loudly to himself. His eyes are strange. I can see them quite clearly in the light of the flaring pitch torch that has been stuck into the gateway of a house by the roadside.

'Whew!' whistles the man, letting go of my arm and giving a little bow. 'That fellow looks dangerous.' I look closely at him now and I'm not so scared of him. He is very tall and imposing, but quite young, and looks just like I imagine one of Jane's brothers to look. He catches my eye and smiles, and his smile is so warm and his eyes so kind that I begin to feel less frightened.

'You're too young to be out alone in the streets of Southampton at this hour,' he says. 'How old are you? Fifteen? What's your name?'

'My name is Jenny Cooper and I'm sixteen,' I say, and I try to sound annoyed and grown-up, but I can hear my voice shaking.

'Captain Thomas Williams, at your service, Miss Cooper.' He bows again and I manage to drop a curtsy. He is very handsome, with jet-black hair curling around his neck and very dark brown eyes. I would like to ask him how old he is, but I daren't. He's probably about the same age as Jane's brother James. It feels so strange, standing there in the street at night with a man that I haven't even been introduced to, a man that I've never seen in my life, and another man, a madman, walking up the street waving his sword, that I start to giggle and then I think about poor Jane lying on the bed muttering, her face red with the fever, and I feel so bad about giggling when my best friend is so ill that I start to cry.

'Are you running away?' He gives me a worried smile, and for a moment looks as though he might move to comfort me, though he can't, of course. It would be most improper. But for some reason I feel that I can rely on him, and I begin to feel better. I shake my head.

The watchman has got to the top of the High Street now. I see him turn round and start to march down towards us.

'Take my arm, keep your head bowed so that your bonnet hides your face, and we'll just stroll along. Try to stop crying, or else I'll be in trouble with the watch.' Captain Thomas Williams has tucked my hand through his arm and he starts to saunter up the High Street, stopping from time to time to look in the shop windows. He doesn't say any more until after the watchman has gone to check on the locked gates of the Assembly Rooms and then he stops and faces me.

'Seriously,' he says, 'I think you should go home. Running away isn't a good idea. I'll take you home now. Where do you live?'

'I'm not running away!' I nearly shout the words and then lower my voice in case the night watchman hears me.

'So where are you off to then?' He's smiling, but he looks a bit worried. I wonder if he's sorry he met me. He probably doesn't want the responsibility of deciding what to do with me.

'I'm going to the post-inn. I want to send a letter.'

'A love letter?'

'No, to my aunt.' I hold up the letter so that he can see the address and he looks surprised.

'Wouldn't the morning do?'

'No,' I say, and I tell him everything.

Tuesday, 8 February 1791

I've been sitting here for hours in the dormitory, thinking all about my midnight walk through the streets
of Southampton as if it were still happening, living
through it all again. I can't decide whether it was the
most terrible hour in my life . . . or perhaps the most
wonderful . . .

But anyway, the letter has gone
to Mrs Austen, and Jane is beginning to seem a little better —
almost as though she knows that
her mother is coming. She has
stopped muttering and tossing and
turning and her eyes have closed. Her breathing is still very loud. It rattles in her chest and now it
is like the sound of a tea-kettle boiling. I get into my
bed and wrap myself in the two thin blankets.

But still I am scared to go to sleep in case when I
wake I find that Jane has died. I have to keep awake
and I will keep awake by writing.

I can't help thinking of what might have happened
to me if I hadn't met Captain Williams last night. I
know that I ran a terrible risk, but it will be worth
it if Jane's mother arrives in time.

There's another thing in my mind, and it seems
selfish to even think of it with Jane so ill, but I can't
help it.

I know that if anyone recognized me out alone in the streets of Southampton at midnight I would be ruined forever. My brother, Edward-John, would be ill from shock if he ever heard of it, and his wife, Augusta, who is always so proper, would probably persuade him to cast me off and send me out to the East Indies or some such place.

I have a nightmare feeling that the next time Mrs Cawley takes us walking in Southampton someone will come up to her and point to me and then the whole story will become known . . .

I must think of other things . . . perhaps I shall write about Captain Thomas Williams. He told me the name of his ship – it is the *Bonaventure*, and he has been out in the East Indies. It is strange, but I felt so at ease with him once we started talking that it was as if I had known him for a long time. He is an orphan, just like me, and that made a bond between us. When I told him that my father and mother were dead, he squeezed my arm just a little. I could feel the muscles of his arm through the wool jacket of his uniform. I suppose that life at sea must be very hard work – he was so big and strong that I felt very safe with him. I loved listening to him telling me about his life at sea and about his far-off cousin who died and left him a property on the Isle of Wight and about his uncle the admiral, and what a stern man he was, though he thought he had done his duty by his orphaned nephew and niece when he placed the boy in the naval college and the girl in a boarding school. I think Captain Williams must be a very good brother because he seemed so worried about his sister, Elinor, who he says looks a little like me, except that her hair is not quite so blonde and her eyes are green. He is so nice. He sounded angry when he told me how unhappy Elinor was at boarding school, where the owner used to tell the girls that they could eat the bread but only smell the cheese. The girls there were starving, he said. I could hear the anger in his voice when he told me about that. I liked him very much when he told me that the first thing he did when he heard of his inheritance was to take his sister away from that school where she was half starving and allow her to live at home, with a governess to teach her.

I couldn't help thinking about Edward-John. I don't think that if he had an inheritance he would want to spend it on me.

But I don't want to think about Edward-John or about Augusta.

I want to think about Captain Williams . . .

That uniform of a captain in the navy suits him so well. The gold braid shows up his brown eyes, and the epaulettes on his jacket make his shoulders look even bigger. His voice is lovely, velvet-smooth like chocolate.

And when we had arrived back at the school, he

escorted me up the steps, kissed my hand and then shut the door very quietly behind me.

I don't suppose that I shall ever see him again, but I will always remember him and how hand-some he looked in his uniform. I've tried to sketch a picture of him — it's not as hand-some as he is but it's a fairly good likeness, I think. Drawing is my best subject.

Oh, and he told me that he can set his timepiece by the mail coaches and my letter to my aunt will be at Deane Gate Inn by daybreak. He got me to write 'URGENT' above the address so that the innkeeper will send the letter over to the parsonage at Steven-ton immediately.

He even waited until I could see with my own eyes the men loading the mail coach with the sacks of mail, including my precious letter. He told me that some of the mail had come from his ship, *Bonaven-ture*, from Southampton docks. He showed me how the sacks were stamped with the name of the ship.

I hope that Captain Williams is right that Mrs

Austen will get the letter tomorrow morning. I hope that she will be here soon. I was so frightened that Jane might die, but now I am more hopeful.

A minute ago, Jane cried out as if she was in pain, but when I bent over her there was no recognition in her eyes. She is still in a very high fever. It seems so strange to see her like this — Jane who is always so full of life. It's only a few days ago that she was bouncing on her bed, mimicking her mother:

'Jane, you are nothing but a hoodlum, that's what you are, madam, and don't you look at me in that saucy way or I'll box your ears. Henry, stop laughing at her; you make her even wilder. Frank, stop that; stop it, I tell you. Charles, I saw that! I shall get your father to deal with you if you're not careful. I declare to the heavens that no woman on earth has such a family! It's no wonder that my poor nerves are in such a state!'

Jane jokes about everything. I think had it not been for Jane and her jokes and her friendship I would never have survived the first few weeks here at this terrible school where we are half starved most of the time.

Her mother will know what to do.

Wednesday, 9 February 1791

Only one more day to go and then Mrs Austen might come!

I did sleep after all and suddenly woke with a start to find Lavinia standing over me saying triumphantly, 'You're in trouble!' I had fallen asleep half sitting up and my journal was still on my knee. Quickly I pushed it under the blankets.

'Why?' I asked. I was scared of Lavinia. Could she possibly have seen me go out last night? Pretended to be asleep and then looked out of the window and seen me walk down the street at night by myself? I could hardly breathe, I was so terrified.

'You didn't close your curtain between the beds. You know that is not allowed.'

'Mrs Cawley told me to keep an eye on Jane.' My heart was thumping with relief as I told the lie. It was all I could think of to say, but at least Lavinia couldn't have seen me leave the dormitory, other-wise she wouldn't have bothered about something as trivial as keeping the curtains closed between the six beds in the dormitory.

'No, she didn't.' Lavinia sounded very sure and she probably was quite certain: Mrs Cawley hates Jane and it was easy to guess that she would never have bothered asking me to look after her. 'You're just a liar, Miss Jenny Cooper. Well, I'm going to tell.'

She bounced away and I could hear her calling

down the stairs. 'Ma'am,' she called, her voice sounding very sweet, 'I'm sorry to report that Jenny Cooper
has broken the dormitory rules.' I got out of bed.
Quickly I bent down and pushed the inkpot and the
quill under the bed. I felt quite sick and dizzy when
I stood up again. I was so tired and the floor was
so cold that my teeth chattered and once again the
water in my ewer had frozen to the sides of the jug.
Another day without washing! Why had we been
sent to this horrible place? My feet were frozen as I
pulled on my long woollen stockings, then I put on my
warm flannel petticoat, and then my gown. I wrapped
myself in my shawl and waited. The other girls
avoided looking at me.

I didn't have long to wait. Mrs Cawley marched
into the room, followed by Lavinia smiling smugly.

'Jenny Cooper,' screamed Mrs Cawley, 'you are a
bad, disobedient girl. You will have to wear the backboard for two hours as a punishment.'

I bowed my head obediently. And then I got an
idea and asked if I could sit by the fire downstairs
while I was wearing the board. I shivered a little and
rubbed my hands together. I didn't need to pretend
to make my voice shake. I am scared of Mrs Cawley.
Lavinia says that once Mrs Cawley beat a girl with a
rod until the girl's back was bleeding. I would die if
she tried to beat me. I hate her.

Mrs Cawley's eyes narrowed when I begged to sit
by the fire, and a sour smile came over her face. 'No,

you won't,' she said vindictively. 'I'll send one of the maids up with the board straight away and she will strap you into it. You just stay here in the dormitory until I send for you.'

'It's for your own good,' said Lavinia after Mrs Cawley had gone. 'You'll never get a husband if you have round shoulders. You should practise standing up tall and then you might grow a little. That cousin of yours is taller than you and she's a good year younger.' And then with a contemptuous glance at Jane she swept out of the room. The other girls followed her, but Amelia, who I've noticed is kinder when she's without her friends, stopped for a moment and waited until Lavinia had gone. Then she whispered, 'What about your breakfast?'

'I don't suppose that I'll get any.' My voice sounded as if I didn't care, and at that moment I didn't. I wasn't hungry; in fact, I felt slightly sick. I wanted to feel Jane's forehead and I couldn't do that while any of the girls was around. Mrs Cawley had forbidden me to touch Jane. She had an idea that no one could catch the fever unless they were touching a patient. Captain Thomas Williams told me that wasn't true; it was breathing in bad smells and something called miasma that gave people fever. I didn't care anyway. As soon as Amelia had gone out of the room, I felt Jane's brow; she was still very hot, but I thought she was a little better. At least she was lying quietly now, not muttering. I pray that when her mother comes to take her home to Steventon she will recover.

The only good thing about the backboard is that I can go on writing. I wouldn't have been able to if it had been Mrs Cawley that brought it, but Becky, the kitchen maid, felt sorry for me.

'I have to strap you into it, miss,' she whispered. 'That's what Mrs Cawley told me to do, but I won't buckle it tight.'

'Thank you, Becky,' I whispered back. I moved a little after she had closed the buckles. It was un-comfortable, but not the torture that it is when Mrs Cawley fastens it. I was able to move my head from side to side.

Becky was nice. She even had a bit of bread in the pocket of her apron that the cook had given to her for me. 'You're just as well off without the stirabout, miss,' she said, taking the bread out and showing it to me. 'Mrs Cawley told Cook that she must make it with just water and oats from now on; she says the milk bills are too high. I'll put the bread here on your cupboard so that you can reach it.'

I took it to please her, but I didn't feel hungry. That was the strange thing; normally I was always hungry.

'Could you pick up my inkpot and quill from under

the bed, Becky? Put them on the cupboard too. I want to practise my handwriting.'

And then Becky was off. I don't know how long ago that was. I don't have a timepiece. There is no sound from downstairs. The young ladies, as Mrs Cawley calls them, will all be in the schoolroom, practising their handwriting or listening to a teacher droning on and on, or spending hours getting in and out of an old sedan chair that Mrs Cawley keeps outside the back door so that her pupils can learn how to do this gracefully, without showing our ankles at all – which according to Mrs Cawley would ruin our marriage prospects forever.

I almost feel like crying when I think now of Jane and her jokes. She has such courage and she can even stand up to Mrs Cawley and mock her openly. I resolve never to be so shy and so worried in the future. Last night, when I went out in the streets of Southampton, I did something that I never thought I would be able to do. I am already becoming braver – perhaps too brave!

When I am married I would like to have lots of children – I would like a family like Jane's, with five boys and two girls. I would allow my daughters to play with their brothers, to play cricket and running races just like Jane is allowed. I remember how shocked I was when she told me about rolling down the green bank behind Steventon parsonage with the boys in her father's school, but perhaps that is why she is so full of courage now, and I am such a miserable worrier.

The doctor has just been in to see Jane. I managed to cover the inkpot with a handkerchief, and my journal is hidden under the blankets. I needn't have bothered though. Mrs Cawley did not come with him, only Becky. He seems worried about Jane. He muttered something about asking Mrs Cawley and I saw his eyes go with an air of horror to the huge fungus on the wall. He must have thought that I was feeble-minded, because when I saw him looking at it I couldn't stop myself giving a little giggle, remembering how Jane had said that it looked as if it were a poisonous ingredient for the wicked potions of the villain in the story *The Castle of the Necromancer*.

Before I could stop myself I felt another giggle escape and then I started to cry. The doctor looked embarrassed and ignored me.

'Tell your mistress that if there is no change by five o'clock I will have to bleed her,' he said to Becky on the way out.

'The time is up, so I can take off your backboard now, miss,' said Becky when she came back upstairs after showing the doctor out. I have written all this in my journal since she unbuckled the backboard and went back down to the kitchen, but the tears are pouring down my face now.

'Don't worry, miss, she'll get better.' She looked anxious, poor Becky. I was sorry to upset her, but I can't stop crying. When my mother was very ill a doctor bled her and it did no good at all. I remember how a vein in her arm was opened and how that very red blood dripped out into a white basin. She died two hours later.

If Jane's mother doesn't come soon, I don't know what to do. Now I will lock up my journal, hide it under my clothes in my trunk and hang the key around my neck. I should go downstairs, but I don't feel as if I have the strength even to get off the bed. Perhaps I am tired after missing so much sleep last night. I will just get in under the blankets and try to warm up and then go downstairs.

The voices are like the voices in a dream.
  'She's asleep . . .'
  'No, she's ill . . .'
  'She's burning with fever . . .'
  'Tell Mrs Cawley . . .'
  'Mrs Cawley, Jenny is ill now . . .'
  'Will I get the doctor, ma'am . . .'
  'Mind your own business, girl . . . get on with your work. Doctors cost money, you know . . .'

And then . . . is it hours later?

That loud knock, that hammering on the front door . . .

Mrs Austen's voice, high-pitched, confident . . .

'I'll have you know, madam . . .'

A mutter from Mrs Cawley.

'Never mind how I know . . .'

'Let me see my daughter, madam . . .'

'And where's Jenny?'

Another mutter from Mrs Cawley.

'Rest assured, madam, that we'll never allow my daughter or my niece to return to this place again. I am taking them both back to Steventon this very minute. Pray give instructions for hot water bottles and fresh straw to be placed in the coach . . .'

Mrs Cawley's voice – now loud and angry.

'Don't think to delay me with demands for fees, madam . . . You should be down on your knees praying that these two girls will recover . . .'

Mrs Cawley again.

'Out of my way, madam! Mr Austen, do you carry Jenny and I'll take Jane . . .'

'You, girl, don't try to carry the two trunks . . . Surely there is someone to help this girl. Where is the manservant . . . ?'

'Mr Austen, give the girl a penny. She looks honest, poor thing. It's not her fault that she works for such a wicked mistress.'

Friday, 4 March 1791

This is the first day that I have been able to write. I can't believe that it is more than three weeks since last I wrote in my journal, more than three weeks since that terrible night when I went out into the night streets of Southampton, more than three weeks since I thought Jane was going to die. I haven't been as ill as her, but I felt too weak to write in my journal and there was always someone in my room, either Mrs Austen, or else Jane's sister, Cassandra, or, during the last few days, when they were sure that they would not catch my fever, my brother, Edward-John, and his wife, Augusta.

And then there was Jane herself.

Not ill, not muttering in a high fever.

Just sitting beside my bed chuckling over a novel.

And I think that made me start to get well again.

Edward-John and Augusta came to see me this morning. I tried to talk to them, but I felt too weak to say much. I hoped they would leave me alone, but Augusta returned in the afternoon. Jane was reading and I was half asleep when we heard her footsteps on the stairs. I knew it was her immediately as Mrs Austen wears list slippers and the boys all wear boots. Augusta's shoes clip along in a neat, tidy way, rather like herself.

I could hear her talking to Mrs Austen about her new gown when they were standing outside my door. 'How do you like my gown, dear madam?' she was saying to Mrs Austen. 'Handsome, I think, but I do not know whether it is over-trimmed. I have the greatest dislike to being over-trimmed . . .'

'I agree with you, ma'am,' said Jane beside me as the door opened and the two came in. Jane's face was solemn and she made little effort to lower her voice. 'There is nothing worse than an over-trimmed gown . . . all that lace and flounces – so very vulgar . . .' And her expression was all innocence as she surveyed the flounces of Augusta's lace-trimmed gown which bounced along in front of her.

I quickly pulled up the blanket to hide my mouth and I saw Mrs Austen glance sharply at Jane, who just gave a wicked grin. Augusta, however, wasn't listening to Jane. She was still talking over her shoulder to Mrs Austen and she was in full flow.

'I said to my *caro sposo* – that's what I call my dear Edward-John. It's Italian for *dear husband*,' she said kindly, glancing across at Jane, who nodded gravely. 'I said to him, just this very morning –

– is my gown over-trimmed?

Augusta

Jenny will confirm,
won't you, Jenny –
"Tell me, dear," I
said to him, "is my gown
over-trimmed?" And he said
to me, oh Lord, I blush
to tell you what he said—'
    'How are you feeling
this afternoon, Jenny?'
interrupted Mrs Austen. She
looked as though she was getting
sick of Augusta and her gowns.
    'Much better, thank you, ma'am.'
    'Of course she is well; you
just lie quietly, Jenny, while we
chat.' Augusta, as usual, talked
non-stop and I felt my head beginning to ache as I
tried to pay attention. Jane had gone over to sit on
the window seat and was busy scribbling away on a
piece of paper while Augusta went on and on about
how popular she is in Bristol and what people said to
her and said about her. After about ten minutes of
this, I felt my eyes beginning to close. Augusta didn't
seem to notice, but went on talking. A minute later, I
heard Jane's light shoes crossing the room.
    'She's very weak, Mama,' I heard her say in a sol-
emn tone of voice. 'I think she needs to rest now,
don't you?' I didn't dare look at Jane in case she made
me laugh.

'We'd better go.' Mrs Austen's chair scraped back and she was on her feet so quickly that I reckon that she had been dying to get away for the last ten minutes. She had no interest in Augusta's tales about her social life in Bristol.

After they had gone, I asked Jane whether she had been writing a story and she told me that she was thinking of starting a novel where Augusta would be a clergyman's wife with a very high opinion of herself, but most of the other people in her town would dislike her immensely. Apparently she was writing down some of Augusta's statements so that she could use them when she started the book.

'Here, stick that into your journal for me and then it won't get lost.' Jane handed me a piece of paper. I read it through and laughed. Augusta hadn't exactly said things quite as outrageous as that, but it definitely was in her style.

My dear old beau – he's quite a titled person, you know – he thinks so highly of me – he even leaves the other men to their port after dinner and comes to join me – I wish you could hear all of his gallant speeches – Lord, I mustn't tell you what he said – but I can assure you that my husband would be quite jealous – but what's a woman to do? I can't help it if he admires me –

I carefully glued it into my journal. Then, when Jane had gone downstairs for her tea, I lay back on the pillow and began to think about Augusta. Why could I not just laugh at her as Jane did?

I'm less frightened of Augusta than I used to be before I went to school and became friends with Jane, but I still have a horrible feeling that she might do me some terrible harm. It's hard to explain it, but deep down I think that she hates me and wishes that I were not part of her husband's family. The problem is that my mother left Edward-John the responsibility for me when she died, and Augusta is always whispering to her friends about what a terrible imposition this was on a young man. It makes me very uncomfortable, but there is nothing that I can do about it. I don't suppose that I will get married either as I have a very small fortune – only fifty pounds a year. In any case, I don't think that I would be very attractive to men. I remember overhearing Augusta telling one of her friends that Edward-John was sending me to boarding school so that I would be educated to become a governess, and when her friend suggested that I might get married Augusta gave one of her horse-like laughs and said – it's funny how I still remember the words: *'My dear! With that low stature and that kitchen maid's nose! – Who on earth would ever marry her?'*

And then I think about Captain Williams and how kind he was to his sister . . .

Saturday, 5 March 1791

My brother and his wife went back to Bristol this morning. Now that I am well again, they said that they were happy to leave me in the good care of my Aunt Austen. Augusta was especially keen on my staying with the Austens. She feels that the country air of Hampshire will be better for me than the city air of Bristol. When I am quite strong enough Jane and I may perhaps go for a holiday to Bristol. Jane thinks that will be exciting, but I have a guilty feeling that I would prefer to stay at Steventon. I think that I will have much more fun here. This house is full of shouts and noisy laughs. Jane's brothers and Mr Austen's pupils seem to spend a lot of their time calling jokes down the stairs or teasing each other.

'We have decided that you won't go back to that school in Southampton again,' my sister-in-law said before she left. 'Mrs Thorpe tells me that there is a very good boarding school at Reading. Her daughter went there. I shall make some more enquiries, but it won't be worth enrolling you until after Easter.'

'Don't you think I'm getting a little old for school?' I tried to make my voice sound grown-up and sensible when I said that. 'Jane and I found that we learned very little when we were at school. We could study better at home. There were hardly any books there, only a few novels from the lending library. Mrs Cawley couldn't even speak French, and the gram-mar she gave us to study was too easy. All we did was learn some spellings and do needlework.' I didn't tell her that Jane had already suggested to her mother that we both be allowed to join the boys in their les-sons with Mr Austen. Mrs Austen was so shocked at that suggestion that she pretended to feel faint. Mrs Austen is a little too tough for fainting, but I think that Augusta, who is very proper, really would faint; the suggestion that we should study by ourselves was a possible one though.

Edward-John was nodding solemnly, but I could see by Augusta's face that she wasn't sure so I said very quickly: 'And of course you would save thirty-five pounds a year by allowing me to study here with Jane. Mrs Austen thinks it would be a good idea.' I kept it to myself that it was really Mr Austen who thought it was a good idea and that Mrs Austen had sighed and said, 'Jenny will never get any work done with Jane distracting her.' She had added though, 'Still, it would be lovely to keep you, Jenny dear,' and I thought that was nice of her.

Edward-John and Augusta looked at each other. Then she nodded her head and said, 'What do you think, Mr C.? I am of the opinion that it would be better, in view of Jenny's health, if she stays here in the country air.'

'Perhaps we might engage a drawing master at

some stage,' suggested Edward-John. 'Mama thought Jenny's drawings very talented.' He shot a quick look at Augusta's protruding green eyes and pursed-up mouth and then said hastily, 'Well, we can think about it when Jenny is quite well again.'

I would have loved to ask for a singing master. I remembered the drawing room that I had seen on that terrible night in Southampton where the young lady was singing and playing, and the expression on the faces of the men who stood around the piano listening to her. However, I also took a look at Augusta's face and knew that it would be ridiculous to expect that she would allow Edward-John to spend an unnecessary penny on me.

'I promise that I'll work hard and give no trouble to Mrs Austen.' I knew by their expressions that I had said the right thing, but inside I felt worried. How long would the Austens, with their big family and their pupils, want to keep me?

After they had gone, Jane came into my bedroom to tell me the news that her brother Frank had bought a new pony for himself from the money he had got when he was on board his ship.

I told her that I got all her brothers muddled up, and she suggested that she help me to draw little pictures of them in my journal and then I would know them all as I met them.

I will start a new page so that as we draw she cannot see what I have written about her!

Jane says I must write exactly as she describes so as to capture her brothers most accurately:

James – the eldest. He is ten years older than Jane – he has blond hair and grey eyes, and his nose and chin are quite neat. Jane says that I have captured his fussy, fidgety look just right.

Edward – adopted by rich relations in Kent. Jane has given me a miniature of Edward to copy, which he gave her as a gift last Christmas. She says he wears a wig to show how rich and splendid he is.

Henry – four years older than Jane. He looks just like her, with hazel eyes and dark curly hair. Jane says Henry is tremendously handsome and all the girls love him!

Cassandra (Jane says I must draw her too). I have seen her quite a few times so I know what she looks like, but Jane says I must

give her a dreamy look as she is in love with Tom
Fowle, one of Mr Austen's pupils. I'm not sure how
I should draw someone in love, so I hope I have it
right.

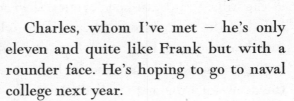

Frank — a year older than Jane (the
same age as me) and a midshipman — I did
my best with Frank's collar, but Jane had
to sketch it for me. I don't think I have
ever seen a midshipman, though I have
seen a captain and I'm sure I could sketch
a captain's uniform.

Charles, whom I've met — he's only
eleven and quite like Frank but with a
rounder face. He's hoping to go to naval
college next year.

I told Jane I thought she was very
lucky to have five brothers.

Jane laughed. 'Five . . . well.' There
was something odd about her expression and a sort
of dryness in her voice.

I just turned back to the page where I have drawn
Captain Thomas Williams. My journal opened automatically at that page and I could see that the corner of the page was a bit dog-eared. I don't think
Jane saw . . .

Sunday, 6 March 1791

Jane's brother Frank came in to see me today. He is on shore leave from his ship, where he is a midshipman. He looked quite like the picture that I had drawn of him, but his hair was even curlier. He is my age and the nearest in the family to Jane.

He was quite like Jane, very chatty and very funny. He just came into my room, sat on the bed and asked me how I was and then started doing imitations of the first lieutenant, who was a silly numbskull according to Frank, and of the captain, who was as old as the hills. Frank stumped around the room to show us what the captain was like on deck when a wind was blowing and how once he stumbled when his legs got tangled in a sail and he lay stretched out on the deck until the mate pulled him to his feet. Frank found that very funny, but said that all the sailors had to pretend not to notice in case they would be flogged for insubordination. Then Frank did a good imitation of the captain lying stretched out on the floor, thrashing about with his legs, trying to dislodge the heavy sail.

'And the helmsman at the wheel was staring out to sea like this.' And Frank blew his cheeks out and tightened his lips so much that the cords on his very brown neck stood out. His face was very brown too, I noticed, and he had nice dark eyes.

'It's a hard life,' he said, but I thought he looked well on it, and very cheerful.

'Not as hard as school,' said Jane promptly. 'We were starved there.'

'Bet you didn't have to eat ship's biscuit,' said Frank, his mouth filled with a slice of cake his mother had sent up to tempt my appetite.

'We had worse! Tell him, Jenny!'

'Fish heads for dinner,' I said. 'And fish tails.'

'And it smelt bad!'

'Tell him about the stinking fish of Southampton, Jane,' I said. I was enjoying Frank's visit. It seems strange, but I have hardly ever spoken to a boy before except my brother, Edward-John.

'Well, Mrs Cawley was reading out from a book where a woman is giving advice to her daughter . . .'

'And she was reading it in a very deep, solemn tone of voice.' I put this in so that Frank could imagine the scene.

'And then she came to this bit – it was priceless . . . She said, *"Belinda, beware the dissipations of London, the idle luxuries of Bath and—"'*

'Let me tell! Frank, listen to this . . . and then Jane said, very quickly, just when Mrs Cawley paused to take a breath, she said: *"And beware the stinking fish of Southampton."* All the girls started to laugh so much that Mrs Cawley sent Jane out of the room.'

'If she were on a ship, she would be flogged with a cat-o'-nine-tails,' said Frank.

I don't think he found Jane's joke as funny as I did. Perhaps boys like broad jokes like people slipping and falling and girls think jokes in word form are funnier.

Frank didn't seem to want to hear any more stories from our school. He produced a pack of cards from his pocket. 'Let's have a game of pontoon,' he said.

I had to tell him that I didn't know how to play. My brother, Edward-John, regards cards as an instrument of the devil. I couldn't help laughing when I imagined his face and Augusta's if they saw me sitting up in bed, my nightcap thrown on the floor, not just playing cards but playing for money!

Neither Jane nor I had any money, but Frank lent us some pennies to bet on our cards. It was nice of him, but he won it all back from us bit by bit. I felt almost well again; it was such fun pretending to have good cards, laying our bets, shouting for another card to be twisted and groaning in agony when we got to more than twenty-one. Jane even got down on her knees and held up her hands in prayer for a nice small card – I wonder what Edward-John would have said to that! He would have thought it blasphemy. And then she screamed in agony so loudly when a ten of clubs turned up that Mrs Austen came in and said it was time for me to go to sleep.

But Frank charmed her until she borrowed some

pennies from him and had a game where she had such lucky cards and ended up laying them all out, one by one, in a five-card trick.

And then she refused to give Frank back his money and told him it served him right for playing cards on a Sunday.

'Dear madam,' said Jane sweetly, 'why did you not remind us if you remembered that it was Sunday? La, I do declare that the day had slipped my memory. Perhaps you should give those ill-gotten gains back to Frank, since they were won on a sacred day like today.'

'Take care that you are not so sharp that you will cut yourself, Miss Jane! Men don't like girls that are too witty. You don't want to be an old maid, do you? Now off you go, Frank. These two girls need to go to sleep.' Mrs Austen's good humour had vanished. As usual, Jane had rubbed her up the wrong way. From what I have seen, Charles and Frank seem to get on well with their mother, and so does Cassandra, but Jane and she are always arguing, and I have to admit that some of it is Jane's fault.

Monday, 7 March 1791

Up to now I had been having all my meals upstairs so that I didn't get cold in the draughty corridors and stairway, but today Mrs Austen said I could come down to join everyone for dinner. The dining parlour was full when Jane and I came in.

I must write down what it looked like, though I hardly saw it in the first few minutes, as I was too embarrassed to look around.

It was a big room, with no carpet, not even rugs: just a wooden floor, marked by the boys' boots. Augusta would have thought it very meanly furnished. A large table made from scratched and battered oak, rather than the modern mahogany, occupied most of the space. Instead of pieces of light, delicate Sheraton furniture tastefully arranged against modern striped wallpaper, as in my brother's house, here there was just a vast, old-fashioned oaken sideboard, with its shelves, cubby-holes and drawers, covering one of the panelled walls.

At the top of the table was Mr Austen, busily slicing meat. Beside him Mrs Austen was putting the meat on plates and adding vegetables and gravy. As she filled each plate, Cassandra carried them, one by one, to the boys, who were sitting on the far side. I hadn't met any of the pupils yet, except Charles, Jane's brother, but they all smiled kindly at me. It looked like a lot of boys and I felt my cheeks becoming quite hot.

'Sit between me and Tom Fowle, Jenny.' Mr Austen gave me a kind smile as I sat down. I noticed that Cassandra gave me a rather sour look. I remembered Jane telling me that her sister was in love with this Tom Fowle, so perhaps Cassandra didn't like me taking the place beside him. Perhaps she normally sat there between her father and her beloved. When she had finished handing out the plates, she went down to the bottom of the table beside Charles, her eleven-year-old brother. She looked annoyed and I felt rather awkward.

'Are you hungry, Jenny?' asked Mr Austen, and I told him that I was starving. Both Mr and Mrs Austen were very pleased at that and Mr Austen insisted on putting an extra slice of boiled mutton and roly-poly pudding on my plate to fatten me up.

It was while I was trying to munch my way through all of this that Cassandra, from the bottom of the table, suddenly said, 'Jenny, how did you get the letter to Mama about Jane's illness? Mrs Cawley couldn't understand how she had heard. Indeed, she said that she had forbidden you to write.'

I choked on a piece of mutton and spent the next few minutes coughing while Jane thumped me on the back and Frank brought me a glass of water from the carafe on the sideboard. I kept the coughing up a bit longer than I needed to; I was hoping that everyone would forget about Cassandra's question, but when I took my final sip of water I looked around the table and everyone, even the schoolboys, seemed to be waiting for my answer. I realized that the subject had been discussed before – probably while I was ill – and now they wanted an answer. I couldn't say that Becky had done it; that might get her into trouble. What could I say? My mind was a blank.

'She tossed it out of the window to a charitable lady who was passing by,' said Jane quickly. She patted me on the back like a solicitous mother and said in a worried way, 'Don't try to talk, Jenny. You'll bring on the coughing fit again and that won't be good for you in your condition.'

All the boys began to laugh then and Mrs Austen scolded them for bad manners at table, and Gilbert East, who is a baronet's son and a great favourite with Mrs Austen, said something cheeky and she rapped his knuckles with a spoon. And then one of the boys proposed that everyone should find a word to rhyme with the word 'rose'. Various suggestions were made and then Mrs Austen, on the spot, made up a long poem beginning with the lines:

This morning I woke from a quiet repose,
I first rubb'd my eyes, and I next blew my nose;
With my stockings and shoes I then covered my toes,

All the boys were proposing various words, like 'froze' and 'clothes', and there was such noise and confusion that everyone forgot about me.

'By the way, Jenny, how *did* you get that letter to
Mama on the night that I was so ill? Charles told me
that it had been sent by the midnight mail; he was the
one that collected the letters that day.' Jane hardly
waited for the door to be closed behind us when we
went up to our room after dinner before she started
to cross-question me.

My heart was hammering. I stared at Jane. I had
almost forgotten about that night and the danger I
had been in, but now it had all come flooding back
into my mind.

'Go on; tell me. I won't tell a soul. I promise you.'

I looked at Jane doubtfully, but then nodded. Surely
I could trust her.

And so I told her the whole story of that night,
about the sailors and about the man with the sword
and about Captain Thomas Williams.

Jane listened to me with her mouth open and she
didn't say a word until I finished.

'That is the most romantic thing I ever heard,'
she said. 'It's as good as anything that Mrs Charlotte
Smith wrote; it's even as good as *Ethelinde, the Rec-
luse of the Lake*. What did he look like?'

I told her all about how handsome he was, about
his black hair and brown eyes and his lovely smile
and high cheekbones and broad shoulders, and then I
showed her the picture that I had drawn.

Jane was very interested in this and she said that

she was going to turn the story of me and Captain Williams into a wonderful romance when she had finished writing *Love and Friendship*. She says that when I talk about Captain Thomas Williams my voice sounds like Cassandra's when she talks about Tom Fowle, which can't possibly be true.

I asked her how many stories she has written and she said, 'A few,' then pulled out the bottom drawer of her chest and I saw that it was absolutely stuffed with pieces of paper that were filled up with Jane's fine handwriting.

'What about this?' she asked, tossing me half a sheet. 'I never finished that but I could write something like it for you. I could just change 'Sir Williams' to 'Captain Williams'. You can stick that in your journal if you like – I've already copied it into my notebook and left a blank page so that I can finish it some time.'

After staying at the Village for a few days longer, Sir Williams went to stay in a freind's house in Surry. Mr Brudenell had a beautiful Neice with whom Sir Williams soon fell in love. But Miss Arundel was cruel; she preferred a Mr Stanhope. Sir Williams shot Mr Stanhope. The lady then had no further reason to refuse him and they were to be married on the 27th of October. However . . .

* * *

I read it with Jane reading over my shoulder, but she didn't seem too pleased with it when she had finished.

'I've changed my mind — throw it away; I wrote that when I was only about thirteen,' she said disdainfully. 'I'd make a much better story of it now.'

'No, I'd like to have it,' I said. I thought I would prefer to have that than to have a story about myself and Captain Williams. Deep down, I suppose I was feeling that I'd prefer to make up my own stories about him.

And then Jane copied some more of her present story into her notebook and I wrote a letter to Edward-John and Augusta. I had just finished it when Jane suddenly said, 'You'll have to marry this Captain Williams, Jenny. That would be just so romantic.'

I laughed at that. 'Jane,' I said to her, 'it would be best if Captain Williams and I never saw each other again. He could ruin my reputation forever with one incautious word.'

'Well,' said Jane, 'I don't suppose we'll go to Southampton again so you should be safe.'

Tuesday, 8 March 1791

I had such fun today. I've just said this to Jane and she said I should write it all down quickly before I forget it. That is what she does. When she thinks of an idea for a story – even if it is the middle of the night – she flies over to her desk and scribbles it down on a piece of paper. Afterwards she reads through it again and if she likes it she copies it into her notebook.

This morning Frank came in just after I had had my breakfast but before I had dressed. I got a bit of a shock when he just banged on the door and then came flying in. The curtains were drawn back from the bed so all I could do was pull up the blankets very close to my chin and try not to blush. I can't get used to being in a house where boys are running around all the time. Soon there will be even more because Henry and James, who are at Oxford University, are expected for the weekend, and Edward, Jane's brother who was adopted by rich relations in Kent, will be coming back from his visit to Europe.

Frank is very nice and most amusing. He and Jane and I were playing cards again yesterday evening, using buttons for money this time. It was great fun as Frank kept trying to cheat and Jane kept tut-tutting and saying things like: 'He is but sixteen years old, but already he has embarked upon a life of crime. His parents brought him up from an early age to have

no principles. I fear that he will end by being trans-
ported to Australia as a convict.'

Frank looks a bit like Jane, with his dark curly
hair and dark eyes — and even at the end of the winter he is very suntanned. He has Jane's rosy cheeks
also, and now they were glowing with excitement.
He came right up and sat on my bed.

'The hunt's meeting at Deane Gate Inn this morning, Jenny. Do you want to come and see us off? Jane
is coming.'

I hesitated and told him I wasn't sure. Though I
had been getting up each day after breakfast, my legs
were still a little weak. 'How far
away is it?'

'Not far and it's a lovely day.'
Frank jerked the blind so suddenly that it flew up and the
knob on the end of the cord
pinged sharply against the
window.

It was a lovely day.
The poplar tree outside
my window had some
tiny green buds on it and
the sun lit the branches
so that they shone gold.
There was a flock of star-
lings whirling merrily
around under a pale blue

sky. Suddenly I felt a lot better and I thought I would love to go out and see the hunt set off. Frank looked very pleased when I told him.

'Good! Get up quickly.' He still hung around, looking out of the window at the woods beyond, as if he thought I would just slip out of bed and dress while he had his back turned. I coughed. I felt very embarrassed.

'Oh, I'll get out of your way so that you can dress.'

Once he was gone, the door slamming behind him and his feet drumming on the wooden staircase, I got out of bed. The water in the pitcher was cold, but I poured some into the basin on the washstand and had a quick wash, drying myself in front of the fire. I put on two petticoats, a flannel one over my che-mise and then my linen one, and I pulled on a pair of new woollen stockings, which went right up to my knees and made me feel nice and cosy. Then I got out my blue muslin gown from the clothes press. It had been washed and ironed, I think, because it was quite clean around the hem. The last time that I had worn it was in Southampton on that terrible night and I remembered noticing a streak of mud on the bottom of the skirt when I hung it up.

Jane and Charles were just coming in the front door when I got to the bottom of the stairs.

'Oh, Jenny, you're coming to see the hunt – that's good.'

'Mama, Jenny is coming to see the hunt go off.' Charles had a high voice that penetrated the whole house.

Mrs Austen popped out from the preserves room, where she and Cassandra were labelling jars of pick- led spring onions.

'It's too far,' she said decidedly. 'You're not strong enough yet, Jenny. That hill is steep.'

'She could go on Frank's old pony,' said Jane.

I felt terrified at the idea because I can't ride, and I said as much.

Frank had joined us by then. 'Anyone can ride,' he said confidently. 'We'll put you on old Squirrel's back – she was my first pony. I'll lead it. Don't worry, Jenny, you'll be fine.'

I asked him why the pony was called Squirrel. To be honest, I was just trying to delay. In one way it was rather fun to go out with all the boys and to have Frank, who was quite handsome, lead me on the pony's back. On the other hand, I was terrified that I might fall off or do something silly.

'I was the one that called the pony "Squirrel's Pony" because Frank used to look like a squirrel on its back – it was far too big for him. He did look funny, perched up there,' said Mrs Austen over her shoulder as she turned to replace the stopper in the big jar of vinegar. 'He saved up all the money that he could earn scaring crows. Then he got a nice tip from a rich cousin and he went straight out and bought the pony when he was only seven years old. I made his first hunting coat out of my red wool wedding dress.' Mrs Austen was smiling good-humouredly at the memory. It's funny how much fonder of the boys she is than of Jane, I thought. She always seemed to be a bit irritated by Jane.

I made a little curtsy to Mrs Austen and said that I would go, if she allowed me. Suddenly I really did want to try to ride, even if Frank was going to lead me. Surely I could manage to sit on a pony's back and be led.

'What happens if she feels faint?' Mr Austen had appeared from his study, following out the older boys, and he looked worried.

'She'll be all right.' Mrs Austen was tired of the subject; she wanted us all to go and allow her to get on with preserving her onions.

'I feel faint; it's the fumes of this vinegar. I wish I could get out in the fresh air for a half-hour.' Cassandra was pouting, standing there with a big apron over her oldest gown and looking as if she wished that she could go too. Her eyes went to Tom Fowle and then she looked away. He was looking at her and both of their faces turned slightly pink. I saw Mrs Austen's eyes go irritably from Cassandra to Tom. But then Jane jumped in between her mother and her sister, her hands clasped and an imploring expression on her face.

'Oh, Cassandra, don't faint whatever you do!'

Jane was pretending to sound alarmed. 'Beware of fainting fits; in my story *Love and Friendship*, Sophia dies after a fainting fit. Her dying words were to her friend, saying, *"Dearest Laura, beware of swoons. Run mad as often as you choose, but do not faint."*'

Even Mrs Austen chuckled at that, and Mr Austen threw back his head and laughed. He rubbed his hand over Jane's dark curls. 'What a little genius this girl is,' he said fondly. 'I love her stories. They are so clever, so humorous. It's a pity she's a girl. What do you think, Frank? Do you think that your sister could beat you at Latin if she were a boy?'

'I don't like Latin,' said Frank. He didn't look a bit worried or jealous of Jane, he just sounded impatient. 'Mathematics is the only subject that is useful to me at sea. That's what they study at the naval college. Come on, Jenny, let's go.'

What fun I am having at Steventon, I was thinking as we all went up the hill together. There was Jane on Frank's pony, teasing Tom Fowle about Cassandra, and Gilbert, with Charles sitting in front of him, pretending that his horse would fall down on the road from Charles's weight. The other students were splashing mud from the puddles over each other. I thought of Bristol and of myself and Augusta sitting in the parlour sewing, or she reading aloud while I was drawing, and it all seemed very dull. And now I was going to see a hunt!

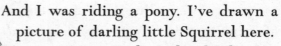

And I was riding a pony. I've drawn a picture of darling little Squirrel here. We were almost late by the time we arrived at Deane and the space in front of the inn was crowded by red-coated riders and dozens of tail-wagging dogs, yelping with excitement.

'Quick, give me my pony!' In his hurry Frank let go of the reins of my pony while he grabbed his own from Jane and they both went over to talk to a boy who was sitting on a grey pony. I got a fright to find myself on my own, but nothing happened.

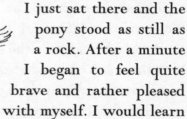

I just sat there and the pony stood as still as a rock. After a minute I began to feel quite brave and rather pleased with myself. I would learn to ride, I planned. Perhaps Frank would teach me, although of course Squirrel was far too small for me; my feet almost touched the ground. Still, it would be fun, I thought, and then I saw one of the red-coated gentlemen smiling at me. I smiled back before thinking and then I blushed. The gentleman didn't look away. I heard him say to the man next to him, 'Who's that pretty girl?' Then I did look away quickly and I didn't hear the reply, but when I looked back I saw that he

was still looking at me.
He smiled even more,
and then took off his
hat and half raised
his whip in a salute to
me. It was lucky that my
sister-in-law wasn't there.
She would have considered
it all very unladylike. The
man had a very handsome
horse though, a big black stal-
lion, and he had a hunting horn in his hand
so he must have been someone important in the hunt.
I wish my picture showed quite how splendid he
looked – I'm never satisfied with my drawings. I
showed it to Jane, who is writing away at her desk,
and she liked it, but I don't think I've made him
handsome enough.

'I wish I was allowed to go hunting,' said Charles
sadly as they all moved away, shouting and laughing.
They were a wonderful sight in the spring sunshine,
I thought, and I wasn't surprised that Charles was
upset not to be going too.

'You know that Squirrel is too old for hunting,'
said Jane. 'She'd drop down dead if you tried to gallop her or jump with her. You'll have to have a new
pony, and you know that Father can't afford to buy
you one.'

I told him he could ride her back home though, if

he liked, because it was downhill all the way to the house and I could easily walk that distance.

Charles was very grateful – he is such a nice boy. When he is happy, his grin seems to go from ear to ear.

As Jane and I walked slowly down the hill together I told her how lucky I thought she was to have brothers like Frank and Charles.

'And Henry,' said Jane. 'He'll be back at the weekend. Henry's my favourite brother. He's splendid; wait until you see him! Alethea Bigg told me that she is madly in love with him.'

I asked Jane to describe Henry again as I gazed over the fields in what I hoped was a nonchalant way. I wondered what Henry would think of me. Life was getting very exciting with all these young men around.

'He's very good-looking – tall and dark-haired,' Jane told me. 'Don't you remember? I told you that when you drew that picture of him.'

'Frank is different to the way I imagined him though. Is Henry as fine-looking as Frank?' I pretended to be looking at something in the hedge so that she wouldn't see me blush.

'Much, much better-looking.' Jane sounded quite scornful. 'And much, much taller. Frank's only a boy; Henry is a man. He's nineteen now. He's a year older than Cassandra. Why, you haven't fallen in love with Frank, have you? Why are you blushing?'

'No, of course I haven't fallen in love with Frank,'

I said indignantly, but I knew I was still blushing. I wish I didn't blush so easily. It's so silly. I remembered that gentleman at the hunt looking at me and I could feel my cheeks getting even warmer. I wondered whether he admired me. I wished that I was not so short and that I had a better nose.

I tried to distract Jane by asking her about the boy on the grey pony, and it worked.

'Oh, that's Tom Chute; I'm madly in love with him.' She didn't blush though, so I think it was just a joke.

Wednesday, 9 March 1791

Today was another good day. The weather was fine and sunny, but very frosty. Mr Austen and his students were working hard to make up for the loss to their studies from the day's hunting, so Jane and I went for a walk by ourselves.

It felt odd to be able to put on our bonnets and cloaks and just stroll out of the front door without saying a word to anyone. Back home, in Bristol, my mother never used to allow me out by myself, not even to a shop a few doors away from our house. She always had to accompany me, and as we had no gentleman in the house we could never go out once it became dark. And of course Augusta was so prim and proper that she didn't walk out without Edward-John or a servant to accompany her once evening came.

But here at Steventon, in the country, it was different. It was so lovely to be able to pick primroses and watch the birds building their nests.

As we went down the laneway towards the church I told Jane how much I admired her house, especially the casement windows. I think they are much nicer than sash windows.

'It's a terrible old ruin of a place.' Jane had to make everything very dramatic. The house could have done with a coat of paint, inside as well as out, but it certainly wasn't a ruin.

'Why are we going to church?' I was surprised at Jane. On Sunday she had begged her mother to allow her to stay at home with me when the others went to church; when I had thanked her, she just told me that church bored her.

'Aha,' said Jane mysteriously. 'I am on the track of something.'

She didn't say any more until we reached the churchyard. Just next to the church door there was a huge yew tree. It looked immensely old – half its branches were broken off and its trunk was as big as a small tower.

'It's hollow inside.' Jane led me around the back and put her hand in. When she took it out she held a sheet of paper, sealed with a blob of sealing wax. She held it out to me.

'Guess who,' she said, pushing it under my nose.

It wasn't difficult. 'Tom Fowle,' I guessed. It was in a large bold hand, written on paper that looked torn from a notebook.

'I suspected this.' Jane was giggling. 'Every morning Cassandra writes a letter and then she makes some excuse to go to the church or to the village,  but she always goes down here. She and Tom Fowle are using this hollow tree as a letter box.'

I was a bit puzzled. I asked Jane why they didn't just hand them to each other — they must meet twenty times every day. Mr Austen's pupils live as if they are part of the family. We meet them at every meal and they are in the parlour every night, playing chess or cards, singing, dancing, or joking and laughing.

'My mother doesn't approve,' said Jane. 'It would be different if it were Gilbert. He's the son of a baronet. Tom has three older brothers; he'll be penniless. He wants to be a clergyman, but it will be years and years before he even has a parish. My father has a parish and a farm but we are still very poor. And Cassandra will have no money. There is no money for any of us. The boys will have to make their own way, but Cassandra and I can't go in the navy, or become clergymen, so we will have to marry money.' Jane sounded indifferent, but I could see how she kicked viciously at a clod of earth while she said, in the sort of high, scolding voice that sounded just like Mrs Austen, *'Affection is desirable; money is essential.'* And then her voice changed again, back to the usual joking tone. 'Shall we play a trick on them? Write something of our own and put it into the hollow tree instead?'

'Put the letter back.' I felt uneasy. Cassandra was the least friendly member of the Austen family. I didn't know whether it was that she thought I was a nuis-ance, or whether she didn't like me very much, but she seemed to look at me in a slightly sour way. I didn't want her to know that I had been spying on her.

'Let's go into the church then.' Jane tossed the letter back as if she was bored with the whole matter.

The church at Steventon was very old, much smaller and older than the churches at Bristol. There was no one there.

'Come on,' said Jane, seizing me by the hand. 'I know where Father keeps the forms for calling the banns. I love the idea of banns, don't you? You see, it might be that some wicked baronet is leading some poor innocent girl astray, pretending to be a young bachelor when really he has a mad wife locked away in the attic of his house. If they call the banns the chances are that one of the neighbours will jump up and say, "I know that Sir John Berkley and he is mar-ried to my first cousin." And then a ghastly pallor will come over Sir John's evil face and he will dash from the church, jump on his horse and ride away, while the gentle girl, Emma, will faint away into the arms of her cousin, who has secretly loved her for many years.' Jane, as usual, had to turn it all into a story while she was fishing out some pieces of printed paper from a cupboard in the vestry. I wondered what her father would say if he found her meddling with church property, but then I thought he would probably just laugh. He was very indulgent to Jane. She was, I guessed, his favourite in the family.

'Who do you want to marry?' she asked.

I told her that I didn't know, because I don't really know any gentlemen.

'I think I'll marry Tom Chute.' Already Jane had picked up a quill from a selection lying on the table, dipped it into the inkpot and begun to fill out the form.

The Form of an Entry of Publication of Banns

The Banns of Marriage

between . *Thomas Chute of the Vyne* . . . . . .
And . . *Jane Austen of Steventon* . . . . .

were duly published in this Church for the first time,

on Sunday . . *Thirteenth* . . . .
Day of . . . . *March* . . . .
in the Year of . *Ninety-one* . . . .

I was going to ask who Tom Chute was, but I remembered that he was the boy on the grey pony who was teasing and joking with her outside the inn before the hunt. Then I asked what Jane knew about him and his family — I felt quite grown-up when I said that. It was true though. You couldn't just marry a man because he made good jokes.

'He lives at the big house called the Vyne. It's not too far from here. It's on the way to Basingstoke.'

'Have you known him for a long time? My mama always said that you should know a gentleman for at least a year before you allow him to pay addresses to you.' I said this jokingly. I was beginning to be able to mention my mother without tears coming to my eyes. I seemed to be living in such a different world now, a world of noise and jokes and boys flying around laughing and talking.

'No, I only met him a few months ago. He will soon come into a large estate and the Vyne. We will probably dine there one evening, so you will see for yourself.'

'How old is he?'

'He's sixteen, just a bit older than me.'

I wasn't sure that you could really come into a large estate when you were only sixteen, but Jane always has an answer for everything.

'Yes, of course you can . . . oh, well, it's his eldest brother really, but he's sickly and cross so Tom will inherit when William dies. I can't stand William. He's always trying to make mock of me. Luckily he lacks the wit to do it with any sense.'

'What does William look like?'

'You saw him yesterday, at Deane. Do you remember the man on the black stallion, the one holding the horn?'

I was glad that it was quite dark in the little vestry so that she wouldn't see me blushing. Then I started to laugh. I told Jane that I didn't think he looked sickly or cross and that I would marry him and then I'd be the one with the big house and the large estate. I told her she could come and stay with me and I'd find her a young man to marry.

'In possession of a large fortune, I hope,' said Jane primly, as I seized the quill and began to fill in another banns form – like this:

The Form of an Entry of Publication of Banns

The Banns of Marriage
between . *William Chute of the Vyne* . . . .
And . . *Jenny Cooper of Steventon* . . . . .

were duly published in this Church for the first time,

on Sunday . . . *Thirteenth* . . . .
Day of . . . . . *March* . . . .
in the Year of . *Ninety-one* . . . . . .

'What about Captain Williams though? Dear, dear, dear, Jenny, what a sad flirt you are – going from one young man to another.' Jane made her voice sound just like Mrs Cawley at the school.

I told her immediately that I didn't even want to think about Captain Williams because he could ruin my reputation forever. Jane nodded wisely and said, 'Very true!' twice.

I would do my best not to think of Captain Williams – not even when I was in bed at night, I decided as we went home, slipping and sliding on the frozen puddles of the lane.

After dinner all the boys decided to have a game of cricket. The ground was hard with frost but the sun was still warm and Mrs Austen said that I could go out if I wrapped up warmly.

'You can bowl, Jane.' To my surprise John Warren handed her the ball. I had thought that we would just be watching, but Frank was sending me up to the top of the field with instructions to throw the ball to Jane if it came anywhere near to me.

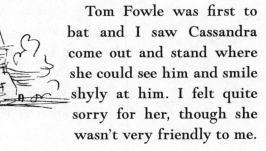

Tom Fowle was first to bat and I saw Cassandra come out and stand where she could see him and smile shyly at him. I felt quite sorry for her, though she wasn't very friendly to me.

I was so interested in watching the
two of them that it was only when
everyone started shrieking 'Jenny!'
that I realized that the ball was
actually at my feet.

Frank, the captain of our team, was very nice to
me. He said that I probably wasn't well yet, so he
sent Charles up to help me in my part of the field.

We had almost finished the game and Tom Fowle
was fielding when Frank hit the ball a tremendous
whack so it went right over towards a row of poplars
on the far side of the field. One
minute we could see Tom running
after the ball, and the next there
was no sign of him. It was Cassandra
who realized first that something was
wrong. She gave a shriek of 'Tom!' and then she set
off running across the field. Jane and I followed and the
others came behind. Tom Fowle was stretched out on
the ground, his head pouring blood, and the colour
was completely drained from his normally healthy-
looking face. His eyes were shut.

Cassandra gasped and then, without a
moment's hesitation, she tore a strip of
muslin from her petticoat and held
it against Tom's dark hair, cradling
his head in her lap. She said nothing, but I think I will al-

ways remember what she looked like in those few minutes before Mr Austen came running up and Tom opened his eyes.

'Slipped on a piece of ice,' said Gilbert nonchalantly. 'You all right, Tom, old son?'

'Cassandra, get up off that wet grass,' scolded Mrs Austen as she came puffing up the field. By this stage Tom had sat up, but Mrs Austen's eyes went immediately to Cassandra's torn petticoat, to the blood-stained strip of muslin around Tom's head and to her daughter's stricken face. Cassandra didn't even glance at her mother. All her attention was on Tom, and her whole soul was in her eyes as she tenderly stroked his hand. It was true love, Jane and I agreed afterwards – no one, remarked Jane wisely, would ruin a good petticoat for a man unless they loved him.

* * *

It's bedtime now and I should be asleep, but I can't sleep. My candle was blown out about an hour ago by Mrs Austen when she came in to say goodnight. I just lay tossing and turning for half an hour. Jane was asleep so I could think my own thoughts. At the moment everything in my mind seemed to be about falling in love and getting married. I was thinking of Cassandra and Tom Fowle and how she had looked when she thought he was injured. I thought about the two of them a lot, of the way they kept look- ing at each other – during meals, when they passed each other on the stairs, when they danced together in the evenings. And then I thought of the handsome William Chute, sitting on his black stallion with the hunting horn in his hand. It's the first time, really, that I seriously thought about falling in love.

In the end I got out of bed and came to sit by the fire with my journal on my knee. There is enough light from the fire to write by. So I've written down the bit about Cassandra and about the fun that Jane and I had in the church, filling out the forms for call- ing the banns.

But in a few years this will all be very serious for us.

I will have to find a husband.

And it will have to be a rich husband, if Mrs Austen is right.

After all, my mother was much poorer than Jane's

father, who is rector of a parish and has a large farm. I know that she only left fifty pounds a year for my maintenance. Edward-John won't want to give me anything when I marry – even if he did, Augusta wouldn't allow him.

I will have no fortune, so who will marry me?

Jane was telling me about a girl who lived near to one of her cousins. This girl was aged barely sixteen when she ran away with an army captain. According to Jane, she was attracted by the soldier's red coat! When her relations caught up with her, the couple had already been living together as man and wife so there was nothing to be done except to get them married as soon as possible.

I just can't imagine!

Thursday, 10 March 1791

It's nice sharing a bedroom with Jane. Cassandra and Jane used to share it, but now Cassandra has her own bedroom as James has left home. I like sharing with Jane; it is good fun to be able to chat together. We stayed awake so late last night, talking and joking — and even after that I had got out of bed and written in my journal — so this morning we both woke up late, and had barely enough time to wash our faces and just smooth our hair before running down to breakfast.

After breakfast I asked Jane to come and help me to brush my hair and said I would do hers for her after that. My mother always said that to have nice hair you had to give it one hundred strokes of the brush twice every day.

When we got to our bedroom, Jane started doing an imitation of her mother scolding the butcher.

'I really cannot think, Mr Baxter, that you can know what you're talking about. How anyone could pretend to be a butcher and sell those pieces of scrap meat for gigot chops, I declare to goodness, I just do not know. These were no more gigot chops than I am a donkey. Do I look like a donkey, Mr Baxter?'

I asked Jane why she did not like her mama. There is something about the way she imitates her mother that makes me feel a little uncomfortable.

'She's not my mother,' said Jane, and her voice was all sort of hissy and low. 'My real mother has been imprisoned in a lonely castle hundreds of miles away. She's been locked up there since I was born. That woman's just my stepmother.'

'What?!' I said, and I must have screamed it because Jane put her hand over my mouth.

'Shh,' she said mysteriously. 'Terrible things can happen in this house. Haven't you read Mrs Parson's book *The Mysterious Warning*? Did you hear that creak last night at midnight? And those footsteps coming slowly up the stairs? Did you hear a dripping sound?'

In a way I found it funny, but in another way I felt uncomfortable. It wasn't really like one of Jane's weird stories where you can tell that, inside, she is finding it all just as funny as you are. Jane actually sounded bitter when she spoke of her mother. I tried to think of something to divert her.

I reminded Jane that since her mother is my aunt — and my mother's sister — then she couldn't possibly be Jane's stepmother. As if my mother would have kept that piece of family news from me! I said all of this in a joking tone of voice. I hoped that she would laugh, but she didn't. She just kept on brushing my hair until she had finished the hundred strokes.

'Ah, mothers don't very often tell their daughters the truth.' Jane's voice sounded sort of hollow. I twisted round again and saw that she was laughing now and I laughed too, with relief. I brushed her hair and then there was the sound of the kitchen door opening.

'Jane, Jenny, come and do your drawing lesson!' Mrs Austen sounded impatient, so we rushed down. She was standing tapping her foot in the parlour. She had promised my brother and sister-in-law that we would do some lessons every day, but really the poor woman had hardly any time for us. She had to look after the pupils' meals and clothing, see to the dairy and the butter making, the vegetables and the baking, and supervise the servants and the monthly washwoman. In reality, she did not have the time to tutor us also. She tried to get Cassandra to take over our education, but Jane argued so much that Cassandra had refused to have anything to do with teaching us. Now Mrs Austen just told us to draw a farm and then she left the room.

I did my best, but Jane did her worst, on purpose. Mrs Austen was not pleased when she came flying in half an hour later. We hadn't done much as we had been discussing Tom and William Chute.

'Jane, your cow looks like a pig and your ducks  look like hens,' she scolded. 'You can just sit there and rub it out and do it again and again until you show some improvement. I declare, I'm quite ashamed of you! Now what is that Betty Dawkins doing with those sheets? I declare to the Lord, she is trailing them on the yard. She must be the worst washerwoman I've ever had.'

And then she went running out of the door, and when we looked out of the window we saw her flying across the yard with her pattens clicking on the muddy cobbles.

I went on with my cow, shading it very carefully. Jane's mama scared me a little. My own mother never used to scold like that all the time. Still, I liked Mrs Austen much better than I liked Augusta, and she was a very busy woman, so it was not surprising that she found Jane a bit of a trial. My mother only had me to look after – not a whole household of about twenty people.

I tried to keep my mind on my drawing and keep the thoughts of my mother out of my head. It worked best like that, I found.

'Look, Jenny!' Jane had been rubbing out, but she had made her cow look worse – now it looked like a real pig with a curly tail and a lot of little piglets in a long line behind it. There was a balloon coming out of one piglet's mouth and it said, *'Mother's cross.'*

'You'd better rub that out,' I said, but Jane is stubborn.

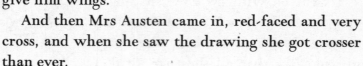

'No, I won't,' she said. 'I think that piglet looks like a little cherub. I'll give him wings.'

And then Mrs Austen came in, red-faced and very cross, and when she saw the drawing she got crosser than ever.

'Jenny, you go up to your room and read a book until I call you. Jane, come with me. I am going to speak to your father about you.'

Jane came in just as I was drawing a picture of Tom Chute. She looked quite normal and she hadn't been crying, so I didn't think that her father was too annoyed with her.

'That's pretty good,' she said, examining the picture. 'Give me your pencil.'

I handed over the pencil and she put whiskers on Tom's face. 'Imagine kissing a man with whiskers,' she said, and we both giggled. I was glad that I hadn't drawn the picture of William yet. I wouldn't have liked that to be spoiled.

'Anyway, the rain has stopped now and I have to go and draw a picture of our house,' said Jane. 'That's the punishment that my father gave me. *I suppose even Jane can draw a house.*' She imitated her mother's high, scolding voice exactly.

I said that I would help her as I didn't want her to get into any more trouble; when Jane is in that sort of mood she gets more and more sarcastic and I get worried about what she might do or say next.

There was no sign of Mrs Austen when we went out and stood in the carriage sweep, so I took the drawing pad from Jane. It would be easier to do the picture myself.

'Four diamond-paned windows downstairs and a door with a porch in front of it in the middle, and five windows upstairs and then three garret windows in the roof,' said Jane, peering over my shoulder. 'Don't forget the two sets of chimneys on each side of the roof. Hurry up; don't fuss. I want to go and do something more interesting.'

I wished that she would leave me alone because she was making me nervous, but I didn't want to suggest that she should go and feed the hens and leave me in peace to finish drawing the house. If Mrs Austen came out now I could hand the drawing quickly to Jane, but if she was not there then I would be in trouble too, and I hate being scolded.

As I shaded the eight-paned windows I asked Jane if she minded being scolded.

'No, why should I? They're all so stupid. I just make up jokes when my mother is scolding me, and then I mimic her to the boys. It's lucky that the boys are here. They are such fun. I like Tom Fowle the best. Last year he pulled me down the three flights of stairs on a tablecloth.'

'I thought you liked Tom Chute.' I determined that no one would pull me down the stairs on a tablecloth. I could understand my mother pitying Mrs Austen. The boys are quite noisy and they do make a lot of work in the house, running in and out in muddy boots. This is a very different school to Mrs Cawley's Seminary for Young Ladies. I suppose the Austens and my brother thought they were sending us to a place that would be like another home for us, because they imagined it would be like Steventon.

'Oh, I'm going to marry Tom Chute and I'll leave Tom Fowle for Cassandra,' said Jane carelessly. 'Why don't you draw one of the casement windows open and Mama shouting out of it at someone? That's the way our house is usually. Give me the pencil and I'll draw her.'

'No, don't, you'll spoil it.' I turned away from her and began to mark in the roof tiles. I hated to rush a drawing, but Jane was in a wild mood and I thought I'd better get it finished quickly. I needn't make it too good; Jane was much cleverer than me, but I was better at drawing.

'You do the front door,' I said, handing the board to her when I had finished the roof. The drawing looked quite nice and I hated to have it spoiled, but I thought it was better that she should be doing something. Any minute now she would get bored and would be off climbing a tree or something. And then her mother would look out of the window and be furious. Jane was funny. One minute she was talking about love and marriage, and the next she was behaving like some sort of boy.

I told Jane not to forget to put nine windows in the top half of the door, trying to sound bossy.

Jane had finished the door in one minute and then went flying into her father's study to give the drawing to him. The sun was coming out so I went to fetch my bonnet. My mother always told me that I should keep the sun off my face or my complexion would get brown.

'Let's go down to the village,' said Jane as soon as she came out. 'We won't need to wear pattens because the ground is hard with all the frost. I hate wet, dull

springs, don't you? And I really
hate wearing pattens.'

I agreed with her. I certainly
dislike wearing pattens too.
I hate the way your foot is
up so high and your ankle
twists.

The road to the village was still nice and dry. Our
feet stayed clean and I didn't get any mud on my petticoat. It was a lovely afternoon, with the hedges or-
namented with tiny snow-white buds of blackthorn
and curling strands of
bright green wood-
bine and the ditches
lined with white and
yellow daffodils. I've
drawn them here in my
journal. They would
make a lovely picture
in watercolours.

Steventon village is a poor sort of place. I suppose
there are about thirty cottages there and they all look
a bit dirty and wretched. Jane seemed to know most
people and even teased a girl called Bet about seeing
her with Mr Austen's bailiff.

And then a boy came up to us. I didn't know how
old he was, but he was strange-looking. He was very

small, as small as an eleven-year-old perhaps, but his face was older. He looked very odd as he came shambling up to us making a strange noise in the back of his throat, just like a cock crowing, with his left hand jerking around as if he had no control over it. I got a terrible fright and jumped back, but he kept coming. He was making for Jane. I was very scared. It looked as if he was going to attack her. And then he sort of threw himself at her. I looked all around, seeking help, but no one seemed to be taking any notice. Two women were drawing water from a well, another was herding her ducks to the pond and Bet, the girl that Jane had joked with, was picking up a little boy who had fallen over.

But Jane didn't seem worried. She was laughing. And then she put her arms round him. She kissed him. 'George,' she kept saying. 'What's the matter, George? Look, here's Jenny come to see you.'

And then she turned around. I was still scared, but I tried not to show it.

'I'm pleased to meet you, George,' I said primly.

'Jenny is your cousin, George,' said Jane, and the boy made his strange crowing noises.

I didn't know what to think. How could this boy be my cousin? My mother had only one sister – Jane's mother – and only one brother who had no children, and my father came from a different part of the country.

Jane had her arm around the boy. She was looking into his face lovingly and then she turned and looked at me. She wore an odd, defiant expression.

'George is my brother, Jenny,' she said quietly.

I'm not sure what I said or how I looked. I remember stammering something stupid like, 'Pleased to meet you, George,' again, but my mind was in a whirl. How could this boy be Jane's brother? I had never heard of him, and he didn't live at Jane's house.

And then I began to feel a bit ashamed of myself, standing there so stiffly and awkwardly. I saw George look at me and I hoped that he could not read my thoughts. Jane was talking to him as though he were a small child, so, on the impulse of a moment, I bent down and picked three tiny wild daffodils and handed them to him.

I think he was a bit puzzled by them, turning them round and round in his hand.

I was glad that I had done it though, because Jane smiled with that lovely smile she has when she is pleased, and then George smiled and then he handed the flowers to Jane and she smelt them and then he smelt them and sneezed, and Jane laughed at the expression on his face and then he laughed and I laughed too.

And the three of us just stood there in the evening sunshine until the girl Bet came up and took George by the hand and led him away, telling him it was time for his supper, and Jane and I were left together.

What could I say?

Even now I am not sure what would have been the right thing to say.

You see, dear journal, I didn't want to hurt Jane's feelings. A thousand questions jumped into my mind, but I didn't want to say anything like, 'How on earth could George be your brother?' or, 'Why is he not living in your house?' or, 'Why has his name never been mentioned?'

Jane said nothing, just stood there looking at me with an odd expression on her face. In the end I just said — and I said it as carelessly as I could, just as though I were talking about Charles or Frank — 'Isn't it funny the way that boys never appreciate flowers?'

And then we both laughed again and Jane said, 'Race you back to the gates.' And we both ran in the frosty air until we were breathless.

When we stopped, Jane slipped her hand inside my arm. I didn't say anything for a moment, but then I asked her whether she wanted to talk about George, but she just shook her head so I didn't say any more.

When we came back from seeing George, Tom Chute was here, chatting with Frank about shooting the crows that were robbing the seed corn from his father's farm. He called out a cheerful greeting to

Jane and she teased him about his coat; I gathered it was a new one, but Jane was pretending that he had robbed a scarecrow for it. I went on ahead of her into the house – I was still a bit shy of all the joking and teasing that went on between Jane and the neighbouring boys.

Mrs Austen was in the hall and she had an invitation card in her hand and a smile on her face, but she waited until Jane came in before showing us the card.

'The Chutes are having a supper dance at the Vyne on Saturday.' She looked quite excited. Mrs Austen loved a dance. When we rolled up the carpet in the evening and the boys danced with Cassandra, Jane and myself, she played the piano, but sometimes Cassandra took over and her mother partnered with someone like Gilbert East or Tom Fowle, looking as if she was really enjoying herself. I must say that for her age she danced in a very sprightly fashion.

'A supper dance!' I could hardly breathe with excitement. Mrs Austen smiled at the look on my face and Jane took hold of both my hands and whirled me round the hall until we were both dizzy.

Friday, 11 March 1791

Something very exciting happened today. Just before supper Jane was looking out of the window and she gave a shriek.

'A donkey! Oh, a lovely donkey! Frank's got a donkey!'

'What?!' Mr Austen got out of his chair. 'He hasn't broken the knees of his new pony!'

'No, he's riding the pony. He's just leading the donkey.' Jane rushed out and I went with her and the rest of the family followed.

'It's for Jenny,' Frank said when he dismounted. 'William Chute gave it to me. He said that Jenny could learn to ride on a donkey. He said that . . .' Here Frank frowned a bit, but then said gruffly, 'He said, "She's a bit shy and nervous, that pretty little cousin of yours. She'll be better with a donkey until she gets a bit of confidence."'

I blushed, but no one took any notice. They were too busy inspecting the donkey, stroking him, looking at his feet, passing hands down his back and estimating how old he was by looking at his teeth. Mrs Austen gave me a sharp, appraising sort of glance – rather like the way that everyone was appraising the donkey, I thought – but no one else seemed to find it strange that a young man should send a present like that to a girl he hardly knows.

* * *

After supper when Jane and I were clearing away the plates Mrs Austen came in, closing the door behind her with a firm bang. Jane raised her eyebrows and said, 'Uh-oh,' under her breath.

'Jenny dear, it was very kind of William Chute to send you a donkey, and I suppose you may keep it, but in general it's not a good idea for a young girl to accept presents from a young man who is not related to her, unless, of course, they are engaged to be married.' Mrs Austen's speech came out in her usual rush of words.

I felt my cheeks turning scarlet with embarrassment.

'A donkey!' said Jane contemptuously. 'Who cares about a donkey? It's not as if he sent her an Arabian mare. Donkeys are two a penny around here.'

'Now, Jane,' said Mrs Austen crossly, 'don't be ridiculous. I'm talking about the propriety of accepting a present from a young man. Young girls like you two have to be immensely careful of your reputation. Nothing scares off a good matrimonial proposal like rumours about a girl being fast.' She lowered her voice to a hissing whisper. 'Men talk together in card rooms and drinking places about girls like that.'

I told her that I didn't mind giving it back. I could hear my voice shaking. Her words made me wonder what she would say if she knew I had walked alone at night with a strange young man through the streets of Southampton. I could even feel my ears burning as I thought of how he had looked at me so gently with his beautiful brown eyes and how he took my hand and tucked it through his arm. Would Captain Thomas Williams talk about me in card rooms and drinking places?

Mrs Austen was looking at me so piercingly that I was afraid that she could read my thoughts. I could feel tears welling up in my eyes.

'You're upsetting Jenny,' said Jane. 'Anyway, if you send the donkey back you make a big fuss of the whole thing.'

Mrs Austen turned her attention from me to Jane. She took a deep breath and I thought she was furiously angry, but then she surprised me by saying, 'I suppose that might be true. Well, I'll get Mr Austen to write a note to William Chute thanking him for the donkey and saying that the two girls will enjoy it. In that way it will divert attention from Jenny. Don't be upset, dear. I have to tell you these things since your poor mother is not here to do it — it's just for your own good. You know it is important for you, as well as for Jane and Cassandra, to get a good offer of marriage.'

And then she was gone, whirling from the room, and we could hear her shouting to the kitchen maid about cleaning out the fire in the breakfast parlour.

'Anyway, she's going to get a bit of a shock about Cassandra,' said Jane, her lips curling in amusement. 'Guess what, Miss Goody-Two-Shoes Cassandra has a little looking glass in her cabinet that I've seen her kissing.

What's the betting that Tom Fowle gave it to her?'

I dried my eyes and laughed. 'And I kissed the donkey earlier. Don't tell your mother that!'

Tonight Jane told me about George.

I had been waiting since yesterday for her to tell me, but I didn't want to push her.

And this was the way our conversation went. It was like a play. It was beginning to get dark, but I didn't light my candle. Jane sat on the window seat — one of those windows that I drew yesterday. As she spoke she played with the catch and sometimes opened and closed the window softly, like someone idly swinging a door. I sat on the bed and watched her face. I could see her because there was still some light, but she couldn't see my face because I was in the shadows.

'You see,' said Jane, 'George was born like that. He was born with something wrong with him.'

I watched the way her mouth tightened and her eyes filled with tears.

'Go on, say something,' she said fiercely.

I couldn't think what to say, and in the end I just asked her why it was such a secret.

'Because my mother is ashamed of him, that's why.' Jane's voice hissed like it does when she is reading out a story about a villain. And then when I said nothing she said impatiently, 'Well, go on, ask me why my mother is ashamed of George.'

I could guess why, but I asked the question all the same.

'Because she cares about money more than anything else! She wants all the boys to be rich and famous and she wants Cassandra and me to marry men with big estates. At least she has hopes for Cassandra — she's pretty and accomplished. If only she can keep her from marrying Tom Fowle, Cassandra might make a splendid match. I don't think she has much hope for me. If I can't even draw a cow, she can hardly say that I am accomplished, can she? And I'm not very pretty either, am I? My cheeks are too red and my mouth is too small.'

I told Jane I thought she was very pretty and that she has a much better nose than I have, but she wasn't listening to me. Her cheeks were bright red now, and her eyes were glittering. I felt like crying. I didn't know what to do.

'How old is George?' I asked. 'Is he younger than you?'

Jane shook her head. 'No, he's older than Henry and older than Edward — wonderful Edward who managed to get a rich cousin to adopt him. That's one of us off our mother's hands.' She was nearly spitting out the words. 'Now she doesn't have to bother about Edward and she can boast about him. That makes her forget that one of her children is deformed and can't speak or read or write. She tells everyone that she has five boys and two girls. I think that she even manages to convince herself of that sometimes.'

'Is that why you pretended she was your step-mother?' I felt very sorry for Jane. Sometimes I feel as if she is older than me, but now she seemed like a little sister who was upset because she was hurt. I went across, sat beside her on the window seat, put my arms around her and gave her a hug.

'I wish she *were* my stepmother.' Jane's voice was choked, as if she wanted to cry but was not allowing herself. She pulled away from me and stood with her back turned. Her voice was hoarse and choked when she said, 'If she were my stepmother, it wouldn't matter that I hate her.'

'But George is definitely your brother, your real brother?' I tried to sound sort of casual, but I had to know the truth. For a moment I wondered if this was just one of Jane's stories. Perhaps she had seen this poor unfortunate in the village and had made up the tale because she was sorry for him.

'Of course he's my brother. I've got six brothers, not five.'

And then Jane ran from the room and slammed the door. I heard her running down the stairs. I guessed that she was going into the privy at the back of the house and that she would lock herself in there until she finished crying.

And I've written all this in my journal. Now I'm going to lock it and I am going to hang the key around my neck.

Saturday, 12 March 1791

Today was a day that I am never going to forget in my life. I have never had a day like it. It all started at breakfast time, when Mr Austen looked up from his book and asked, 'Who's going to walk up to Deane Gate Inn to meet James and Henry from the New-bury coach?'

'I'm going riding with Harry Digweed,' said Frank.

'What about you, Jane and Jenny? Will you go?'

'Yes, let's, shall we, Jenny?' Jane sounded enthu-siastic. I was glad to see that she looked herself this morning. I nodded happily. It was very exciting meet-ing people off the stagecoach. I even enjoyed going with Jane to collect the letters from Deane Gate Inn.

'I'll come too then,' said Frank, suddenly chang-ing his mind. 'Harry won't mind what time I arrive. His mother can never get him out of bed in the morning.'

'And me,' said Charles.

'You'd better wash your face first,' said Jane smartly.

'Dear, dear, look who's talking,' said Mrs Austen, but she was smiling as she said it. She was in a very good mood. She was excited that James — her favour-ite son, according to Jane — was coming for a visit. She hadn't seen him for months. I gathered that James studied very hard, unlike Henry, who, apparently, liked to amuse himself and to attend every ball in the neighbourhood.

The coach was late, so we needn't have hurried. When it arrived we saw James and Henry sitting up in front beside the driver. They were glad to get down and to walk with us. They said they were frozen as they had set off in the early morning, but they were both in very good spirits. I had a good look at them so that I could compare their likenesses with the pictures in my journal.

And this is what they look like. They are both quite tall and they both had greatcoats, which they took off and slung over their bags as they walked along. James has the small thin nose and pale skin of his father and he has blond hair — I don't know the colour of Mr Austen's hair because he is always wearing a wig. Henry is quite like Jane in appearance, dark-haired and dark-eyed. Both were dressed in the same way, in well-fitting white trousers, a blue coat with a stand-up velvet collar, and a white shirt with a high stock tied round the neck in a loose bow. They both wore their own hair and they wore it quite long, almost touching their shoulders. I've tried to do a picture here of them and I think it's quite good.

Henry gave Jane a great hug when he descended. She is obviously his favourite. Jane was so excited to see him and straight away started to tell him about all of her latest stories. James wasn't so interested in her. I thought I liked Henry better than James. He was very friendly to me and paid me some compliments, telling me how well I looked and that he liked my cloak and that the blue bonnet suited me.

'I've decided on a play for our end-of-team taster production, Frank,' said James, as we all went at a brisk pace down the hill. 'It's Sheridan's *The Rivals*. There are parts for everybody in it and I've written a prologue and an epilogue. I've been in touch with Cousin Eliza and she has promised to be Mrs Malaprop.'

'She will be excellent, won't she, Frank?' Henry had an amused grin. I thought he was probably like Jane in his sense of humour as well as in appearance. 'No one can be as funny as Eliza.'

'And Cassandra will be Lydia.'

'Then you'll have to have Tom Fowle as Captain Jack Absolute,' said Henry with a little of his mother's decisiveness. 'Tom's not much of an actor, bless him, but he will play the part of a lover of Lydia very well indeed.'

So everyone knows the secret about Tom Fowle and Cassandra, I thought. It was highly unlikely that Mrs Austen didn't know it also.

'What about me and Jenny?' asked Jane. James was definitely not Jane's favourite brother, I thought. Her voice was quite sharp.

'Well, I'd forgotten about Jenny, but I thought you might be the maid,' said James carelessly. Even though he is quite handsome, I didn't think he was as nice as Henry.

'Who's going to act the part of Julia, then?' Jane sounded quite pert and James clicked his tongue disapprovingly at her.

'Don't say that Father has allowed you to read *The Rivals*,' he said with a stern look. 'I must say that I think he should supervise your reading. There are parts that are quite shocking. I've cut them out of our production.' He sounded so prim when he said that, and Jane made such a comical face, that I found it hard to hold in a fit of the giggles.

'Dear, dear,' said Henry with a wink at Jane. 'She's got a point though, James. Who is going to be Julia?'

I was looking at Henry with interest because I remembered Jane saying that he was her favourite brother. She was right – he was very handsome – taller than William Chute, although he was years younger. He saw me looking at him and gave me a very wide smile and a quick wink. I looked away quickly; I could feel one of my embarrassing blushes coming on.

'I thought of Frank.' James gave his young brother a sidelong glance. 'He could wear one of mother's old gowns.'

'Well, you can think again.' Frank sounded quite alarmed. 'My voice is broken now.' He was so upset that his voice rose and cracked and he turned very red. James looked dubiously at him and I had to bite my lip to stop myself from laughing. There was no way that Frank, with his breaking voice and moustache fluff around his upper lip, could pass for a girl.

'Perhaps Charles then. And I will be Sir Anthony Absolute, the wealthy baronet.' James smiled to himself; his good humour had come back. He seemed to fancy the part of a baronet.

'What about Jenny for the part of Julia? Wouldn't she be lovely?' enquired Henry. 'Are you good at fainting, Jenny?'

I said that I wasn't. I remember that I almost shouted it. Or perhaps it was more like a squeak. I definitely didn't want to act in a play and I didn't think that I would be able to faint. I said that they should let Jane be Julia and I would be the maid.

'No, Jenny will be perfect as Julia,' said Henry. 'I'm going to be Faulkland and I am madly in love with you. Don't worry, Jenny. I'll help you to learn your words. We'll make a great pair.'

I didn't say any more after that. I liked the idea of

Henry helping me to learn my part in the play. And I quite liked the idea of him pretending to be in love with me.

'What do I have to say as the maid?' demanded Jane.

'Not much,' said James. He was frowning. I felt a bit uncomfortable. I think that he didn't like all his arrangements being upset.

'I'll make some more up then. I'll make up something funny. The maid could be made very amusing,' said Jane.

'And I don't mind being a servant or something,' offered Frank.

'In fact, you'll do anything as long as you don't have to wear a dress; it wouldn't do for the sailors on board the good ship *Perseverance* to find out about that,' joked Henry.

'By the way, Frank,' said James carelessly, 'I was down in Southampton with the two Portsmouths, Newton and Coulson, and they took me on board one of *Perseverance*'s sister ships, I think it was the *Bonaventure*. The captain gave us dinner, and I must say I thought it was a very smart, well-run ship.'

'What's his name?' asked Frank. He was always intensely interested in anything to do with the navy. He was always talking to me about it. That must be where I had heard the name *Bonaventure* — it seemed familiar to me.

'Oh . . .' James snapped his fingers with the air of

a man who has a lot to think of. 'One of those ordinary names: Thompson — Jameson — Williamson — no,
it was Williams, Captain Thomas Williams. Come to
think of it, I almost forgot' — he turned to me and
I could feel the palms of my hands icy with cold
sweat — 'yes, he knows Jenny — at least, when I told
him that I lived at Steventon, he asked me whether I
had a cousin called Jenny Cooper.'

It was amazing that he couldn't hear the thumping of my heart — that they could not all hear it.
The beats sounded so loud to me that I even expected
the mare and foal who were cropping the grass in
the field over the hedge to lift their heads and stare
at me.

'How many guns had she, James?' I began to be able
to breathe a little again when Frank asked that question. I clutched Jane's hand, and when she squeezed
mine back I knew that she understood the danger I
was in.

'I don't know — I never looked.' James sounded
bored with the whole subject, but he was still half
looking over his shoulder as if waiting
for me to say something. I stared fixedly
at the star-like shape of a tiny golden
celandine on the opposite side of the
road. Jane let go of my hand and
moved up next to her eldest brother. I
dug my nails into the soft part below my
thumbs while I listened to her.

'James, I don't want to be just a maid. Why can't I be Mrs Malaprop? I could do it just as well as Eliza. Why do you have to be the one giving the orders all the time? Why can't we all choose our favourite parts?' Jane had a very petulant tone and now no one was looking at me.

'Well, you can't, and that's that! The trouble with you, Jane, is that you always think that you can get your own way. I agree with Mother. It's time that you started to behave like a young lady, not a spoiled child. Aren't you supposed to be in school or something?'

'My dear man, I'm too busy with my writing for things like school,' said Jane primly. 'I am just about to embark on writing a play in three acts, which I shall dedicate to you, James, and I hope that it will make you ashamed of your ill-temper to such a talented person as myself.'

Even James had to laugh at that, and then Henry took his arm and began asking his advice about a new horse that he was going to buy from John Portal, one of the neighbours. James, of course, had plenty of advice to give, and Jane and I gradually got further and further and further to the rear of them as we lingered to pick some primroses.

'Oh, Jane,' I said, when we went up to our bedroom to wash our hands, 'what will I do? Do you think that Captain Williams has told James all about me?'

'No, I don't think so.' Jane dried her hands on the

towel by the fire and tipped the water into a pail below the washstand. She looked quite calm when she turned round and I began to feel a little better. 'No, I'm certain that he didn't. James would have looked quite different. He's a very fussy, pernickety sort of man, but he didn't even seem very interested. If he had heard anything like that he would have been on to Mama instantly with a big, long, pompous letter and when he met you he would have looked at you like this.' And Jane tilted her nose in the air and looked down it with such a self-important and haughty manner that I had to smile.

I smoothed out the soft petals of the primroses and shut them between the leaves of an old book, and began to feel hopeful that Thomas had not told James how we met, and I asked Jane if she agreed.

'Thomas!' teased Jane. 'Oh, so he's Thomas! Don't you know that it is considered very fast for a young lady to use the first name of a young man? My dear creature, you quite make me blush!'

Jane could always make me laugh, but I pleaded with her to tell me what to say if James asked me about Thomas in front of his parents. I couldn't imagine Mrs Austen being diverted by Frank's questions about gun ports.

'You could say, "La, my dear cousin, my acquaintance is with admirals, vice-admirals, rear admirals, all kinds of admirals, but as for the inferior ranks I know little: post-captains may be very good sorts of men, but to tell you the truth, I don't know one from the other.'''

She made me giggle, but I begged her to think of something that would be believed by her mother. I was feeling much better though. It did look as if Thomas had said nothing about meeting me at midnight. I promised myself that I would have a look at his portrait in my journal and see whether I could make him even more handsome. I would stick the primroses into my journal once they were pressed and I would think of him every time that I looked at them.

'Or you could just open your eyes very wide and say, "I'm not sure, Aunt. Perhaps he was one of Augusta's visitors." Don't worry about blushing – you often do blush when my mother asks you a question. Now let's go down and see if there's any toast left. I'm hungry again after the walk.'

As soon as James and Henry had had breakfast, we all went out into the barn where the play was going to take place. I could see that they had set plays there before because there were some pieces of old furniture, carefully covered over with straw, and a pair of old curtains were in a box at the back. Henry started to paint the scenery on big pieces of board, and Jane and I were set to work sweeping the stage while Charles and Tom Fowle put out some benches for the audience.

'I've got some small parts for the Terry children and for the Digweed boys,' said James.

'Just so that their parents will come to watch your play,' said Jane. 'That should build up the audience numbers — otherwise we might just have our dear parents and no one else.' I thought that was quite funny and I giggled, and then I was sorry because I thought James looked cross.

'Why don't you read the play to us while we're working, James,' said Henry, starting to paint a blue sky across the top of the board. The lime wash wasn't quite dry, but he worked some white into clouds and it made the blue sort of hazy and the sky looked very realistic. I told him that I thought it was very clever and he gave me a lovely smile and told me that the play was set in Bath so he was going to do two sets of scenery, one outside the houses in the Crescent and one drawing-room scene.

'Well, this is Jenny's bit.' James gave me a fright. I didn't know that I would be called upon to say anything so soon. I had a feeling that James wanted me to be useless so that he could cast someone else. My mouth was dry and I could say nothing. He frowned a bit and then he said the words again and looked at me impatiently. Henry repeated them in a very high-pitched voice and that made everyone laugh so I relaxed a bit and repeated the sentence.

Then James read Jane's bit. It was just, '*Yes, madam.*' Jane didn't like that and she put in a funny bit about hiding the book that I had been reading and getting out a boring book by Dr Johnson instead.

'Oh, why not,' said Henry when James objected. 'It's quite amusing.' So Jane went on putting in funny bits and by the end of a quarter of an hour her part was bigger than mine.

'Now you must say this in a very weak tone of voice, Jenny,' ordered James. 'Say, *"I think that I am about to faint."*'

I repeated the words but they didn't satisfy James. 'Your voice must be weak but clear,' he objected. 'You'll never be heard in the back row if you speak like that.'

'We haven't got a back row,' shouted Charles, 'and we're not having one either, because I'm going out now. I promised to help John Bond with marking the new lambs.'

'Try it again, Jenny,' said Henry, busily putting the finishing touches to a stately house.

I tried again, but I knew by the frown on James's face that he didn't think much of it.

'Now, Jane, you say, *"Oh, my dear mistress has fainted."*'

'That's boring,' objected Jane. 'In any case, the audience can see – even the back row, if there's going to be one – can see that she's fainted. Why should I say that? It isn't interesting or funny, and it doesn't tell anything new.'

And then she clasped her hands together and shrieked, '"*Oh, my dear mistress, don't faint to that side; that's not your best side. Faint to the right and then you will be in a good position when the gentle-men come in."* That's better, isn't it, Jenny? Go on — say your bit again.'

I said it, and it did sound much better this time, probably because I was trying not to laugh and that made my voice sound all quavery and when Jane said her lines then I collapsed in a heap, as elegantly as I could, but making sure that I was on my right side, and Henry clapped, sending a shower of green paint spots over his scenery.

Today was a very busy day. Now it is night-time and Jane and I have brushed each other's hair and we are here in our bedroom; Jane is on the bed with her writing desk balanced on her knee, reading from a book and scribbling on a piece of paper, and I am sitting at the washstand, writing in my journal. We have two candles in our room now. Jane asked her father whether we could and he immediately said yes, so Jane fetched another one with-out asking her mother.

'We need two because I like to read and Jenny likes to write in her journal or draw,' she said to her father. I felt very nervous be-cause I think that my aunt, Mrs Austen, is someone who has rules, and that one of her rules is one candle for each bedroom. But Jane is right; we do need two candles.

'What are you reading?' I asked.

'It's a book about teaching people who can't hear and can't talk how to spell out letters using their fingers,' she said briefly. 'I found it in Father's library. Look, it has pictures of how you make the shapes of the letters with your fingers and thumb. I was thinking that if I could teach George his letters, he could talk on his fingers. You see, I have tried and tried to teach him to talk, but he doesn't seem able to learn.'

I said I thought that if he learned his letters, then he could learn to read also – more to please her than anything else. I'm not sure that George, from what I have seen of him, would be able to read. I told Jane that I would help her teach him.

Jane's face lit up and she gave me a big smile. 'Shall we start tomorrow?'

I came across to her bed and peered over her shoulder.

'The A looks a bit like an apple with a stalk standing up,' I said. 'We can start with that. We'll bring him an apple so that he knows what it's all about.'

I was just going to put this journal away when I remembered that Mr Austen, when he heard about it, told me that I should write down my thoughts as well as the day's events.

Let me see . . .

I suppose I'm thinking that it must have been sad

for Mr and Mrs Austen to have a child like George, someone who will never grow into a man like James or Henry. And how Mrs Austen is so fond of James, and Mr Austen is so fond of Henry. I wonder . . . are they extra fond because they are comparing these two, who are so handsome and clever, with poor George? I wonder too if they ever feel sorry for George. He doesn't seem very well looked after down in the village. I think he just shambles about all day. When I saw him he was not properly washed and his hair wasn't combed. If he were well cared for, he would have a look of Charles. He has lovely eyes, and when he saw Jane, they lit up.

And then I start to think about Henry. He is very nice. He paid me a lot of attention today. He admired my hair and how blonde it is. He praised my blue eyes and told me that they reminded him of sapphires. He told me that I am the perfect height, and that he doesn't like girls who are too tall. When we rolled back the carpet in the evening and Mrs Austen played some tunes for country dances, Henry was my partner for all of them and Jane teased me about him.

He looks so very handsome, with his black hair tied behind with a black velvet ribbon and his hazel eyes smiling at me, that I would love to draw a proper picture of him. From the first moment that he arrived, he has paid me attention.

'Isn't Jenny looking so much better?' That was the

first thing he said to his mother when we arrived back from Deane Gate Inn.

'You were raving with fever when he saw you the last time.' Jane made it sound very dramatic. 'He was the one that carried you into the house. And he knelt by your bed and sobbed, "My own dear love, don't you know me?"'

I felt myself getting as red as if I still had a fever, but Henry just laughed and pulled Jane's dark curls. 'Jenny was beautiful even then,' he joked, and then both he and James went into the parlour to have some breakfast and we all followed to talk to them.

'How's the romance getting on in *Jack and Alice*?' enquired Henry, while James told his mother all about Oxford. 'You know about Jane's novel, I suppose,' he said to me. He probably just said it to include me, because everyone knows about Jane's stories.

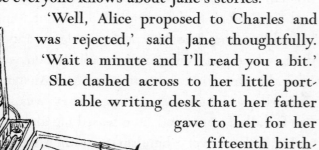

'Well, Alice proposed to Charles and was rejected,' said Jane thoughtfully. 'Wait a minute and I'll read you a bit.' She dashed across to her little portable writing desk that her father gave to her for her fifteenth birthday. She took out her notebook and read aloud in a very dramatic way:

'However, I was determined to make an end to the matter and therefore wrote him a very kind love letter, offering him with great tenderness my hand and heart. To this he returned an angry refusal, but thinking it might be rather the effect of his modesty than anything else, I wrote again offering my undying affection.'

Henry was laughing and I giggled also. Jane was very good at imitating the style of the romances that she loved to read. I wondered what Henry would think of my journal and then I felt myself blush, despite myself. I wish I could learn not to blush. I am always doing it.

Jane has just asked me what I was writing and when I told her it was about reading out to Henry about Alice, she tossed me over a piece of paper.

'Here, you can stick that in your journal,' she said.

I read it through and raised my eyebrows. I told her I didn't think that James would like the dedication. I believe he will think Jane is laughing at him, mentioning his two plays like that.

The Visit

A comedy in 2 acts

Dedication:

To James Austen Esq.

Sir,

The following Drama, which I humbly recommend to your Protection and Patronage, tho' inferior to those celebrated Comedies called 'The School for Jealousy' & 'The Travelled Man', will I hope afford some amusement to so respectable a scholar as yourself, which was the end in veiw when it was first composed by your Humble Servant

the Author.

'Well, Henry liked the dedication that I wrote for him. He said that he would pay me a hundred guineas.' And Jane tossed me another piece of scrap paper.

I asked her whether Henry did pay her a hundred guineas, but I laughed as I asked it and she just laughed as well. From what I've heard of Henry and his spendthrift habits he probably couldn't spare a hundred pennies.

To Henry Thomas Austen Esq.

Sir

I am now availing myself of the Liberty you have frequently honoured me with of dedicating one of my Novels to you. That it is unfinished, I greive, yet fear that from me, it will always remain so, that as far as it is carried, it should be so trifling and so unworthy of you, is another concern to

Your obliged Humble Servant,

The Author.

Messrs Demand & Co. - please to pay the demand of Miss Jane Austen Spinster the sum of one hundred guineas on account of your Humble Servant.

H.T. Austen

105.0.0 pounds

Sunday, 13 March 1791

Yesterday was a wonderful day – the day of the supper dance.

Let me see what I can remember about the Vyne. The house is very big and old-fashioned. Mr Austen told me that that sort of building with the timber beams showing is called Tudor.

The house was full of guests. The Lefroys and Portals and Terrys and Digweeds were there, as well as the Chutes, of course.

When we went to take off our wraps and cloaks in Mrs Chute's bedroom there were three sisters there and Jane introduced them to me. Their name was Bigg and Catherine was the same age as Cassandra, Elizabeth the same age as me, and Alethea the same age as Jane. All of them were dressed very fashionably in gowns of fine soft silk with a sheen. I've drawn a picture of the three of them here.

Catherine

Elizabeth

Alethea

'Jane!' screamed Alethea when we came in. 'I so wanted to see you. What's this I hear about you nearly dying at boarding school?'

'I was carried out of there unconscious,' said Jane dramatically. 'And so was Jenny. We were left for dead.'

'I knew that!' Alethea's eyes were sparkling with excitement. 'I kept asking Papa to bring me over to see you. I know all about it. Wait until you hear!'

'What?' asked Jane. I could see that she was excited. I almost felt a little jealous. It was obvious that Alethea and Jane were great friends. I took a few steps back and waited.

'Have you heard what happened after you left?' Elizabeth took part in the story.

'It was a scandal,' said Catherine to Cassandra. 'Mrs Cawley didn't want anyone to know, but then girl after girl took the fever and parents started rushing down to Southampton and removing their daughters by post-chaise.'

'Maria Bertram wrote to Catherine,' said Alethea.

I said nothing. I remembered Maria and Julia and the insults that they heaped upon me. I remembered their sneers at my poor education and their peals of laughter when I couldn't put together the jigsaw of the countries of Europe and how they had jeered at my lack of artistic knowledge.

'Well, Maria wrote and told us everything,' said Elizabeth, 'and apparently Mrs Cawley had to close the school. Maria and Julia go to a very good school in Bath now.'

'I like your new gowns,' said Cassandra politely to Catherine. She obviously didn't want to spend the evening talking about boarding schools.

'We shouldn't be wearing them really,' said Catherine, 'because they are intended for the Basingstoke Assembly Rooms ball next fortnight.'

'But we begged and begged and in the end Mama said that we could as long as we made very sure to spill nothing,' said Elizabeth primly.

Alethea was whispering something in Jane's ear. I could just hear the words, 'Mama . . . Catherine . . .' And then something about William Chute and then both Jane and Alethea collapsed into fits of giggles and I could see Jane whisper something back in Alethea's ear. Under all the giggles I could only make out one word and that was 'Cassandra'.

'They're made from sarsenet, you see,' Elizabeth was saying, glancing down at the glossy material.

'And they won't wash,' added Catherine.

'So don't you dare make me laugh when we're at supper, Jane,' threatened Alethea. I think she is the one that Jane likes the best. I liked her too as she seemed to be more fun than her sisters, even though I felt a little jealous that I was not part of the whispering and giggling.

'The Biggs must be very rich to be able to afford silk for their girls,' I whispered to Jane as we went out to the hall to greet Mrs Chute and her sons.

'I don't care for the colours too much though,' Jane whispered back with a shrug, and I agreed with her. Catherine had a very bright purple, Elizabeth a strange shade of green and Alethea wore blue — but a very dark blue.

'Muslin is nice when it's new,' said Catherine with a slightly disdainful glance at my gown.

I felt embarrassed. My best gown is more than two years old. It still fits me because I haven't grown at all in that time, but it has been in the washtub so of- ten that it has a washed-out, limp appearance.

'William Chute is here tonight,' whispered Eliza- beth to Jane. 'He's just back from a visit to London. I declare he gets handsomer and handsomer. They say that he doesn't care for balls, only for hunting.'

'I prefer Tom,' said Jane bluntly. 'Cassandra can have William.'

Cassandra gave her a condescending smile and moved away to talk to Catherine. She wasn't listen- ing to Miss Bigg though. Her attention was on the door, and in a moment it was opened and Mr Austen and the boys came in. Cassandra moved towards them, and Tom Fowle's face lit up with a big smile. I saw Mrs Austen's eyes go suspiciously to the two of them, but Jane was by her side in a moment.

'Mama, can't we have some new gowns? These old

muslins are as limp as a piece of lettuce, and mine's far too short,' whispered Jane in her mother's ear. 'Look at the way Elizabeth Bigg keeps twirling to show off the twill weave.' Jane's whisper was very loud, and Mrs Austen frowned at her as we went up to curtsy to Mrs Chute.

There were only three of the Chute family – as well as Mrs Chute, I mean. Our host was William Chute, the man who sent me a donkey; he's the eldest son, the squire. Jane keeps saying that he will die soon because he's sickly and cross and then Tom Chute will be the heir to the estate and she will marry him.

However, I think that's just Jane having fun. William certainly didn't look sickly or cross. He gave me a great welcome and smiled at me when I thanked him for the pretty little donkey, but mostly he just chatted away to Henry and Frank about hunting and about the rumour that a couple of highwaymen were hiding out in the woods outside Steventon. They seemed very excited about that and talked about getting up a party to get rid of these menaces to the stagecoaches.

As well as William, there are Mary, who is older even than Cassandra, and Tom. At seventeen, he's the youngest of the family.

Tom is great fun. I'm not surprised that Jane likes him so well. All during the supper before the dance Mrs Austen and Mrs Chute were having a whispered conversation and Tom and Jane were imitating them, nodding their heads and pinching their lips and saying things like, *'I would never have believed it'*, *'And after all I did for her!'* and *'. . . in my own kitchen, too.'*

'What's the joke, Jenny?' Henry gave me a fright. Mrs Austen stopped whispering and turned round to look at me. Tom and Jane looked like a pair of owls, staring at me with round, serious eyes, and that made me want to giggle even more, especially as I overheard Jane saying to Tom, *'Dear child – she has not been out in such exalted society as this before. She is very young.'*

'She's thinking of how she's going to play the piano for us in a minute,' said William.

'I – I don't play the piano,' I stammered, feeling quite alarmed, although I thought it pleasant of him to try to get me out of an embarrassing moment.

'Let's start the dance,' said Henry. He looked across at me and smiled. I thought that no one in the world could smile like Henry. The smile starts at his mouth and lights up his whole face and then spreads to his bright hazel eyes, which become very soft and dreamy. His gaze lingered on me for a moment and then he turned his smile on to his mother and asked her to play the first dance. Apparently there was a servant in the kitchen with a fiddle who would play the rest of the tunes.

And then, while Mrs Austen was exclaiming about

how out-of-practice she was, Henry whispered across the table. 'You'd like to dance, Jenny, wouldn't you?'

Henry is very good at getting his own way. In a minute, we were all in the long drawing room, where the furniture had been moved to the sides and the floor waxed to a high shine. I'm not sure how I managed to get from the dining room to the drawing room; I was so excited at the idea of dancing, especially with Henry. My legs felt weak, almost as though I were ill again. Henry took my hand, his skin feeling cool to my hot palm, and led me in and then went over to talk to his mother. There were two servants there with fiddles, but Mrs Austen, looking quite good-humoured, sat down at the piano.

'Dance this one with me, Jenny,' said Henry. He held out his hand and I took it. I couldn't believe that he asked me first – before any of the Bigg girls or Mary Chute or anyone. My cheeks were bright red, I know – I could even feel the lobes of my ears glowing. Jane was chatting to Tom Chute as if he were Charles or Frank and she didn't blush at all. She mustn't care anything for him, I thought.

I had three dances with Henry, one with Frank, one with William Chute and then another one with Henry. Jane danced two dances with Harry Digweed, but after that she went back to Tom Chute and they danced together for most of the rest of the evening. Whenever I overheard them they were going on with their game of pretending to be two gossipy old ladies,

saying things like, '*Did you ever know such a thing?*'
and '*Wait till I tell you what she said*' every time
they met and crossed hands in the dance.

'Are you coming to the ball at the Assembly Rooms
at Basingstoke Saturday fortnight?' William asked
me when I was dancing with him.

I told him that would be up to Mr and Mrs Austen
and then he said something rather nice.

'Oh, Henry will make sure that you come! He told
me that he was going, and I don't think that he will
want to go if you are not there to dance with him.
Henry always wants to dance with the prettiest girl
in the room.'

I wondered if he was just being polite, or if he
really did think that. I looked up at him doubtfully.
Perhaps he was just joking. In my mind was always
the memory of my sister-in-law, Augusta, saying to
one of her friends, 'Jenny is such a thoroughly un-
attractive girl, no manner, no style. I declare it em-
barrasses me to take her out with me. Only my duty
to Edward-John persuades me to sacrifice my own
comfort.'

'Don't you believe me?' asked William
as I looked at him uncertainly. 'Prettiest
girl in the room — you'll be the belle
of the ball at Basingstoke!'

I must remember to tell Jane that
I don't think William is cross and
sickly at all. I think he is very nice.

After that I danced with Henry again for the last dance of the evening. I couldn't think of anything to say. I wasn't good at dancing and talking at the same time like Jane did with Tom Chute. Henry didn't say anything either, just smiled at me and pressed my hands gently when we were doing the two-hand turn. I was glad that I didn't have to talk. I was too busy looking at his face. There was something about the way that he looked at me with a half-smile that made my heart thump very fast. From time to time I thought of saying something to break the tension, but I didn't. We stood up opposite Tom Fowle and Cassandra and they didn't say anything either, just gazed into each other's eyes. It was very romantic.

What does Henry think about me? I was wondering about that all the way home in the coach. I thought that he liked me, but I knew that his mother would not approve of his paying attention to me. I was afraid that she might think I was fast if I encouraged him. Earlier in the evening when William Chute brought me back to her after our dance, she had patted me on the arm approvingly and told me that I was looking very well. But all the time as the coach bumped and jolted its way down the road towards Overton and then turned down the narrow laneway from Deane to Steventon, she hardly said a word to me.

All through the journey I kept wishing that I weren't always worrying and being anxious about things. I wish I were more like Jane and just looking for fun all the time. She never seems to care when her mother's in a bad mood — she just laughs and jokes and takes no notice.

And then . . .

When the coach arrived back at Steventon parsonage, Frank and Charles jumped out from the seat at the back. Henry handed out his mother and Tom Fowle handed out Cassandra. They went up the steps side by side while Jane jumped out, taking no notice of Henry, and ran up after Cassandra.

And then, after the others had gone into the house, Henry put out his two arms and lifted me down.

And he held me close for a moment and then he kissed me very quickly.

Not on the hand.

On the cheek.

I don't think that I have ever been so close to a man before. Men smell so different.

I wished that I could stay outside in the starlit garden, just stand quietly by myself and think about everything that happened this evening — think about dancing with Henry — think about Henry kissing me — think about what William Chute said about my being the prettiest girl in the room, even prettier than the fashionably dressed Bigg girls — think about dancing with . . .

Think about Henry . . .

I couldn't though. I had to walk ahead of Henry and go through the porch and into the best parlour.

As soon as we came into the room I thought Mrs Austen looked at me rather critically. I quickly moved away from Henry and went over beside Jane, who was telling her father all about the evening.

'Did you have a good time, Jenny dear?' Mr Austen was so kind to me always.

I told him that I had.

'Not too tired?'

I exclaimed that I could have danced twenty dances more without getting tired, and I think I must have said it very loudly, because everyone looked over at me.

'She was looking very well tonight.' Mrs Austen came across and joined us. 'William Chute paid her a lot of attention. He told his mother that she was the prettiest girl he had seen for a long time.'

'He was only being polite.' I had a quick look at Henry to see if he was jealous of William Chute, but he didn't seem to be interested. And then I felt embarrassed that I had looked at him. I hoped that he hadn't noticed, and I felt my cheeks burn. I knew it was stupid to be always blushing like this, but Mrs Austen didn't seem to be annoyed. She was looking at me in a pleased sort of way. Actually she made me feel quite uncomfortable as her eyes moved up and down. I wished that I were a bit taller.

'This child needs a new gown,' she said eventually.

'What do you say, Mr Austen? Perhaps all of the girls need new gowns. Jane's is too short and Cassandra's has faded and Jenny's—'

'Of course, my dear. Whatever you think best.'

Jane was beside me now, squeezing my hand. I squeezed back. I knew what she was going to say.

'Mama, could we all go to the Basingstoke Assembly Rooms? There's a ball in two weeks' time. The Bigg girls are going and the Chutes. Oh, please say that we may – please, please, please, please!'

'What do you think, Mr Austen?' I knew that Jane had won when Mrs Austen made a pretence of consulting her husband. She is always the one who makes the decisions. She wouldn't have asked him unless she had made up her mind.

'Well, my dear, I would certainly enjoy a game of cards with some of my old friends. The Harwoods should be there and Hugh Digweed and the Portals – we'll make a whist table or two, I dare say.' Mr Austen beamed his gentle smile at Jane's excited face.

'Well, in that case, Mr Austen, perhaps we will hire the coach and go to Basingstoke for the ball.' Mrs Austen did her best to sound like an obedient wife.

Jane and I threw our arms around each other. We were both laughing with excitement. It was a great feeling. I'd never felt so happy in all my life.

'And the new gowns?' enquired Jane. 'Could they be made by a dressmaker?'

'We'll see,' said Mrs Austen, and she gave a broad smile.

'Oh, Mama!' For a moment I thought Jane was going to kiss her mother – she never seems to do this – but she just gave her a lovely wide smile and Mrs Austen smiled back and tugged at one of Jane's dark curls just as Mr Austen did sometimes.

'My mother thinks that William Chute has fallen in love with you,' said Jane as soon as we were safely in our bedroom.

I told her not to be silly, but she put on a very wise, elderly look and told me that he would be a very good match for me.

'Think of the property,' she said solemnly. 'A fine house, a great estate – do you think that you could fall in love with him?'

I giggled, but then I stopped and thought about it. William Chute was very nice but . . .

'Well, what would you say if he proposed to you?' enquired Jane. Her head was on one side and she was looking at me the way you look at someone when you want to capture their likeness to draw a picture of them.

I told her I wasn't sure, and she nodded briskly. 'My dear Jenny, that answers the question. If a lady doubts whether she should accept a man, then she certainly should not do so.'

I was glad that she hadn't asked me whether I

would accept Henry if he asked me. I'm not sure that I would have told her the truth. My feelings for Henry are very private. And I'm not yet sure what they are, exactly!

There is one more thing that I must write.

When I saw Jane and her mother looking at each other in such a friendly way, I felt a terrible sort of pain. I suppose it was jealousy. I miss my mother so much. My feelings and my sorrow got hidden while I was with Edward-John and Augusta. They were so critical of my mother that I never wanted to talk about her. I even stopped myself thinking of her, but now, suddenly, I miss her terribly. For a moment I almost hated Jane for having a mother and father while I have neither.

There was something else that I thought also.

I realized that I had always been feeling guilty when I was staying with Edward-John and Augusta — guilty that I didn't do or say the right thing, guilty that I was a nuisance to them.

But now I have stopped feeling guilty.

They should have been nicer to me, I decided. I did my best not to be a nuisance. I tried hard to please them both. Despite what Augusta whispered to her friends, I probably wasn't an expense to them, since Edward-John had charge of my income from Mama's estate.

I know a bit more about money and what things

cost these days as Mrs Austen is always adding up her accounts in a loud voice and calling Frank to help her. The sum of fifty pounds a year should have more than covered my food and laundry and no one ever thought to buy me new clothes. If Mrs Austen can run a large house and feed her big family on not much more than four hundred pounds a year (Jane told me that is what Mr Austen gets from his position as rector and his farm and the school), then Augusta and Edward-John could not have been out of pocket on my account.

Now I shall lock up my journal and go to bed and dream of the ball at Basingstoke.

And Henry will be there . . .

Monday, 14 March 1791

The Austens' cousin, Cousin Eliza, arrived from Basingstoke this morning just after we finished breakfast. She is going to stay a week, she said.

'I shouldn't have come; I have a hundred things to do, but I couldn't resist a play,' she declared, leaping out of the post-chaise and waving her hands around. She has a strong French accent, though she was born in India and has lived half her life in England. Her hat, with its feather, looked quite French, I thought, and she kissed everyone on two cheeks – she even kissed Jane on two cheeks and then a third time. 'Jane,' she cried in a very foreign way, '*mon chou chou*, how you have grown! And Henry, my cherub, la, I declare you are a man now, Henry.' And then she was off on another round of kissing. Even I got

kissed and my curls patted. Apparently she is a coun-
tess; Henry, for fun, keeps calling her *Madame la
Comtesse*. Her husband is a French nobleman. She
shed tears when she spoke of him, because he is over
in France and as she said herself in her French accent: 'These are revolutionary times.' And
she rolled the letter *r* so that it sounded
as though there were six *r*s at the beginning of *revolutionary*. Even the king and
queen of France are in danger, apparently.
Eliza shed a tear for them too, dabbing at her eyes
with a beautiful, lace-trimmed handkerchief.

*handkerchief
lace-trim*

And then a minute later,
she was whispering behind her
hand with Henry, telling some story
which sounded very scandalous – I
overheard words like 'her bedroom' and
'he was hiding in the closet!' I saw Jane
move her chair a little nearer – so as to pick
up details for her novels, I suppose.

We had great fun today practising for the play.
James's friend John Portal was the villain, Sir Lucius
O'Trigger, an Irish baronet; he had to carry me in
his arms when he was abducting me. I was very embarrassed in the beginning, but he made a joke of it,
pretending that I was too heavy – although he carried
me very easily, as he is very tall and strong. Henry
shouted out, 'Lucky man!' when Mr Portal said that

about my being heavy, and James got annoyed with both of them. No one took any notice though, and Henry winked at me. I do think that Henry likes me. I'm glad that Cousin Eliza is going back to London next week. Henry isn't paying me nearly as much attention as he did yesterday. I'm not as good at flirting as she is. Cassandra says that it is abominable that a married lady should flirt in the way that Eliza does, but Jane said that she has to keep in practise as her husband is across the sea in France.

'Don't be silly, child,' said Cassandra with a superior air. 'Women don't flirt with their husbands.'

'And that's why married women have to have lovers, I suppose,' said Jane. She sounded thoughtful and her face was very serious, but I could see that she was trying to shock Cassandra, who is very prim and proper.

I wish I could flirt. I would love to say witty things to Henry and have him laugh the way that he does with Cousin Eliza. I'm just not good enough at making jokes, or else I am too shy.

Cousin Eliza is a born actress. Even after breakfast this morning, when you would think she would be tired after her long journey from London, she was doing a minuet with Henry around the sitting room, declaring that 'He is the very pineapple of politeness,' and slipping slightly on the polished wood, and the sunlight streaming in through the two casement windows behind her made her look as if she were on a stage. It was like a play that I once saw at Bristol. I made up my mind that I would try to be like Eliza – sophisticated, clever and amusing, the sort of person that would attract men. Of course, she was brought up in India and then France so I might not be able to be as stylish and elegant as she is. Jane and I had a talk about it in our bedroom. We tried waving our hands around and introducing a few words of French into English sentences. And then we practised walking the way that Eliza walks, sort of sweeping around. Of course she had a train, even on her walking gown – it looked so elegant with her stylish spencer fitting so tightly around her bosom and her large hat with a feather in it. I have never seen a hat like that before.

'Men fall at her feet all over Europe,' Jane said with an air that impressed me very much, but then she spoiled it by adding, 'even my father,' and that made us both giggle.

We both pinned our wrappers to the shoulders of our gowns and stuck a couple of new quills in our hair. Then we tried sweeping up and down the bedroom saying, 'la' and *'chérie'* to each other. We both decided that a train certainly made you feel much more elegant – especially as we had to keep our noses in the air in order to prevent the quills falling out of our hair.

And then Jane whispered to me that she had seen Eliza kissing Henry – on the lips too! And that the kiss lasted for ages!

I thought of how I would feel if Henry kissed me like that; I felt quite jealous of Eliza but I didn't want to show it, so when I saw Jane looking at me I said that Eliza had a way of pursing up her lips and perhaps that was what made Henry do it, and Jane nodded wisely. 'That's the secret of sophistication,' she said. 'You must always look as if you are ready to kiss a man once you are alone.'

'What about a girl's reputation though?'

'Perhaps it's better to get married first,' said Jane thoughtfully. 'If you were a sophisticated widow with plenty of money left you by your husband, then you could do what you wanted.'

Monday afternoon, 14 March 1791

Mrs Austen was in very good humour this afternoon. About twelve o'clock, when I began my usual chore of dusting and polishing the sideboard, rubbing up the brass handles on the many drawers and trying to work around the books and papers and cricket balls and spinning tops and an old doll belonging to either Jane or Cassandra and all the other items that littered the shelves and cubbyholes of that huge piece of wall furniture, she stopped me.

'Never mind about that now, dear,' she said. 'Jane, leave the kettle – it can do without a polish for once. Go upstairs and put on your bonnets and cloaks, the two of you; we're going shopping at Overton.'

'We're getting new gowns!' exclaimed Jane.

Mrs Austen nodded. 'Make haste,' she said. 'We should go in the next few minutes. Where is Cassandra? We'll miss the coach. I declare she takes longer over those hens every day.'

'Here I am, Mama.' Cassandra came in with pink cheeks and the three of us went clattering upstairs to get ready.

'Such excitement!' exclaimed Eliza, coming out of her room and smiling with amusement. 'Ah, at your age there is nothing so exciting as a new gown!'

'Are you coming, Eliza?' asked Jane.

'*Chérie*, I would love to, but I am only here for a

few days and I feel that I owe it to your brother to give all of my energies to the play.'

'She's a great performer,' said Jane, grinning as I closed the door of our bedroom behind us. 'She sounds just like a classical actress wedded to her art. I bet she just wants to flirt with Henry.'

'Or James,' I said.

'Or both,' said Jane. And we giggled, but I kept thinking that I hoped Eliza would flirt with James, not Henry.

Overton is a small town compared with Bristol, but still it holds all the shops necessary to the people who live in the countryside around. There are five grocers, two butchers, four tailors, seven shoe-makers, one hairdresser, two breeches makers, a clockmaker and two millinery and haberdashery shops. As soon as we had got down from the coach and Mrs Austen had expressed a hope to the coach-man that there would be clean, dry straw for our feet to rest on when we returned, we went straight to Ford's, the biggest shop in the town.

'You've come just at the right moment, ma'am,' said Mrs Ford when Mrs Austen explained our er-rand. 'I've just got the pretti-est selection of muslins, new in from Bristol.' She bustled off and was back in a moment with her arms laden with a rainbow of stuff, all lovely pale colours: lavenders, yellows, pinks, blues and delicate greens.

'I was thinking of pink for all three,' said Mrs Austen bluntly. 'It would save money.'

Cassandra made a face, and I took my eyes reluctantly from a sky blue. I love blue, and my mother always told me it suited me best of all.

'Why do Jane and Jenny have to have pink?' Cassandra sounded quite upset. 'If we are all dressed the same, it will make me look about fifteen. You know pink suits me best, but I don't want us to look like triplets.' She picked up a pink and gazed at it longingly.

'That's a lovely colour, Miss Austen,' said Mrs Ford. 'That's a true shell pink. It will go very well with your complexion and your grey eyes.' She took her eyes from Cassandra and glanced from Jane with her dark hair and her dark eyes to me with my blonde curls and blue eyes.

'This would look good on Miss Jane,' she said, picking up a primrose-yellow muslin and holding it against Jane, turning her around to see her reflection in the large cheval looking glass that stood on the floor next to the counter.

'I like that much better than the pink,' said Jane with conviction. 'I'm sick of pink.'

'Well, don't have a new gown then,' said Mrs Austen drily. 'Wear your old one.'

'How can I?' Jane clasped her hands dramatically. 'Dearest Mama, you know that I look like a half-grown pullet in that.'

I could see that Mrs Ford was trying hard to keep a smile off her face, and one of the young assistants in the background was giggling. I kept my lips tightly pressed together and did my best not to smile at the thought of Jane like one of those lanky half-grown chickens that struts around the farmyard with its long legs and small body.

'Well, we'll take seven yards of that pink,' said Mrs Austen, 'but, Jane and Jenny, you'll have to agree on a colour.'

I immediately said that I didn't mind the yellow, though my eyes were still on that lovely blue. It was like the sky on a fine winter's day.

Mrs Ford held up the yellow doubtfully against me and then shook her head. 'Not her colour,' she said decisively. 'That makes her look far too pale.'

'Well, let's have blue for the two of them,' said Mrs Austen. 'You don't mind, Jane, do you?'

Jane shook her head, but she still looked longingly at the primrose-coloured muslin. Mrs Ford did not bother holding up the blue against her. Anyone could see that it wasn't her colour.

'It's a pity they are not more alike in colouring, ma'am,' she said to Mrs Austen. 'You're right, of course. If you can get something to suit both, you'll save at least a yard on the making up. Wait a moment – I've got an idea. Where did I put those sprigged muslins?'

'They're in the back room, under the tamboured muslins, Mrs Ford,' called one of the girls, going after the flying figure of her employer.

Mrs Ford didn't run back though. She walked slowly and carefully, bearing a brown-paper parcel reverently in her arms.

'There you are, Mrs Austen, ma'am. This came from London yesterday.' Slowly and gently she stripped off the folds of brown paper.

And there on the counter was lying the most lovely stuff for a gown that I had ever seen in all my life. The cloth was so beautiful, of the finest cotton, and woven so softly, that it looked just like Indian muslin. It was whiter than any snow could be and the tiny sprigs were not of a colour but were silver. Mrs Ford picked it up, and as she moved it on to her arm the light from the oil lamp caught it and made it sparkle.

'It's just like frost on snow,' I said eventually, and Mrs Austen gave me a pleased grin.

'See how it will suit both of them, ma'am.' Mrs Ford held it up to Jane. 'Look, it makes the dark hair and eyes look even darker, and isn't it lovely with those rosy cheeks?'

134

And then she held it against me and I looked at myself in the mirror and all the young lady assistants crowded around smiling and whispering praise. I looked at myself and felt that I looked like something from the land of dreams. Only a princess could have a gown as beautiful as this one.

'We'll take twelve yards,' said Mrs Austen decidedly.

After dinner, Jane and I slipped out down to the village. Jane had managed to put a basket under her shawl and in the basket she had a nice ripe apple from the orchard at Steventon. I had done a drawing of an apple and I had written the letter A beside it. I had also copied the finger shape of the sign language from Mr Austen's book.

George was pleased to see us. He snatched the apple from Jane immediately and started to eat it in huge chunks. I was quite shocked — I didn't expect him to have good table manners, but it seemed almost as if he were starving. He even ate the core of the apple and the little stalk on the top.

Then we showed the picture and the sign for apple, but it wasn't a success. He just kept poking in Jane's basket to see whether she had another one hidden there.

'Tomorrow we'll just show him the apple and then we'll keep it until he makes the sign,' I said to Jane as we walked back from the village. 'He'll soon get the idea.'

It was so funny today when we were passing the shrubbery – we were walking on the gravel sweep and we were not talking; I think we were both thinking about George – when we suddenly heard a sound – someone saying, 'Shh!' very quietly. Jane looked at me with a grin and put her finger to her lips. We both walked on until we came to a laurel bush, and then Jane ducked behind the large green leaves and I followed her. We stood there very silently for a moment.

'They're gone.' It was Cassandra's voice.

Jane put her finger to her lips again and began to steal deeper into the shrubbery. I followed her, trying not to laugh. We passed a few more evergreen bushes and then stopped. In the centre of the clearing was a huge rhododendron bush. It was a very old one and the branches with their peeling bark splayed out sideways, just a couple of feet above the ground. The bush was covered with small fat flower buds, their tips just showing purple, but deep within the leaves was a flash of pink. Hardly daring to breathe, we came a little closer and there, right in the centre, were Tom Fowle and Cassandra. They had made a little nest with heaps of old sacks and a couple of cushions. They were just lying there, not kissing, not touching, just lying there side by side looking at each other. I tapped Jane on the shoulder and turned and started to go back. Somehow

I couldn't bear to disturb them. They looked so in love with each other.

'Don't tell,' I said to Jane when we were going in through the door.

'Of course I won't.'

But during supper, once Mrs Austen had gone out, Jane couldn't resist saying to her father, 'Papa, Jenny and I have been thinking about doing some nature study – perhaps starting off with trees and bushes. Do you think that is a good idea?'

Mr Austen, of course, did, and went into a long explanation about deciduous trees and evergreens – he recommended books and he even told us we would find some excellent examples of evergreens in the shrubbery.

Jane nodded thoughtfully and said, 'That's just what I was thinking myself today. Like rhododendrons, for instance.'

It was good luck that Mrs Austen was out of the room because Tom Fowle went bright red and Cassandra blushed a rosy pink. It was funny, because she kept trying to shoot Jane angry glances, but then she would look at Tom and her face would get all soft again. I'm beginning to like Cassandra. I hope things work out for her.

Tonight Jane was busy with her notebook while I was doing my journal. I had just finished writing all of this when she said, 'Look at this. You can stick it in your journal. I might use it in a story some time.'

Mrs George Austen
The Parsonage,
Steventon.

Dear Madam,
            We are married and gone.
                        Tom and Cassandra Fowle.
- -

Her Highness Madam Austen, having read
this letter which, of course, sufficiently explained
the whole affair, flew into a violent Passion and
having spent an agreeable half an hour calling them
all the shocking Names her rage could suggest to
her, sent after them 300 men with orders not to
return without their bodies whether dead or alive,
intending that if they should be brought in the latter
condition, to have them put to death in some torture-
like manner, after a few years' confinement.

Tuesday, 15 March 1791 .

We had just finished breakfast and Jane and I were airing our bedroom when the dressmaker, or mantua maker, as Cassandra grandly called her, came around. We saw her on the sweep when we looked out of our bedroom window. She was a small woman with a pale face and rounded shoulders and she was carry-ing a flat basket in her hand.

Jane and I were downstairs before she reached the front door.

'Miss Jane Austen,' she said, dropping a curtsy. 'Miss Cooper,' she said to me, and then as Cassandra came out of the dining room, she dropped another curtsy and murmured, 'Miss Austen.'

'Come in, Mrs Tuckley, come into the best parlour. Mrs Austen is there.' Cassandra was very grand to-day. I don't think that she has quite forgiven Jane and me for spying on her and Tom Fowle in the rhodo-dendrons yesterday – she wouldn't speak to us for the rest of the day.

'She should thank us,' Jane had said this morning when we were brushing our hair. 'If we don't tease them, he might never declare his intentions to Papa.' She lowered her voice and hissed, 'He might abduct her by midnight in a post-coach and then she would be ruined.'

The idea of decent, kind, shy Tom Fowle abducting

the very virtuous Cassandra had made us both laugh so much that Mrs Austen tapped on the ceiling of the parlour below and told us to hurry down.

'I've just brought some patterns today, ma'am,' said Mrs Tuckley. 'I thought that the young ladies could choose the styles that they like and then I could make sure that you had enough material and I could start work first thing tomorrow. I should have the gowns ready for a week on Saturday with no trouble, because my niece is coming to help me tomorrow and she is a good, fast worker.'

'The young ladies can do their share also,' said Mrs Austen firmly.

Jane made a face, probably only because she is in the middle of her novel *Love & Freindship* (as she spells it). Jane is very accomplished with her needle, better than I am.

'Let's see the patterns,' she said, lifting the cover off the basket.

'Jane!' reproved Mrs Austen.

'We have seven yards of pink muslin for me and twelve yards of white muslin for the two young girls to share between them,' said Cassandra to Mrs Tuckley in a very matronly manner.

'Two young girls and one elderly one,' whispered Jane to me, and we both had a giggle at that. I stopped first because I feared it wasn't very polite to Mrs Austen when she was going to such a lot of trouble for us.

'These are the paper patterns that I made from the Misses Biggs' new gowns,' said Mrs Tuckley, bringing out some large shapes of brown paper from her basket. 'These ones are from Miss Bigg's gown, these are from Miss Elizabeth's gown and these from Miss Alethea's gown.' While she was talking to us she was able to sort out the patterns in a moment although they all looked the same to me.

Cassandra didn't look too pleased at that. 'Catherine Bigg will be at the Assembly Hall's ball at Basingstoke; I don't want to look the same as her.' I could see that Mrs Tuckley was looking a bit worried so I picked out some black silk ribbon from her basket.

'If this was to be plaited across the top of the bosom it would look very unusual and different and it would go well with the pink,' I said, and Cassandra even smiled at me.

'You are very artistic, Jenny,' she said approvingly.

Mrs Tuckley looked relieved. 'I'll slot it in and out of the muslin, Miss Austen.'

Cassandra nodded graciously. She liked the very polite way that Mrs Tuckley talked to her and the way that Mrs Tuckley was always so careful to give her, as eldest girl in the family, the title of Miss Austen while Jane was just Miss Jane. Cassandra will probably make a very good mistress of a house when she and Tom Fowle get married.

'Here's Elizabeth's pattern for you, Jenny – she's about your size.'

As soon as Jane handed it to me, I couldn't help giving a cry of delight. 'Oh, it's got a train on it!'

'They've all got trains.' Mrs Tuckley was looking at Mrs Austen a bit nervously. Mrs Austen had pursed her lips and was looking disapproving. 'Don't worry about that, ma'am. The young ladies will be able to help each other to pin them up before they start dancing so the material won't get spoiled.' She was talking very quickly now. No doubt she was anxious to use these patterns, as they would save her quite some work. I was anxious too. I had never had a gown with a train before, but I could just imagine how fine I would look as it flowed behind me when I walked down the long passageway at the Assembly Rooms that Jane had told me about. Perhaps Henry would hand me out of the coach, which was to be hired for the evening, and we would walk in together, the tips of my fingers just resting on his arm, perhaps with a blue ribbon holding back my curls – if I can get my hair to stay in curl – and the train whispering along the ground behind me.

Now I must write about George. Today was a success. We fed him the apple slice by slice, and each time we made him make the sign with his fingers. In the beginning we had to position his fingers, but once he got the idea that he would only get the apple if he made the sign, he did it himself. Bet came along while we were teaching him and she asked what we were doing. Jane told her that we were teaching George to read and she just laughed and went away.

I said to Jane that I thought Bet was unkind, but Jane shook her head and told me that Bet could not read herself and probably thought it was a very hard thing to do.

'She's just jealous perhaps,' I said when we were walking home, but Jane wouldn't agree. That's the nice thing about Jane. Once she gives her friendship she won't let anyone say a word against a friend, and Bet was a friend of hers.

'Bet and I were brought up together until I was three years old,' she said. 'She's my foster-sister.'

I was amazed at that and she nodded. 'Yes,' she said. 'My mother left us all down in the village until we could walk and talk and dress and feed ourselves. She only took us back when we wouldn't be a nuisance to her.'

She didn't say anything for a while. Then she added, very sadly, 'And George never learned to do anything, so he was just left down in the village.'

Wednesday, 16 March 1791

'Jenny, this is something that I've had for you for a long time. I took them from your poor mother's jewellery box before *Madam* (Mrs Austen always called Augusta *Madam*) could take them for herself.' As usual, Mrs Austen was in a rush. She took a box from her reticule, handed it to me, put down her teacup, finished her pound cake in two bites, pushed open the breakfast-room door and in a moment was outside shouting orders to the gardener to be sure to get more potatoes planted today than he managed to do yesterday.

The breakfast room was very quiet after she left, Mr Austen sipping his tea and reading a poem by Cowper, Henry frowning over a piece of paper from his pocket with some figures on it and Jane scribbling in her notebook. Cassandra had gone to feed the hens and all of the other boys had gone into the schoolroom. Cousin Eliza was having breakfast in bed as she did most mornings.

I opened the box very slowly. It was a beautiful box, made of thin sandalwood covered in blue silk. I had often admired it on my mother's dressing table.

But I had never seen it opened before. It had always stayed locked.

The box was full of pale blue glass beads. They glistened in the

light of the pale winter sun that came through the
breakfast-room window. I couldn't stop myself giving a cry of delight. Everyone looked at me with
surprise. There was a piece of paper on the top of the
box with the words 'Beads from my wedding gown
for Jenny's first ball gown' written on it. I've stuck it
in here as I don't ever want to lose it.

Beads from my Wedding Gown
for Jenny's first ball gown.

I felt very sad for a moment after I put the note
down; no doubt my mother had kept these glass beads
from her wedding gown in memory of my father.
'What's the matter, Jenny?' asked Jane.
I couldn't speak, but I handed her the piece of yel-
lowed paper. She glanced at it quickly
and Henry looked over her shoulder.
'What colour is your gown,
Jenny?' Henry put away his figures and looked at me kindly.
I told him about the white
sprigged muslin, almost whispering the words because I was just
thinking how beautiful the gown
would look if the beads were
sewn all over it. I would have to
talk to Mrs Tuckley about it.

Jane and I rushed upstairs to fetch our work baskets, and as we came out of our bedroom again we saw something strange. Henry was going upstairs very quietly, making no noise on the wooden boards, and we saw him turn the handle of Eliza's door and slip inside without even knocking. Jane looked at me and raised her eyebrows and I did the same back, but I didn't know what to think. We tiptoed downstairs, and as we passed Eliza's room we could hear them both laughing and joking.

I've decided that I don't really like Cousin Eliza very much. I think she is a shallow, insincere sort of person. I don't believe that she cares for Henry. I think that she is just leading him on.

It's night-time and Jane and I are in our bedroom. We should be in bed, but we are both writing, she in her notebook and I in my journal. I have just finished writing about the gowns and I am trying to think of something else to write in order to fill up the page. Jane is writing very fast. I think she is very clever. She is almost a year younger than I am, but she can write much more quickly.

I'll ask Jane to read out what she's writing so I can finish my page . . .

She says she has finished copying and has tossed the piece of paper to me. Here it is:

It may now be proper to return to the Hero of this Novel, the brother of Alice, of whom I believe I have scarcely ever had occasion to speak; which may perhaps be partly owing to his unfortunate tendency to alcohol, which so completely deprived him of the use of those faculties Nature had endowed him with, that he never did anything worth mentioning. His Death happened a short time after Lucy's departure & was the natural Consequence of this heavy drinking.

When he died, his sister became the sole inheritress of a very large fortune, which as it gave her fresh Hopes of rendering herself acceptable as a wife to Charles Adams, could not fail of being most pleasing to her – & as the effect was joyful, the cause could scarcely be lamented, so she did not mourn her brother.

I read it through and laughed, but then I asked Jane how she could write about things like love and marriage when she had never been in love.

'I've never been drunk either,' she said, 'but I can write very well about that.'

I told Jane that for all I knew she was drunk every night before I came here, and that it was a good job I was such a good moral influence on her, and she laughed.

Then I asked if she would ever write a love story with Eliza as the heroine.

'Oh, Eliza is not in love,' said Jane impatiently. 'She just flirts. That's different. Flirting is great fun. What about you? You're in love with Henry, aren't you? I know by the way you blush.'

I said that I thought Henry was in love with Eliza, but Jane just laughed at me.

'He's just flirting too,' she said. 'Henry is a terrible flirt; everyone knows that. There's a difference between flirting and being in love. Real love is what Cassandra feels for Tom Fowle.'

I wish Eliza would go back to London. I'm sure Jane's right and that Henry is just flirting with her – but I wish she would go.

Oh, and I forgot, we taught George the sign for the letter *B* today. He learned it by having bits of bun.

Thursday, 17 March 1791

One of Augusta's many letters arrived this morning. Mrs Austen passed it to Eliza with a grin, and
Eliza read out bits of it with great spirit and soon
she had the whole table rocking with laughter, as she
skimmed down and picked out the choicest snippets
in her wonderful French accent.

*'My dearest husband — He really is engaged from
morning to night — There is no end of peoples coming to him, on some pretence or other — The magis-
trates, and overseers, and churchwardens, are always
wanting his opinion. They seem not able to do any
thing without him. "Upon my word, Mr C.," I often
say, "rather you than I — I do not know what would
become of my drawings and my piano, if I had half
so many people calling on me" — Bad enough as it is,
for I absolutely neglect them both to an unpardonable
degree — I believe I have not played a bar this fortnight — But I have so many calls on my time — Mrs
John Colwell, herself, called on me yesterday. "Mrs
Cooper," she said, "you are such a good charitable
person — I declare to goodness that I actually saw
you speak to one of those poor creatures that came
to hear your husband preach"— pray tell Mr Austen
that Mr Cooper means to pay him the compliment of
posting the book of his sermons to him . . .'*

'Well, that's very kind . . .' Mr Austen sounded a
little taken aback.

I told him that I thought his sermons were better than my Edward-John's — I wanted to reassure him because he is always so nice to me.

'Still, to have a published volume of his sermons! And such a young man too! There's writing ability in your family, my dear.' He gave a nod at his wife, who preened herself; she is good at writing funny poems, I must say.

'Jane will be the writer of this family,' said Henry, and Jane looked very pleased.

After dinner Jane asked Susan if she could have a tiny slice of cake. She had been making herself useful in the kitchen and complimenting the cook on the dinner so I wasn't surprised when the cake tin was opened and a slice given to her. I had already prepared my drawings so we went straight down to the village.

There was no sign of George anywhere around. He wasn't near the pump, nor hanging around outside the inn. We went to Nanny Littleworth's house, but she hadn't seen him for a while.

And then we found him on the lane to the church. He was lying on the ground, on his side, and he was twitching. There was still enough light to see how his eyes rolled in his head and how his lips were covered with froth. He was having a fit. But it wasn't the sort of fit that Augusta would have; this was a real fit. I had never seen anyone have a fit before and it seemed terrible.

I think I will always remember how Jane dropped to her knees beside him and cried over him as if it were the end of the world. I couldn't stop crying myself. And then Mrs Littleworth came along and told us both to go home immediately. Bet was with her, and it was Bet who lifted up Jane and walked us to the gate of the parsonage.

'He'll be fine tomorrow, he'll be fine,' she kept saying in her country voice. 'He doesn't mind. He's used to it and we're used to it. Now, go home the pair of you, and for God's sake don't say a word to your mother about this. Promise me, Miss Jane, and you, Miss Jenny, nothing must be said, or it will be trouble for my mother.'

Jane and I cried the whole way up to the house, and now I am crying again.

I must stop crying or else I will just start thinking about my mother's death and Jane will notice. I've told her that I don't like talking about it and she doesn't ask me any questions, but I think it upsets her when she thinks I am unhappy. Even though she and her mother fight from time to time, I think that she finds it a terrible thing to imagine being someone like me with no family – I can't count Edward-John, as I don't believe that he cares anything for me. We hardly knew each other before he married and came back to Bristol, as he lived in Berkshire.

And now I'm going to try to stop worrying about this by thinking about the ball at Basingstoke Assembly Rooms.

The gowns are progressing very well. They've been cut out and the side seams have been sewn so that now we have an idea of how beautiful they will look. Mrs Tuckley pinned them around us today, and tomorrow she will sew the seams in the bodices so that they will fit us snugly. I just can't wait. Every time that I think about dancing in the Assembly Rooms in less than a fortnight I feel little thrills running up and down me. I think it will be the most wonderful night of my life. Even Cassandra is excited. She goes around singing to herself and exchanging small, secret smiles with Tom Fowle. Jane and I think that being in love must be very good for the complexion; Cassandra looks very nice these days, with lovely pink lips and pink cheeks – even her hair seems to curl more beautifully.

Friday, 18 March 1791

This morning at breakfast Henry had a little parcel beside him.

'What's that, Henry?' asked Jane as soon as she saw it.

'Curiosity,' teased Henry. 'Just something that I bought at the mercer's shop yesterday when I was escorting Cousin Eliza to Overton.' I saw him give a quick, joking look at Eliza who was at the breakfast table for once, pouring out the coffee she insists on having for breakfast. She blew him a kiss, and Mrs Austen scowled, though Mr Austen just laughed.

'A pair of gloves,' guessed Jane, but Henry shook his head.

'He's got six pairs of gloves already,' said Gilbert East.

'A cravat then,' persisted Jane.

'And he's got a drawer full of them,' said Tom Fowle's brother William.

'In any case, I am hoping that Jane will make me a cravat if there is a square of muslin left over from her gown,' said Henry. He didn't really need another cravat, I guessed. He was always beautifully dressed, and this morning he was wearing a snowy white one knotted under his chin in the latest style.

'I will if you show me what you've got there.' Jane kept on pestering him until he undid the twine and took out two beautiful bandeau-style ribbons.

'Something for you girls to wear in your hair on Saturday night,' he said. 'There's a pink one for you, Cassandra, that should match your gown.'

'Oh, thank you, Henry.' Cassandra rushed over and admired herself in the looking glass.

'And the red one for Jane — matches her rosy cheeks.' Henry pinched Jane's cheek. She wriggled away, but she was pleased with the bandeau. It was made from silk, like Cassandra's.

Cassandra was still admiring herself. She had a quick look at Tom Fowle and a smile passed between them. I think Tom really loves her. There is a look of adoration in his eyes. I made a promise to myself not to laugh at them any more, no matter what jokes Jane makes. I feel very sorry for the two of them and hope that Mrs Austen will allow them to get engaged. I'm sure Mr Austen won't mind. He seems to like Tom Fowle very much.

'And this is for Jenny, to match her beautiful blue eyes.' I was so busy looking from Mr Austen to Tom Fowle that I got a shock when Henry opened the parcel a little more and slid out a gorgeous bandeau made from the deepest and softest blue velvet. I couldn't say anything; I loved it so much.

'Let me put it on.' In a moment Henry had it around my head and had pulled one of my curls forward. He placed one hand on my shoulder while he was arranging my hair and I could feel myself tremble. I wished that we were alone and that the whole of the breakfast table wasn't staring at us. He was so close to me that I could feel a warmth coming from him and could see that his dark eyes had little flecks of light in them. I felt myself moving closer to him and then jerked back.

'Come on, look at yourself.' He was smiling down at me, smiling just the way that he smiles at Cousin Eliza. I didn't dare look at her. I didn't dare look at anyone. I was too embarrassed to move and I knew that I had started to blush when he touched my hair.

So Henry unhooked the looking glass and brought it over to me, putting one finger under my chin and turning my head slightly so that I could see myself perfectly in the glass.

'Very nice,' said Mrs Austen drily. 'Now, girls, thank Henry and put these upstairs until Saturday night. Jane, your satin slippers definitely need cleaning before the ball, and, Jenny, you had better check yours also.'

'You do mine, will you, Jenny?' said Jane in an offhand manner. 'I must do my practising.'

She went off without saying anything else and I was a bit puzzled.

I wondered if I had offended her – or perhaps she thought the velvet bandeau was a better present than her silk ribbon.

I didn't think about it too much, though. All the way up the stairs I could feel the tingle of a beating pulse in the place where Henry had put his finger, just on the soft place under my chin.

Something very embarrassing happened later on. I was dusting the breakfast parlour after lunch while Jane was practising the piano. The boys hadn't gone back into the schoolroom yet. They were all shouting and laughing and making a great noise on the stairs.

And I overheard a conversation.

And it was about me.

And I didn't move away as I should have done.

I just stayed there with the duster in my hand, listening.

It was my aunt and my uncle in the study next to the breakfast room. They had been talking for quite some time – about vegetables and about Mr Austen's farm, I think – and I had been taking no notice.

And then I heard my name.

'Mr Austen,' my aunt had said. Her voice, as usual, was the voice of someone who is in a rush and has something of importance to say. It is a very high-pitched voice – like a corncrake, Jane says. It's the sort of voice that easily goes through walls.

'Mr Austen,' she said. 'I wish you would have a

word with Henry and tell him to stop flirting with Jenny. He'll turn that girl's head.'

Mr Austen must have said something. I just heard a murmur.

'Nonsense,' said my aunt. 'She's no child. She's sixteen years old. That's just the age when girls get all sorts of silly notions about love into their heads.'

One of the boys shouted something and then they all went running out of the hall door. I could hear the noise of their boots on the steps, and through the window I saw them running across the grass towards the field. Sometimes they played ball for a while before lessons began.

Now that they had gone, everything was quiet so I could hear Mr Austen's voice quite well.

'They would make a lovely couple, Jenny and Henry, he so tall, dark and handsome and she so small, blonde and pretty – lovely girl, lovely hair, lovely eyes, sweet-natured, too; she would make a perfect wife.' From the sound of his voice I could guess that he had a smile on his face.

'Nonsense!' Mrs Austen's voice was even more high-pitched than ever. 'Don't talk such nonsense, Mr Austen. Both of them will be as poor as church mice. How could they get married? They won't have two pennies to rub together.'

Mr Austen was saying something about how they had married without many prospects, but I didn't wait to hear any more. I slipped out of the breakfast room, replaced the duster on the shelf of the cupboard under the stairs and tiptoed up to my bedroom. I was glad that Jane was still playing the piano; if she had been in the bedroom I know she would have asked me why I was so flustered. When I got to the bedroom I leaned first one cheek and then the other against the icy coldness of the window glass.

Me marry Henry! I had never imagined that anyone would even have thought of that. I wondered whether to talk to Jane about it, but then I decided against it. I thought she was a bit short with me, a bit abrupt – perhaps she is a little jealous because Henry, her adored brother, gave me such a beautiful present and made such a fuss of me. I resolved that I wouldn't mention Henry to Jane. I didn't want her to think that I was a flirt like Eliza.

I wasn't sure whether Jane would want to go down to the village today, but she did.

George was pleased to see us. He ran up straight away, and now that I wasn't so scared of him I could hear that he was saying, 'Jane.' I tried not to look away, but to look at him. He was occupied with Jane so I could really look at him without feeling embarrassed. I began to think that he really did look like one of the Austen family. His hair is brown and curly, just like Jane's hair, and although his face was dirty and one side of it is a bit twisted, his eyes are the same green-brown colour as Jane's, and as Mr

Austen's eyes also. There was an expression in them that made me very sad. They looked as if he were trying to say something, but couldn't: almost as if he were inside a cage and trying to get out. I wondered why he couldn't talk. He seemed to be able to make noises and I suddenly thought it must be terrible if he thought he was saying words, but yet no one could understand them.

Funnily enough, he seemed to be brighter and better today. Perhaps Bet is right – perhaps having a fit is like a very severe sneeze and then feeling your head clear. Now that he has got over the fit, George feels better.

Jane had another slice of cake and we taught him the sign for the letter *C* with very little trouble.

On the way back I suggested to Jane that the next time we see him we should go over the three letters again and make sure that he knows them. I couldn't think of any food beginning with *D* so I thought we might skip that and go on to *E* for egg. The Austens keep their own hens so it is always easy to get hold of an egg.

Sunday, 20 March 1791

James arrived so early this morning that he was in the house before any of the family was up. He had taken the overnight coach from Oxford. Mrs Austen wanted him to go to bed after breakfast, but he wouldn't. He said that he had come on purpose to practise the play and that he wanted to have a really good practise because this was Cousin Eliza's last day.

'I want everyone there – no one going off to shoot crows,' he said, glaring at Frank.

Actually Frank was quite good at the practise today. Cassandra was being wardrobe mistress and she dressed him up as Fag, the servant, in an old, slightly ragged coat of Mr Austen's. He was very funny as the servant.

'*Rich!*' he declaimed, sounding, except for his half-broken voice, just like his father in the pulpit. '*Why, I believe she owns half the stocks! Zounds, Thomas! She could pay the national debt as easily as I could my washerwoman! She has a lapdog that eats out of gold – she feeds her parrot with small pearls – and all her curl-papers are made of banknotes!*'

James and Eliza were funny too. I thought they acted very well together. Jane couldn't stop laughing when James said, in very prim tones, after Mrs Malaprop was complaining about Lydia (Cassandra), '*It is not to be wondered at, ma'am – all this is the natural consequence of teaching girls to read. Had*

I a thousand daughters, by heaven! I'd as soon have
them taught the black art as their alphabet!'

'Time for church, everyone,' said Mrs Austen, putting
her head round the door and grinning at the way
that Mrs Malaprop was mixing up words with other
words that sounded like them, like calling *particu-*
lars 'perpendiculars'.

   'Oh, Aunt dear, I have such a headache. I vow it is
a true migraine.' Eliza clasped her hand to her forehead dramatically, as if she were still in the middle
of the play. 'Oh dear, I so hate to miss church, but I
fear I cannot go.' And then she staggered off with a
quick look over her shoulder at Henry. Jane grinned
and nudged me.

Henry came with us all along the lane to the church,
but I didn't see him in church, though I turned
around a few times to see whether he was standing
at the back.

   When we came back from church though, there
was no sign of Eliza, and Henry said he wanted to
practise the scene with me, and that was good. I lost
my shyness as I was determined to be as like Eliza as
I could (but without the French accent) and it was
so lovely afterwards, while Jane was playing on the
piano, when Henry whispered in my ear some words
from the play: *'Let music be the food of love.'*

* * *

After dinner, Cassandra, Jane and I went up to the guest bedroom to help Eliza to pack her clothes as she was returning to London that evening.

I said very politely to Cousin Eliza that it was a shame that she had to go back especially as she was returning a few days later, and her answer gave me a shock.

'Ah, but, *chérie*, I must go back to my poor little boy.' She pronounced the word *little* as 'leetle'.

I said that I didn't know she had a little boy – I wondered why no one had mentioned him. And then, since she had called him 'poor', I asked her politely whether her little boy was unwell.

'Poor angel! He is never well! But I have found a physician that will give a new treatment.' She was mopping her eyes with her handkerchief and Cassandra was shaking her head and frowning at me so I said no more. A minute later Eliza had gone to the window, laughing gaily and calling down to Henry. She accepted his invitation to come and see the new horse that he had bought and went clattering down the stairs on her high-heeled French shoes.

When she had gone out, Cassandra told me the story of Hastings, Eliza's son. Apparently he was now aged about four or five, but he had not been normal from the age of ten months. He suffered from fits from an early age and could not stand or walk unaided, though Eliza and her mother had managed to teach him his alphabet, according to what Eliza told her uncle.

'The trouble with Eliza is that she is so stubborn. She will not admit to herself that the child will never progress. She insists on keeping him with her and trying every cure that comes up. Last year it was sea bathing – goodness knows what it will be next year. She should find some responsible person to care for him and then just put him out of her life.' And Cassandra sighed in an elderly fashion over her cousin's obstinacy.

I said nothing, but I did not agree with Cassandra. I found myself admiring and liking Eliza more than I had done before.

I vowed to myself that if I had a child who had problems, like George or little Hastings, I would not abandon it, but would love and care for it tenderly and to me it would be the most precious child in the world.

At the end of the day, we all walked up the hill to see James and Cousin Eliza off on the stagecoach – Henry was going to stay on at Steventon for the week.

And this time I was the one that suggested to Jane that we go and see George on our way back and get on with his lessons. We didn't have any food for him, but I had my sketchbook with me and I thought he might like to see the stagecoach that I had drawn. He nodded when he saw that, but on another page I had a picture of a gun, which I had drawn for Frank in my sketchbook, like this, and George was more interested in that. As soon as he saw it, he said, 'Bang!' instantly. Jane tried to get him to make the sign for the letter G, but he would not do it, just kept saying, 'Bang!' and smiling as if he wanted us to be pleased with him.

'I think that is fine, Jane,' I said after a while. I could see that she was getting upset and George was beginning to look at her in a worried way. 'I think it's even better that he says "bang". That means something to him. It probably means that he can hear a little, also, if he can hear a loud sound like a shot. He's probably not completely deaf. Good boy, George, good boy,' and I patted him on the back and Jane threw her arms around him and kissed him.

Monday, 21 March 1791

When we finished our lessons this morning, Frank gave me the usual riding lesson on the donkey. I was getting on well now, and Jane could perfectly well have done it, but Frank insisted that he was the one to teach me. Cassandra is probably right about Frank. He was bored. He couldn't wait to get back to his life at sea. He and Jane kept arguing about the best way to teach me.

When we came back in, Mrs Tuckley was there and I explained to her about the new beads. She looked at them dubiously and said they would take a long time to sew on and that I should think very carefully about whether there would be time for them.

'You'll need to count them, Miss Cooper,' she said with a sigh as she slipped her thimble on to her finger. 'Then you'll have to plan where to put them. There may not be enough to arrange all over the gown.'

I got a pewter plate from the sideboard, opened the box of glass beads and began to count them carefully, one by one, on to the plate.

Jane had promised to help me with sewing on the glass beads, but I was surprised when Cassandra joined us. The only problem was that she took charge immediately.

'Make sure that your hands are clean, Jane,' she said in a very elder-sister way. 'Now, Jenny dear, how are we going to arrange these exquisite beads?'

That was a question that didn't need an answer as Cassandra carried on almost without drawing a breath.

'I think that the best thing would be to make a triangular shape down the back and widening out to completely cover the train. I would say there aren't

enough to cover the whole of the back of the gown and they need to be close together to attract the eye instantly.'

I hurriedly said I thought that was a wonderful idea, as I could see Jane opening her mouth to object. And I did really think it was a good idea. The train was my favourite part of the gown and I liked the notion of attracting attention to it — this is what it will look like.

We had quite a nice time sewing together for the next hour before Cassandra had to go and help her mother with the dinner. Jane made up a story about a young man, possessed of a good fortune, of course, who had come to the neighbourhood in order to rent Freefolk Priors, a large empty house near Steventon. Once he arrived he fell in love with the prettiest girl in the neighbourhood, Cassandra Austen. He proposed on bended knee in very flowery language (Jane was good at making up ridiculous marriage proposals) and she accepted.

'What did I say?' enquired Cassandra. She was laughing and in one of the best moods that I have ever seen her.

'Just what you ought to, of course; a lady always knows what to say.' Jane always has a smart answer for everything.

'Cassandra!' shouted Mrs Austen.

Cassandra got obediently to her feet. 'The only problem, Miss Jane,' she said, poking Jane in the shoulder with her forefinger in a friendly way, 'is that Freefolk Priors is already let – to a General Mathew.'

'A general!' Jane was impressed.

'Aged about sixty . . .'

Jane made a face at that.

'And,' continued Cassandra, 'he has no son – just one unmarried daughter – Anne – aged thirty-two and on the shelf. Mama is quite excited about this. General Mathew is the Commander-in-Chief of the Windward and Leeward Islands and Governor of Grenada. Just remember that!' And then she rushed off to the kitchen.

'Imagine!' I said to Jane. 'Thirty-two years old and on the shelf! She must feel very miserable.'

'I wouldn't care,' Jane said. She tossed her head and looked as if she would not care. 'I'd stay at home and write books and make lots of money, just like Miss Burney.'

Then her mood changed. She began to look thoughtful. 'So that's why Mama sent James to call on a General Mathew. I was wondering about that. She was very particular about brushing his coat and tying his cravat.'

We looked at each other with eyebrows raised. 'Well, well, well,' I said, but then I shook my head. 'He's too young for her; she's ten years older than him.'

'*My dear Jenny*,' said Jane, imitating her mother's voice perfectly, '*equality of age may be desirable, but money is the essential.*' She changed back to her normal voice and said, 'I bet you that this Anne Mathew has a fortune of her own. James may be the eldest and a great scholar, but he's going to be a clergyman and all he can hope for is a parish. Having a general as a father-in-law will help with that.'

After dinner it was raining so Jane and I couldn't go down to see George. We spent some time making more drawings for him. We got as far as *O* in the alphabet and I wished that we could get an orange for him to eat, but I never saw oranges at Steventon parsonage. The Austens seemed to eat only the fruit and vegetables that they grew themselves. It was a pity though, because I felt that my picture of an orange would not be understood by him unless he had tasted one once.

'Perhaps Henry would bring one from Overton,' suggested Jane. 'You ask him. He'll do it for you.'

'No, he won't.' I could feel myself going red as usual.

'Yes, he will.'

'No, he won't!'

'Yes, he will.'

'No, he won't!'

We went on like this for about five minutes, both of us getting weak with laughter, and I suppose we were getting louder and louder because Mrs Austen popped her head in to ask what on earth we were doing.

'Jenny would love an orange; she always eats oranges in Bristol, and I told her that Henry would get one for her.' Jane kept a very straight face at this and I pretended to look at something out of the window. When I turned round, Mrs Austen was looking at me with an odd expression on her face.

'Bless me, child, if you want an orange your uncle will get you one when he goes to Basingstoke tomorrow,' she said abruptly, and went out.

I was mortified that Mrs Austen would think that I was criticizing the food I get here, but Jane said it wasn't that; it was mentioning Henry. She had a thoughtful look on her face, almost as if she had just realized something.

I didn't want to hear anything more though, so I

ran out and called to Charles to come and have his drawing lesson from me. He had drawn about forty horses already on his slate and he was beginning to be quite good at shading the curves and getting expression into the horse's eye. Today, I planned, I would allow him to use a page of my sketchbook, and if it was good then we would frame it.

After supper tonight we had music and dancing as usual. Mrs Austen insisted on everyone changing partners after the first set. Cassandra, I noticed, was then paired off with Gilbert East, the baronet's son, I was paired with Tom Fowle's youngest brother, and Henry with Jane – the rest of the boys just paired up together, and there was a lot of fun about that, with Tom Fowle calling Charles a sweet maiden.

And then it was all change again – Jane took over the piano and Mrs Austen grabbed Henry while Frank firmly took my hand.

'Jenny . . .' said Frank as he twirled me expertly around. 'Jenny, tomorrow would you be able to come out for your riding lesson before breakfast, while Jane is practising?'

I told him I would without waiting to hear the reason. Frank and Jane were quite fond of each other, but they always argue, and Jane has a habit of telling Frank exactly how he should be teaching me and he doesn't like that, probably.

Tuesday, 22 March 1791

My riding lesson with Frank went very well this morning — he seemed to be pleased that Jane wasn't hanging around criticizing or making jokes. He told me all about his life at sea and his hopes of becoming a lieutenant. He said that the first lieutenant was hopeless and that he was sure he could do the job much better.

Then he seemed to get a bit embarrassed and started talking about the ball at the Assembly Rooms. He asked me if I was looking forward to it.

I just said, 'Oh yes,' and I immediately started to think about Henry, and when I next looked at Frank I thought he looked a bit sulky so I apologized quickly and asked him what a first lieutenant did on a ship.

Frank is very nice. I wish that he were my brother. He's the same age as me, of course, but I think of him as younger. Jane always says that girls are much older than boys of the same age!

After we had put the donkey away and fed her, Frank went off to see whether breakfast was ready, but I stayed outside for a while. It was windy, but not really cold. I liked the damp, fresh smell of the country air. Everything was nice and quiet except for the noise of the hens' beaks tapping their large metal dish. It was Cassandra's task every morning to let them out of their house. Jane told me that she used to help Cassandra, but in the past few weeks her sister had told her that she would prefer to do it on her own. There was no sign of Cassandra anywhere this morning, but oddly enough I heard a giggle from the hen house.

I was just going to go in for breakfast when I saw Mrs Austen come out of the kitchen. She came out very fast and hadn't stopped to put on her pattens; she still had her list slippers on. They were too big for her and just flapped around her feet. She didn't see me standing there, but headed straight for the hen house, bustling past the feeding hens, who scattered with squawks of dismay and then came running back to their dish again.

'Cassandra!' Her voice pealed out and there was an uncanny likeness to the squawk of a disturbed hen. 'Come out of there directly, the two of you.'

I should have gone indoors straight away, but I was standing just beside one of the laurel bushes and I thought it might be best to stay there in case I attracted attention to myself. I was very embarrassed though when I saw Tom Fowle follow Cassandra out of the hen house. He looked very silly, with a sheepish face and a couple of white chicken feathers sticking to his hair. (I did a sketch for Jane to show her just what he looked like – she thought it was very funny so I've stuck it into my journal here.)

'Go inside for your breakfast, Tom,' said Mrs
Austen in a very severe tone. 'I'll get Mr Austen to
deal with you later on.'

Tom gave one glance at Cassandra and then went
off as quickly as he could. After a moment I heard his
large feet crunching the gravel on the carriage sweep
in front of the house. He probably felt relieved that
it was Mr Austen who was going to deal with him.
I think all of the boys were far more scared of Mrs
Austen than of her husband. I heard Gilbert East
say once that Mr Austen was the easiest and kindest
schoolmaster that anyone could ever have.

'What have you got to say for yourself, young
lady?' Mrs Austen sounded choked with rage as
she faced Cassandra. Her back was towards me,

but I could tell by the twitch of her head how angry she was.

'We love each other.' Cassandra was braver than I would have been. She faced her mother without going red. She wasn't crying either.

I took two steps backwards, very gently. I would try to escape while they were occupied with each other. It would be terribly awkward if one of them chanced to see me standing there listening to their private conversation.

'Nonsense!' I heard Mrs Austen say as I reached the second laurel bush.

'He wants to marry me.' I had reached the third laurel bush when Cassandra said that. Her voice was defiant and quite loud. A movement from overhead took my attention and I saw Jane up there. She was sitting on the window seat of our bedroom and the window was slightly ajar. She must have finished her piano practise and gone upstairs to air the room before breakfast. She would be listening to everything with great interest.

'Cassandra, just you listen to me,' screeched Mrs Austen. Her voice was so loud that even the hens seemed to be impressed, and they gathered around her as though she were preaching a sermon to them — or else perhaps they thought she was calling them for a second meal. I moved to the fourth laurel bush. I would go in by the front door, I planned; I would just steal along the side of the house and keep on the moss beside the wall so that my feet didn't touch the gravel.

I couldn't help overhearing though. Mrs Austen's voice was getting louder by the minute. The whole house must be hearing the words.

'No money . . . no prospects . . . What will you live on? . . . after all I have said to you . . . ashamed of yourself . . .'

Cassandra tried to say something about love, but her mother interrupted her.

'Love!' she said scornfully. 'I tell you this, Miss Cassandra, love will vanish pretty quickly when you have ten children in a couple of pokey rooms. That boy is going to be a clergyman. It's his only future. He can't marry for at least ten years, not until he makes a position for himself, finds a patron, gets a parish. And where will you be in ten years' time? Answer me that, pray. You'll be an old maid, a very poor old maid. Your father can do nothing for you; nothing, do you understand? You must marry money.'

And now I was at the kitchen door. The cook was frying eggs for breakfast; the spluttering of the hot fat had probably prevented her from hearing any- thing, but the parlourmaid and the kitchen maid were whispering and giggling in the corner by the scullery. I brushed past them and rinsed my hands under the tap there and then slipped into the breakfast parlour. Jane was already there, looking demure, but her hazel eyes were sparkling with excitement.

Cassandra didn't come in to breakfast. Mr Austen asked where she was and Mrs Austen told him that Cassandra had a headache. I saw the boys look at each other; Tom Fowle turned red, and Jane nudged my foot under the table. Mr Austen, I thought, was probably the only person in the house who didn't know all about the hen-house drama this morning.

'I feel sorry for Cassandra,' I said to Jane as we began our lessons. I twirled Mr Austen's globe as I thought about Mrs Austen's words. Life was hard for girls without money, I thought. Unless a rich man asked their hand in marriage, they were doomed to be old maids and that wasn't a pleasant thought!

'I wish I were a boy,' said Jane as if she had read my thoughts. 'Frank has great plans to be rich. First he is going to be the best midshipman in the navy – so good that his captain will immediately recommend that he become a lieutenant – and then he will be such a good lieutenant that he will catch the eye of some admiral, and the admiral will recommend that he become a captain and get his own ship. And then he will capture some Dutch ship and get lots of prize money and he will be very rich . . .'

I nodded, my eyes on the globe, looking at all the places where Frank would sail in his ships – the East Indies and the West Indies, the Atlantic Ocean and the Pacific Ocean. '. . . and then he will be able to marry whosoever he likes.' It would probably take about ten years for Frank to get to that position, I thought. It was just as well that I was not in love with him or I too would be an old maid by the time he came home rich and triumphant. Who would I marry though? I didn't think that Mrs Austen would like me to marry either Henry or Frank, and I didn't really know any other young man.

And then a sudden thought crossed my mind. It was more of a picture than a thought, really.

And the picture was of a very handsome young man in naval uniform, with black hair, high cheek-bones and brown eyes and a voice that was as soft and warm as chocolate.

But I didn't really want to see Captain Thomas Williams again, did I?

I couldn't see him again.

I just couldn't.

It was impossible.

Unthinkable.

If I did, I would be disgraced forever and my repu-tation would be in tatters.

Even if he said nothing to the Austens, what would he think of a girl who allowed herself to walk through the streets of Southampton at mid-night with an unknown man? I imagined those brown eyes filled with scorn and I knew that I definitely did not want to see him again. How miserable – if only things were different. If only I had been cleverer that night, hidden myself better – not been such a coward as to stand in the middle of the pavement staring, like a frightened mouse, at that madman whirling his sword. I wish I didn't keep remembering Captain Williams. It's so stupid; I hate myself.

I'm going to turn back the pages of my journal and look at the sketch I made of him. At least I have that.

'Look at this,' said Jane. She had been scribbling on a piece of paper while I was daydreaming and now she was copying it into her notebook where she keeps her stories. I read it over her shoulder and said that she would have to change the name of Cassandra because she would be upset if she read it – everyone reads Jane's stories notebook.

'I'll change it to Rebecca then in my fair copy – you can have the one that says Cassandra, because no one reads your journal.' Jane was writing busily as she spoke.

'There you are,' she said, tossing it over to me when she had finished.

So I've put it in here. I'll have lots of Jane's written works before this journal is finished.

'Lovely and fair one,' said the noble youth, 'not withstanding your forbidding squint, your greasy curls and your swelling back, which are more frightful than imagination can paint or pen describe: I cannot refrain from expressing my raptures and asking you to marry me.'

Alas for the passionate young man, Cassandra's mama did not approve of the match on account of the tender years of the young couple, Cassandra being but 36 and the noble youth little more than 63. It was agreed that they should wait a little while till they were a good deal older before embarking on matrimony.

Wednesday, 23 March 1791

Mrs Austen is still in a bad mood today. She was very cross with Jane this morning. She says that she has no accomplishments except piano playing.

'You can't sketch, you have no interest in cooking or managing a house; you just spend all of your time making up jokes and scribbling silly stories,' scolded Mrs Austen.

'Well, I don't care,' said Jane. 'I won't want to get married to a man who would want me to be a house-keeper. I shall marry a man with a good fortune.'

'Jane . . .' said Mrs Austen. She said the words slowly and solemnly. 'Don't be silly. It won't be up to you to choose a husband. A man will choose you, and no man of fortune will choose a silly girl without any accomplishments who spends all her time making jokes and allowing boys to slide her down the stairs on a rug. I know you are not yet sixteen, but you must think of the future. Your father cannot afford to give you a dowry. If you wish to marry well, you must be willing to make yourself attractive to a young man of fortune. Why can't you be more like your cousin? Look how polite she is and how beautifully she draws. I'll tell you this, Jane: she's the sort of girl that men like. You're just a silly tomboy. The Lord forgive me, but I have no patience and no time to deal with this child!'

And then she slammed the door and went out.

'I don't care,' repeated Jane, opening the door again. And then, very loudly, she shouted after her mother, 'I don't care; so don't bother talking to me. I shall make my living by writing novels, and thousands of people will buy them, and that's that.' She slammed the door shut and scowled at me for a minute and I felt terrible. I wished that Mrs Austen hadn't said that about me.

However, Jane being Jane, after a minute she began to grin and she scribbled a few words on a piece of paper, which she crammed into her pocket. Then she jumped up and said cheerfully, 'Come on, Jenny, let's go out.'

When we had put on our bonnets and were coming down the stairs we saw Cassandra go into Mr Austen's study.

'Tom Fowle is in there, and my mother also,' whispered Jane. We looked at each other.

'I hope they don't send poor Tom away,' said Jane as we went down the avenue towards the gate. 'I like Tom.'

'And he and Cassandra are very much in love,' I said. I felt very, very sorry for them.

Mr Austen had brought an orange home for everyone. Jane had decided that she would be the one to give the orange to George as he was her brother, and I said that in that case I would share mine with her.

George was glad to see us. He was getting used to

all the strange things that we did, and I noticed that his eyes always went to the basket when we arrived.

Today I took out the picture of the orange first. I was really proud of it as I had copied it from the real fruit and blended the paints very carefully until I got the exact colour. As I had guessed, he didn't take too much interest, but I formed my fingers and thumb into a round shape and kept saying 'orange', while pointing to the letter *O*, and he made an attempt at making the sign after me.

But when Jane peeled the orange and popped a slice in his mouth, he was amazed by the taste. I don't think he had ever eaten anything so strange. For a moment he stood very still and I thought he was going to spit it out, but then he chewed and swallowed and opened his mouth for more. After every few slices we made him point to the letter and make the sign with his own fingers and thumb. By the end of the time we were sure that he knew the sign for the letter *O*, and we tested him on a few more. He remembered *A* for apple, *E* for egg and *C* for cake, but that was all.

'Still,' I said to Jane as we walked home, 'now he knows four letters of the alphabet and a month ago he didn't know any; perhaps by Christmas he will know them all.'

Mrs Austen was in a much better mood at dinner time, and what was even more surprising was that Cassandra was looking very well. She was smiling to herself and being very helpful to her mother.

'I'll help Mary with the clearing up, Mama,' she said when everyone had finished. 'You go and have a rest.'

'We'll help too,' said Jane virtuously. She carefully closed the door after the last of the boys had gone out and came back over to the table and started to pile the dirty dishes on the tray.

'Come on, Cassandra, tell us what is happening,' she coaxed.

For a minute Cassandra hesitated. I felt awkward because I thought she would tell Jane to mind her own business, but I think she was so happy that she wanted to tell someone about it.

'You mustn't say a word,' she said warningly.

'Your secret is safe with me, young maiden,' hissed Jane. I thought this would annoy Cassandra, but it didn't. She just laughed.

'Well, Papa talked to Mama last night and then he talked to Tom again this morning and then we all talked together. Papa was very nice.' Cassandra's eyes filled, though her lips curved in a smile; she was halfway between laughter and tears. She looked very pretty, I thought.

'Go on,' said Jane. She didn't normally hug her sister, but she did so now. And Cassandra hugged her back.

'We've promised to wait,' she said. 'We're going

to be engaged, but not married. Tom told Papa that he does have some prospects. He has a distant cousin who is a lord — Lord Craven.'

'He never spoke of that before!' Jane sounded impressed. Her stories were full of lords.

'Tom's not like that.' Cassandra smiled gently and blushed a little. 'He never boasts. He only mentioned it to Papa today. He said that Lord Craven has promised to get him a place as a chaplain on one of his ships going to the West Indies. When he comes back Lord Craven will do his best to get him a parish.'

Jane asked her when they would be able to get married, and Cassandra told her that it would probably not be for five or six years yet. She still looked very happy about it, but when Cassandra carried out the tray to the kitchen, Jane and I agreed that the time was far too long.

'Perhaps Lord Craven will die and leave Tom ten thousand pounds,' said Jane cheerfully.

'Shh!' I said, energetically dusting the crumbs from the tablecloth. I could hear Cassandra coming back.

'You sit by the fire and we'll do the work,' said Jane solicitously, taking the copper kettle from her sister. 'People need to rest after an emotional shock, and being proposed to is probably the greatest shock that any girl can have.'

'I must find out what he said,' she muttered to me

as we carried out the kettle and teapot to the kitchen. 'How can I write romantic novels unless I know what they say on such occasions?'

I said that it was probably private, but Jane didn't look as though she were listening.

'Cassandra,' she said when the tablecloth had been folded and put away in the drawer, the fireplace swept and new wood put on the fire.

'Yes, Jane.' Cassandra was in a happy dream, staring at the flames.

'What did Tom say when he proposed?' asked Jane pleadingly.

For a moment I thought Cassandra would tell her to mind her own business. On a normal day she certainly would, but she didn't. 'He said, "How many hens will you and I have when we are married?"'

I could see Jane opening her mouth to exclaim: *What!* So I frowned at her and said very quickly, 'And what did you say, Cassandra?'

'I said, "Oh, Tom!"' And Cassandra smiled even more at the memory.

As soon as the room was tidy we left Cassandra to her happy dreams and went upstairs to our bedroom.

'Well,' said Jane as soon as the door was closed. 'I must say that I can write a better proposal than that.' She went across to her writing desk, took out a half-sheet of paper and picked up her quill. 'I'll tell you

one thing, Jenny,' she said over her shoulder, 'I'm going to make sure that all my heroines fall in love with
a man who can propose properly.'

'And who are in possession of a good fortune, of
course,' I said quickly. This 'possessing a good fortune' was by now quite a joke between Jane and myself.

'What do you think of this for a proposal?' Jane
tossed over her piece of scrap paper when she had
finished and I stuck it into my journal.

> 'And now, my adorable Laura,' said the
> amiable young man, taking my hand tenderly, 'when
> may I hope to aspire to receive that reward for all
> the painfull sufferings I have undergone in the
> course of my Attachment to you, to which I have
> ever aspired? Oh! When will you reward me with
> Yourself?'
> 'This instant, Dear and Amiable Edward,' I
> replied.
> We were immediately united by my father who,
> though he wasn't a clergyman, had always intended
> entering the church.

I'm not sure what Mr Austen might think of the idea
that he wasn't really a clergyman, but at least this
time she had written Laura instead of Cassandra.

Thursday, 24 March 1791

Frank was a bit shy and embarrassed when we met in the stables this morning. Sometimes he's quite brotherly, but at other times he seems uneasy with me when I am by myself. We had a good lesson though. Frank was very encouraging about my progress as a rider. He wanted me to come with him to Deane Gate Inn for the letters, but I didn't feel confident to ride my donkey on the road.

When I went indoors, after he had gone, Jane was still practising the piano so I found Charles and suggested that he give his framed picture of the horse to his mother.

Mrs Austen was very pleased with Charles's drawing. She praised it and immediately got John Warren to knock a nail into the wall in the breakfast parlour so that it could be hung up where everyone could admire it. She's a funny woman; she can be so cold, but also so warm and friendly. She tried to kiss Charles, but he didn't want her to in case the other boys laughed at him, so she kissed me instead and told me what a good girl I was and what a comfort it was to have me. I wish she would act like that to Jane, and then Jane wouldn't be so prickly with her.

But then a minute later, when Henry came down to breakfast and jokingly kissed my hand and told me how pretty I was looking, I saw Mrs Austen look at me with quite a different expression.

The parlourmaid was just bringing in the dish of eggs when Frank arrived back. There was one letter for Henry. He took it reluctantly from Frank's outstretched hand, made a face over it and stuck it into his pocket immediately. There was also one for Mrs Austen. She left hers lying on the table while she was making the tea and then opened it while she was munching through the dry toast that was all she ever ate for breakfast.

'Who's your letter from, my dear?' Mr Austen was always very obliging. He knew that his wife loved to gossip about her letters.

'From Mrs Portal.' Mrs Austen was very thoughtful. The letter was a short one, but she read it through again. I was opposite her at the table and I thought it was probably the third time that she had reread it.

'John's mother?' Henry looked up. 'Perhaps she thinks that I didn't give enough money for his horse. He's her darling only son, you know.'

'No, it's nothing about a horse at all,' said Mrs Austen. She scrutinized Henry from his glossy hair to his well-brushed coat.

'Who is your letter from, Henry?' teased Frank, and Henry gave him an angry look. Jane had told me that Henry was living at home for a while as he had got into debt and owed money to lots of trades-men and a lodging-house keeper in Oxford. I saw Mr Austen look at Henry in a worried way and then at

his wife. She, however, was taking no notice of anyone, but had gone back to staring at her own letter
as if she was planning something. When she spoke,
it was still in that thoughtful manner.

'I was thinking that we would ask the Portals
to drink a dish of tea with us tomorrow evening.
Henry, I wish you would ride over there and take a
note from me, inviting them. The young people could
have a dance with all of you afterwards.'

'What young people?' asked Frank. 'There's only
one — just John.'

'They have a visitor.' While Mrs Austen spoke, her
eyes rested on Henry, tall and handsome, his morning
coat spotless as always, his white silk stock neatly
knotted around his neck, his leather boots polished
(by Charles) to a high shine. When she spoke again it
was directly at him and her voice was low, impressive
and full of meaning. 'A Miss King.'

Jane looked at me and I looked at her. Jane's lips
formed the words 'possessed of a good fortune'.

I gave her a smile, but I felt a little hurt at the way
Henry so quickly got to his feet, checked himself in
the looking glass at the top of the room and then
waited attentively while his mother rapidly wrote
the note, sealed it and handed it to him.

'Take it over to Laverstoke House yourself,'
she said. 'Make sure that you give Miss King my
compliments and say that I am looking forward to
meeting her.'

Friday, 25 March 1791

The Portals didn't come to drink a dish of tea with us today. Henry brought back a polite note saying that Miss King was tired after her journey and wanted to reserve her energies for the ball at the Assembly Rooms in Basingstoke. Mrs Portal hoped that Mrs Austen and her charming family would be present. Henry had not met Miss King, as she had been upstairs when he called. Apparently Mrs Portal had spent some time trying to persuade her to come downstairs, but Miss King had not appeared, although Henry had spent half an hour there making polite conversation in the drawing room.

At lunchtime Mrs Austen seemed to be turning matters over in her mind.

'How did you like William Chute, Jenny?' she enquired casually.

I replied carefully that I thought him very pleasant, but I could feel my cheeks getting red.

'He danced with you, didn't he? Usually he's keener on playing cards than dancing. His mother despairs of him. He's thirty years old and no sign of a wife. And there he is, the master of such a fine property.'

'He danced with all three of the Bigg sisters too,' said Jane promptly. 'Do you think that he will make an offer for every one of them as well as for Jenny?'

'Don't be ridiculous, Jane,' said Mrs Austen automatically.

'They're going to the Assembly Rooms ball tomorrow night, you know,' said Jane warningly. 'And their little brother, Harris, is going too. That's probably a plan. They think that William Chute will be fond of children and Catherine will lead Harris by the hand up to William Chute and then cast down her eyelashes, and William Chute will immediately think what a beautiful mother she will make for his children, so he will propose.'

'Harris Bigg is a confounded nuisance,' said Henry. 'He almost lamed my mare the last time I had her out. He managed to fall off his pony just in front of me. He's the clumsiest child I have ever known. I think he might be a bit simple.'

I wondered what Henry thought about his own brother, George. Jane had said that she was the only one that cared. It seemed strange to me. I had only known George a few weeks, but I was fond of him and I worried about him.

'Harris Bigg! He's younger than me!' Charles stopped eating for a moment, but then carried on again. He still looked indignant, but he liked his food.

'So?' Henry was in a sour mood this morning.

'Well, why can't I go?' Charles swallowed his mouthful.

'You'd have to wear white gloves,' said Mr Austen warningly.

'And no one would dance with you,' said Frank.

'I'll dance with Charles,' I said boldly. Mrs Austen smiled at me affectionately and Charles stuck his tongue out at Frank.

'Save me a dance, Jenny, also,' said Henry. His voice sounded very affectionate and I could feel the warm colour rushing to my cheeks. I looked down at the table and then looked up again. He was still watching me with a smile on his face. I wondered if he thought that I was pretty. I wished that it was just the two of us there in the parlour by ourselves. We had never been alone since that night after the Chutes' dinner party. What did he feel when Mrs Austen talked of William Chute dancing with me? Perhaps he was jealous and that was why he asked me to save him a dance at Basingstoke. If only he knew! William Chute would be nothing to me if only Henry cared for me. But did he? I made myself remember how he flirted with Eliza and forgot me when she was around, but I couldn't help my heart beating very quickly and I hope that nobody noticed that my breaths were short.

'You'll be wearing your new gown, will you?' asked Henry softly. His head was quite close to mine and he seemed to be trying to catch my eye.

'We're hiring a carriage, and Henry and Frank can go on the back. I suppose that Charles could fit in there with them,' said Mrs Austen.

'I don't want to go on the back; Henry and I will ride,' grumbled Frank, to my relief, as my aunt had begun to eye me in an irritable way with Henry still smiling at me, and my cheeks were hot with embarrassment. Now she turned her annoyance on Frank.

'You will do no such thing,' she said decisively. 'We don't want you arriving with mud-splashed breeches. And what about your shoes? You would have to carry them with you. You can't dance at the Assembly Rooms in riding boots.' She wasn't looking at Frank now but at Henry.

'Would you powder your hair, Henry?' she enquired, tilting her head as she surveyed him carefully. 'It would look very good.'

I had to bite my tongue to stop myself exclaiming. I liked Henry's dark hair, tied behind his neck with a plain black ribbon. Powdered hair always looked so artificial.

'Certainly not,' said Henry sternly. 'I have enough expenses without having to buy hair powder, especially now that they are talking of putting a tax on it.'

'Still' — Mrs Austen was trying to console herself — 'I dare say that many young ladies these days may think it looks old-fashioned.'

'Don't worry, Mama.' Henry stooped and gave her a kiss. 'I won't disgrace you. Charles will polish my new shoes with the buckles on them — won't you, Charles?'

'Oh yes,' said Charles eagerly. I guessed that Henry would give him sixpence for doing it. Jane told me that although Henry was in debt, he was always very generous to Charles, and Charles, like Jane, adored him.

'How's James going to get there then? He's coming too, isn't he?' asked Frank, who was still annoyed.

'James,' said Mrs Austen with a small smile, 'will be going with General Mathew and his daughter, Anne.'

'Really?' Mr Austen looked surprised but Mrs Austen distracted him by asking him had he finished with his newspaper – knowing that he hadn't, of course.

'What shall you wear, Mama?' asked Cassandra. She was very careful of her mother's feelings these days, I noticed. Poor girl – she was so relieved at being allowed to consider herself engaged to Tom Fowle.

Mrs Austen laughed. 'I think my yellow silk will have another outing,' she said. 'It's an old friend of twenty years and I wouldn't want to neglect it. Thank God I am too advanced in years for this new fashion of straight-down muslin gowns. I like a gown with a good wide skirt.'

'Jenny,' said Jane later on, 'I was thinking that we might try to dress up George one day, especially now that he has got used to having his hair combed and his face washed. There is an old suit in the theatre dressing-up box. My mother made it for Frank a couple of years ago when he was acting the part of a parson.'

I asked her if she was sure that it was worth both-
ering George about a small thing like clothes. She
didn't reply for a moment, but when she did her answer sent goose pimples down my back.

And this is what she said:

'I'm thinking of bringing him over one day next
week and showing Mama and Papa how he can read
some of his letters.'

Saturday, 26 March 1791

Cousin Eliza and James arrived on the stagecoach this morning. They hadn't told their time of arrival so they drove from Deane Gate Inn by post-chaise. Jane and I were out in the garden gathering daffodils when the chaise, driven by the post boy, skidded across the gravel of the sweep and pulled up in front of the hall door. Eliza was laughing and so was James. He didn't often laugh; I realized that when I saw him now. He handed Eliza out of the chaise with quite an air of a man of the world, and Eliza dropped a splendid curtsy to him. He whispered something in her ear as she rose up gracefully and she said, 'Fie, fie, Sir Anthony!' and they were both laughing as they went up the steps.

I wondered whether Henry saw them.

Jane and I still had a last fitting for our gowns this morning and we had to help with the sewing of the hems, so we didn't join in the rehearsals in the barn. I kept wondering how they were getting on and who Eliza was flirting with — Henry or James?

Eliza was in great good humour at dinner time. Mr Austen laughed so much at one of her tales that a button flew off his waistcoat and Mrs Austen had to sew it on again.

After dinner, Cassandra, Jane and I tried on our new gowns so that Mr Austen and Cousin Eliza could see them. Jane wanted the boys called in, but neither Cassandra nor I agreed with her. I think Cassandra wants to surprise Tom Fowle tomorrow night – and I want to surprise Henry. Cousin Eliza said that she will wash and dress our hair in the latest style from Paris and that we should not let anyone see us until the transformation (she pronounced it in the French fashion) had taken place.

Cassandra took off her gown quite quickly and went back downstairs just as the boys were coming out of the schoolroom. Jane and I stayed chatting with Cousin Eliza and listening to her talk about Marie Antoinette, the Queen of France, and the things that used to go on in the court before this revolution came along.

Cousin Eliza had great plans for doing our hair. She went to her trunk and got out some trim-mings for Jane and me. There was a red velvet rose for Jane and a beautiful blue velvet one for me. I explained that Henry had given us a ribbon each for our hair. I could feel myself getting red, but although the velvet rose was nice, I still wanted to wear his gift. Cousin Eliza didn't mind in the least. She helped us to trim our gowns with the roses instead. They were sewn to the left shoul-der and they looked lovely there.

She said that we were two of the prettiest girls in England and that the young men would be queuing up to dance with us. I hope she is right. I really only know two young men, Henry and Frank.

Frank is very nice, though he's quite young. He probably will dance with me, but I hope that Henry dances with me also.

Eliza then gave us both a little card to record the names of our partners. It was small enough to go in the smallest reticule and it had a tiny little silver pencil attached to it.

'And you must have a fan,' she said suddenly. She went over and rummaged in her trunk and eventually she found two of the most beautiful fans, made so finely of ivory that they were no thicker than a pencil.

'There you are,' she said triumphantly. 'These come from my beloved France. The one with the little pink rosebuds on it for Jane, and the one with white and gold lilies for Jenny.'

'It's lovely, but it's just that I don't want a fan dangling from my wrist all the evening,' said Jane, handing hers back.

'But, *chérie*, you don't dangle your fan from your wrist; you use it, *mon enfant*. Don't you know the language of the fan?'

Jane and I looked at each other and we both

raised our eyebrows. 'No, we don't, Eliza,' said Jane. 'Tell us.'

'Dear, dear, dear, *ma pauvre petite*! Your poor *maman*, Jane! She is so busy with the meals and the washing she has not time to teach the young girls the things that matter.'

'Tell us, Cousin Eliza, please,' I repeated. I couldn't ever imagine Mrs Austen, with her work-worn hands and her battered features, fluttering a fan in front of her face. If we were going to learn, it would have to be from Eliza.

'There are so many things you can say with a fan!' Eliza spread her hands in a very foreign way and then took my fan from me. '*Regardez, mes enfants!* Like this' –

she half folded her fan and put her head on one side – 'you say, "I'm not sure," and then, like this' – she folded up the fan and turned its left side upper-most – 'this says, "Call tomorrow," and . . .'

'Jane,' screamed Mrs Austen from the bottom of the stairs, 'where did you put my shawl? I declare to the heavens, you are the untidiest girl I have ever seen or heard of in my life! Come down at once and find it.'

'Wait till I come back – I want to hear all the rest.' Jane slammed the door behind her and went clattering down the stairs.

When she was gone I asked Eliza how men knew how to understand the language of the fan. Did someone teach them? I was thinking about Henry, and the strange thing was that I think Eliza might have been thinking about Henry too when she answered with a slight smile on her beautifully rouged lips.

'*Chérie*, a wise young man will always get an experienced lady to teach him the language of love.'

For a few minutes neither of us said anything, but then as we heard Jane's footsteps running up the stairs, Eliza said, very softly, 'Jenny, Henry is sweet and good-natured, but he is a young man, and young men love to play games. Do not get too serious. You have fun while you are young.'

And then Jane whirled back into the room and Eliza gave us more lessons on the language of the fan until we were quite perfect – though I could never imagine myself unfurling my fan in that dramatic gesture that meant: *I love you!*

'I'm going to have such fun teaching Tom Chute all about this!' said Jane in the end.

But I'm not going to have to teach Henry, I thought to myself; I think he probably knows it already. Did

I mind? I decided not to think of it any more. Cousin Eliza was just having fun with Henry. Perhaps I should do the same.

Before we left, Eliza told us both to come to her room after supper.

'Her first ball is the most exciting event in a young girl's life,' she said dramatically. 'You come here to my *chambre* after supper, and I will get you ready. You will bathe here —' She gestured theatrically towards the hip bath by the fire. It had a screen half around it, but I could see a basket full of little jars and bottles on a stool. 'And I shall shampoo your hair with my special shampoo from India. My godfather, Warren Hastings, brings me a present of some every time he visits England, so I shall shampoo and dress your hair and then you can have a little rest. One should always rest before dancing — and then you will come back in here and don your new gowns. And then the ball!'

'Thank you very much, Cousin Eliza,' I said, and Jane hugged her.

'I shall enjoy it hugely,' said Eliza. 'You must go now, *mes petites*. I shall take a little *promenade* over to the barn to run through my part again.' She slipped on her cloak and pulled the large hood over her head.

I don't know who she is going to practise with as James has already left for General Mathew's place. She and Henry don't have a scene together.

I could hardly eat any supper as I was so excited and so nervous, and Jane was almost as bad. As soon as the meal was over and the table cleared, we slipped upstairs, telling Mrs Austen that we were going to have a rest. First of all we went into our bedroom. It was still bright out of doors, but the room was dim and the two white and silver gowns hanging on the closet door gleamed with the shimmer of moonlight.

'I can't believe that it is going to happen, can you?' I asked Jane, but she just said, 'Grab your towel and wrapper before Cassandra comes along to see what we are doing.'

We tiptoed down the stairs, taking the steps cautiously one by one so that the wood did not squeak. Just as we got to the bottom of the flight, Sukey, the kitchen maid, came toiling up, carrying two heavy pails of steaming hot water, one in either hand. Jane opened the door for her and then we went in. The room was already steamy, with a huge glowing fire, and it smelt of rich and exotic scents. As we came in, Eliza was emptying a small bottle of bright red liquid into the water already in the bath. Sukey poured first one pailful and then the second one and the red liquid swirled in cloudy whirls and coils, the vivid colour changing to a dusky pink. The air was filled with a sweet fragrance and then Eliza added a hand-ful of lavender to the water and the clean, sharp smell blended with the perfume of roses.

'Thank you, Sukey,' said Eliza gently. Sukey looked almost bewitched by the scents, but she pulled herself together and bobbed a curtsy. 'Here you are,' said Eliza, handing her a coin. 'Come back with two more pails in half an hour.' And then, Eliza being Eliza, she took a little scented muslin bag from her basket and handed it to the kitchen maid. 'Put that under your pillow tonight, Sukey, and you will have sweet dreams.'

'Thank you, ma'am.' Sukey bobbed another curtsy and went towards the door, taking one last look at the steaming bath before closing the door quietly be-hind her.

'Now, *mes petites*, we have to decide on a soap for you.'

'We brought our soap, Eliza,' said Jane, holding out the scummy white bar that lived on our wash-stand.

'*Mais non! Mais non!*' Eliza was getting more French by the moment. She took the soap from Jane, smelt it and put it down with a shudder. 'No, that coarse lye soap is *terrrrrible* for your delicate skins. How could your *maman* give you such a thing?

203

Voilà!' And Eliza went in behind the screen and came out with two bars of soap and held them out. Jane touched the orange one, but I only had eyes for the second piece of soap. It was a pale green, shiny and smooth and glossy. I sniffed the bar, and Eliza handed it to me with a smile. I held it up to the light from the window. It was completely translucent and it smelt wonderfully romantic and aromatic — like pine needles under a hot sun.

'Mine smells of oranges,' said Jane, sniffing hers.

'You have chosen so well, my children,' enthused Eliza. 'I knew that the green would suit Jenny's character — shy, like a little violet in the moss be- side a spring — and you, my Jane, this is your scent — sharp, exotic, spicy — just like your personality.'

First Eliza washed my hair with her special In- dian shampoo. She rubbed and massaged my head and then showed me in the looking glass. I had white foam like a whipped syllabub all over my head, almost like a very curly wig, and I smelt of incense.

While I bathed, Jane had her hair shampooed and then she bathed. Eliza insisted that we use her thick Turkish tow- els, not the thin, hard towels from our bedroom, and while we sat, wrapped in these, in front of the fire, she styled our hair.

Mine was pulled back from my face, with just one little curl hanging over my forehead. Then Eliza fastened the rest of my hair with a little ribbon of rubber on the back of the crown of the head and allowed the whole weight of it to flow down my back. While the hair was still damp, she quickly wound strands of it around spills of paper and tied them tightly with rags.

'Leave them in place until after your gown is on. I myself will brush it out and fasten the blue velvet bandeau. You will be ravishing, *ma petite*!'

And then Eliza went to work on Jane's hair. First she sprinkled it with an exotic oil that filled the room with its spicy smell and then she wound each curl around her finger, brushing it and holding it in place until it dried before going on to the next.

'I shall just take some of this back hair to form *un petit chignon*,' she cried. 'Ah, now, it starts to come together. *Voyons,* we will make you a little dark-haired rose.'

And the amazing thing was that Jane's head did look like a rose — like one of those huge French roses with hundreds of curled petals. I told her how pretty she looked — she couldn't do the same for me with my hair all screwed into corkscrew spirals, but I had complete confidence in Cousin Eliza.

'And now, *mes enfants,* go back to your room and sleep. I will wake you before the carriage comes and help you to get dressed. But sleep now.'

Jane is asleep as I write this, but I couldn't sleep. I wanted to write down everything about that extraordinary hour in *Madame la Comtesse*'s room. When I am old, I will read these pages again and I will remember what it was like.

The Assembly Rooms
at Basingstoke

Sukey taps at the door and we both wake with a start. She puts fresh wood on to the fire, lights the candles, and then goes out with a last look at the two beautiful gowns. 'Jane, help me with my stays. Lace them tighter . . . tighter. They should push the bosom up.'

I can hardly breathe, but then Jane opens the laces a little. 'You look fine,' she says. 'At least you have a bosom to show off. I wish my bosom would grow a bit. I'm going to stuff a couple of Cassandra's torn silk stockings inside my stays.'

I slip on my chemise and then my finest lawn petticoat. I wear my shortest petticoat. I don't want any of it to be seen under the gown. The gown is too beautiful.

And then Eliza appears with her hair in curling papers and wearing a very becoming wrapper of lace; she seizes the two gowns and we follow her to her chamber, which is lit by at least twenty candles. She hangs up the gowns and then shakes a little more of that spicy, aromatic oil over Jane's hair and brushes her curls once more.

Then Jane has to sit very still with a piece of old muslin over her head to absorb the extra oil while Eliza takes out my curling papers and brushes each fat ringlet over her finger and arranges Henry's bandeau carefully, pulling forward a couple of curls over my forehead. She brings over the looking glass and I think that I look years older, that my hair is blonde and beautiful, that my eyes are large and even bluer than my velvet bandeau. I don't even notice my snub nose.

Then Eliza slips our gowns over our heads very carefully, produces two pairs of superfine white elbow-length gloves from her trunk, hands us our fans and our reticules. Last of all she leads us over to a full-sized cheval looking glass – the only one in the house, I think – and we both tell each other how lovely we look.

'That gown really suits you. I think white is your best colour,' I say to Jane. 'I like you better in white than in pink.'

'I'm glad we forced Mama to agree to short sleeves, aren't you?' Jane was admiring her bare arms.

'I love them.' But I was too busy looking over my shoulder, admiring the shimmer of blue light from the beads on my train, to bother about my arms.

'Sit on the bed, *mes enfants,* while I dress,' says Eliza, and we sit and admire how swiftly she gets ready, patting her lips with a piece of damp red leather from Brazil (so she told us), brushing out her curls, dusting her face with some talc and pulling on a pair of superfine silk stockings before taking a gown of shimmering lilac from her press.

'The coach from the inn has arrived.' Charles is clattering up the stairs, his voice high with excitement.

'Let's go,' I say, opening the door and looking out.

Charles is wearing a pair of white gloves; they are far too big for him and look quite comic next to his young-boy skeleton suit.

'Don't forget you promised me a dance, Jenny,' he says. He looks so sweet with his well-brushed hair that I feel quite motherly towards him. He sounds a bit anxious so I smile reassuringly at him as I drape a lace shawl lent by Eliza over my shoulders. Mrs Austen says that I will be cold, but I don't want to spoil the effect of my lovely gown with my old blue cloak.

In the end, Mr Austen, Henry and Frank have gone to Basingstoke by stagecoach with the other boys from Mr Austen's school. It is just as well; I'm worried about my gown as Jane and I squeeze next to Eliza, while Cassandra, Charles and Mrs Austen sit opposite. I wish I didn't have to sit down; I'm worried in case I lose one of the glass beads, although Jane and I sewed them on as firmly as we could. It seems an age before we arrive at Basingstoke.

When we get out of the coach we have to walk up the stairs. Luckily they are laid with a beautiful red carpet so I allow my train to swish up behind me, though Mrs Austen, Cassandra and Jane hold theirs up.

The Assembly Rooms are grander than I could ever have imagined. The ballroom is painted in red and gold. The ceiling is embossed with curls and scrolls of stucco, all crusted in white. Four great chandeliers, their diamond-shaped crystal droplets flashing in the light of the hundreds of beeswax candles above, hang from the ceiling, and in their light, gowns – pink, white, green, blue – revolve in the dance.

I can't walk in. I can't follow the others. I just stand, looking, until Henry comes back to me.

'Come on, Jenny,' he whispers, taking my arm. 'You look lovely. They're just finishing the cotillion and then they will have a country dance. You'll be my partner, won't you?'

And then we are in the line facing each other and the music has begun. We move to and fro. Other couples are talking but we are just dancing: just dancing and look-ing at each other. His eyes are fixed on me.

And then we take hands and Henry swings me around and around. He is smiling and I start to smile too.

And then I see Eliza. She is dancing with a foreign-looking man. They pass down the row in front of us and they are both chattering in French. They act like old friends and he is calling her *'chérie'*.

And then Henry and I thread in and out of the line, going down to the bottom of the row and then back again. For a moment, Jane and I are briefly opposite each other. She doesn't even see me; she is too busy laughing with the Irish cousin of the Lefroys.

Now Henry takes my hand and we join with Gilbert East and a girl called Charlotte Palmer, who are the couple nearest to us, and we whirl around in a circle.

And then the music stops and everyone stands laugh-ing and chatting.

'Henry!' It's a fine young gentleman in a red coat with gold epaulettes on the shoulders and a high gold collar. 'Henry, what's the news? What did your father say? Will he be able to come up with the money to buy you a commission?'

A commission? Suddenly I stop smiling. Does Henry really want to join the army?

'Frederick!' Henry is a bit uneasy. He looks at me and then across at his mother, sitting on a sofa by the wall.

'Come on, Jenny,' he says, 'you look a bit tired after that dance. I'll take you over to Mama so you can have a rest.'

I'm not tired, but I allow him to walk me across the room. He is the most handsome man in the room, I think proudly, admiring the glossy black of his evening coat and the snowy whiteness of his cravat.

'Jenny! Is it time for our dance?' Little Charles is jumping up and down with excitement. Quickly he takes his white gloves out from his pocket and does his best to pull them as high as possible so that his fingers can come some way near to the tips of the gloves' fingers. He is so excited that I feel ashamed. If Henry had wanted to go on dancing with me, I would have forgotten all about the poor little fellow.

'Quick,' I say. 'The music is starting. Let's take our place in the line.'

I see a few people smiling when I join the line and face my little escort. His face is pink with excitement and he bows to me in a very courtly way. Gilbert East bumps into him purposely, but Charles takes no notice. He is concentrating very hard and I see his lips counting 'one, two, three; one, two, three' as we whirl around.

'The next dance is mine, Jenny,' says Henry as we cross over. I feel his gloved palm touch my bare arm for an instant, above my elbow. Even though my gown is so light and I didn't obey Mrs Austen and wear a flannel chemise, I suddenly feel very hot.

'Do you like dancing?' asks Charles in a very grown-up manner.

'I love it,' I say. I hope he won't keep talking to me; I want to think about Henry. I needn't have worried; even those few words make him miss his step, and he goes back to counting, his lips moving silently. Jane is dancing with Tom Chute. They are having a good time; as I'm not talking I can hear them making funny remarks to each other as they stand at the end of the row, waiting their turn to go up to the top again.

'A fine sight, ma'am,' says Tom. 'It makes one proud to be a part of this great civilization where such sprightly dancing takes place.'

'Nonsense, my dear man,' says Jane, imitating her mother's voice as usual. 'Every savage can dance.'

'There's Anna Terry over there,' I say to Charles when the dance has finished. 'Why don't you go and ask her to dance?' Anna Terry is younger than Jane and she looks a bit bored, leaning up against the sofa where her mother is sitting.

Charles eyes her doubtfully for a moment; I fear that

he will want me to dance with him again, so I quickly say, 'I've promised the next one to Henry.'

He nods and saunters off towards Anna in a very 'man-of-the-world' fashion. I don't look after him though, because I am looking for Henry. This will be a beautiful dance, a dance to remember. I know that by the slow, sweet music that is coming from the violins.

And everything is perfect. Henry doesn't want to talk either, so we just move silently through all the figures of the dance, going forward, reversing, bowing, curtsying, threading our way in and out, crossing over, the skirt of Henry's frock coat brushing against my hip as we pass one another.

And then the dance is over. Henry and I are standing beside the refreshment table and I am drinking a small glass of wine. I don't like it much, but I drink it because Henry has fetched it for me. He is standing so close to me. I remember the time that he lifted me from the coach in his arms.

And then that friend of Henry's, the officer, comes up with a very fashionable lady. She is wearing a jaconet dress, and the muslin is the finest and softest that I have ever seen. It fits her like a glove and it is cut so low that I can see most of her bosom. She is the only young lady wearing a hat, and a splendid hat it is, beaded all over and crowned with some very tall ostrich feathers. It makes her look even taller than she is – she towers over me. I don't care. Tonight I don't mind being small. I don't mind not having a hat. I like the way that Jane and

I are wearing our hair. And I like the velvet ribbon and the feel of the curls falling down my back. Henry likes them too, I think. I felt him touch my curls once when he was leading me back to my place.

'Miss King,' says the officer, 'may I present my friend Mr Henry Austen.'

I know who she is now. She's the heiress from London, the one who is staying with the Portals at Laverstoke House. Jane overheard Mrs Austen yesterday, joking about her to Henry and telling him that Miss King has a fortune of thirty thousand pounds.

And now Henry is bowing over her hand. 'May I have the pleasure of the next dance, Miss King?' he enquires.

I feel my cheeks burn. I put down the glass of wine. I don't know what to do. I had assumed that Henry would dance with me next. The officer has gone back to his own party and I am left standing there feeling awkward. I have a quick look around for Jane, but she is with the Lefroy party. Perhaps I should just walk across the room and go to sit beside Mrs Austen. Perhaps that was my last dance and I shall spend the next three sitting out. I start to move away, but then Henry suddenly remembers me.

'My cousin Miss Cooper, Miss King,' he says, and we both bow stiffly at each other. I can see her looking me up and down, perhaps trying to assess what my gown cost or how old I am.

Then Henry beckons to Frank. Frank instantly comes

214

across. He gives Henry a glance and then turns to me.

'Dance with me, Jenny,' he says. He sounds uncomfortable and self-conscious. I wonder whether Henry has teased him about me, although we have often danced together at Steventon. Now he's awkward with embarrassment. I put my hand in his though. At least it gets me away from Henry and Miss King.

Frank is not much of a talker; he is too busy looking around the room to see if there is anyone from the navy present. He spends all of his time talking just about the navy, and he is always going to visit naval men. While we are waiting for the music to begin he tells me all about how someone he knows captured a French frigate – or perhaps it was Spanish – and all the officers got a fortune.

'When do you leave to join your ship?' I ask him politely as we meet in the centre, but he has gone, moving around Tom Fowle with a cheerful grin.

I give up trying to talk. It leaves me time to watch Henry and Miss King. He is smiling at her in just the same way as he smiled at me, bending his head and then laughing at something she says. I suppose she is very witty, not shy and quiet like me.

'Guess what,' says Jane as I move around her on my way down to the end of the row.

'What?' I slow down a little. I don't suppose Frank will miss me.

'Fanny Dashwood opened the ball with Mr Wickham and now she is dancing with William Denn. They say that she is going to jilt Mr Wickham,' Jane hisses in my ear and then we part, she moving up the room still opposite the Irish cousin of the Lefroys, and me going down opposite Frank. I can see that she is using her fan energetically and he is laughing aloud as she explains it to him.

'You're looking lovely, Jenny,' says Frank, as he holds my hand and twirls me around.

I smile at him and think it is nice of him to make the effort to compliment me, but his head has twisted around almost before the words are out of his mouth.

'Who's that?' he asks. 'Look, Jenny, the chap who has just come in – the fellow in the blue coat. Who's that, I wonder?'

He doesn't expect me to know, or even to answer him.

But I do know who it is.

It is a tall, black-haired, handsome young man wearing the blue uniform of a naval officer, his coat opened at the top to show the white ruffled shirt. It is Captain Thomas Williams.

I just can't believe it. I never expected to see him again in my life. What is he doing here? Why isn't he in Southampton? Or why isn't he on his ship? I am glad that I am holding Frank's hand, otherwise I might faint. What am I going to do? What if he sees me? What if he tells someone about me?

Frank and I have danced to the end of the line and now it is our chance to talk. I look at him and he looks at me. We both begin to say something at the same time, but Frank's remark is probably more interesting than mine.

'Do you know, Jenny, a fellow told me that Captain William Parker has got forty thousand in prize money after only ten years of being in command of his own ship.'

'Really,' I say, trying to control the panic in my voice. 'That sounds a lot of money. How did he get all that?'

Frank gives an impatient sigh. 'By capturing frigates, of course! Each petty officer and midshipman gets his share. Freddie was only a midshipman on his last voyage, but he got seven hundred and ninety-one pounds as his share of the prize money . . . and eight shillings and a halfpence,' he added after a minute. At any other time this would have made me giggle, but now I am too worried about Captain Williams.

I wonder what the prize money for the captain was, but I don't ask as we have started to dance again. Is there any way of avoiding Captain Williams? He's bound to tell everyone where and how he met me. What will Mrs Austen say if she hears that I was out in the streets of a rough place like Southampton at midnight? What if Augusta gets to hear of it? I close my eyes at the terrible thought.

'Jenny?' Suddenly I realize that the music has stopped and that Frank has asked me a question.

'Sorry, Frank, what did you say?' My voice sounds as distracted as I feel.

'Would you like me to take you back to Mama?' Two

other naval officers have joined Captain Williams and I can see that Frank is itching to join their group.

'No, don't worry about me, Frank. Look, there's Jane over there. I'll join her.'

Jane has left the Irish Lefroy cousin. I rush over and seize her by the hand.

'Jane,' I whisper, 'help me. I'm in terrible trouble. I don't know what to do. He's here.'

'Who? The love of your life? The man that has your heart? Oh, Jenny, Jenny, show him to me, I pray.' Jane's eyes are sparkling with fun; obviously she has not understood the situation.

'Jane!' I hiss. Usually I find it funny when Jane talks like the characters in Mrs Radcliffe's novels, but now is not the time.

'What's the matter, Jenny? You've gone as white as a sheet.' Jane's voice changes: she knows that this is not a joke.

'It's that man,' I whisper. 'He's here.'

'What man?' Jane looks all around the crowded Assembly Rooms.

'The man at Southampton. The man I told you about. The man I met when I went to post the letter to your mother.'

'What! The one waving the sword?' Jane stares over at a crowd of scarlet-coated army officers who are laughing uproariously at some joke.

'No, not him.' Quickly I duck beneath one of the huge parlour palms. Its fronds make a dark cave from which I can peer out. I can still see the naval officers. Frank has joined them now. 'No! The other one – Captain Williams the naval officer.'

'Well, you'd better keep out of his way,' says Jane, looking all around her. 'Anyone except me would die of horror if they knew that you were out at midnight in the streets of Southampton without a chaperone.'

'Oh, Jane, what will I do?' I am in despair. I can't spend the rest of the evening hiding under a potted palm.

'I think you'd better go and sit by Mama for the next dance. He won't notice you there; young men are looking at the young ladies on the dance floor, not at the old ladies by the wall,' says Jane wisely. 'Walk on this side of me. Keep your face turned towards the wall. Here, link your arm in mine.'

'Is he looking?' I whisper.

'Which one is he?' Jane speaks in her normal tone.

'The black-haired one.'

'He's quite handsome.'

'Quite handsome!' He's as beautiful as a god, I think, but I don't say it aloud. I can see Jane smiling though, so I think she is just trying to tease me.

'Well, very handsome. I see what you mean about those cheekbones. He probably is a man of property. His breeches are very white. That shows the wool is of superfine quality,' says Jane, sounding like Cassandra in one of her instructing moods. 'No, he's not looking. He's chatting to Frank.'

I keep my head turned away and Jane links me so tightly that we are almost like one girl as we move through the room.

'My dear creature, let us keep together; let no man come between us.'

Jane is getting as much fun as she can out of the walk down the room, but I feel my legs trembling and I can't help peeping around Jane to see if the dark head and the splendid lace shirt of Captain Williams are turned in my direction.

Mrs Austen is not best pleased to see us. Mr Austen has gone to play cards in the card room and his wife is enjoying a good gossip with an old school-friend of hers, a Mrs Allen.

'Very rich indeed,' she is saying in a penetrating whisper as we draw near. 'It would be just the thing for him. He's always had a way with him, you know. Could always charm the birds out of the trees. I . . . Yes, girls?' Her tone to us is quite sharp.

'Jenny is tired,' says Jane. 'I thought she could sit the next dance out here with you.'

'Sit here, my dear.' Mrs Allen is probably getting tired of the conversation about Henry and the very rich Miss King, because she makes room for me on the sofa beside her.

'Come on, Jane.' Tom Chute comes up and takes Jane by the hand. She puts her fan into the 'maybe' position and then they both laugh uproariously. I envy her. She

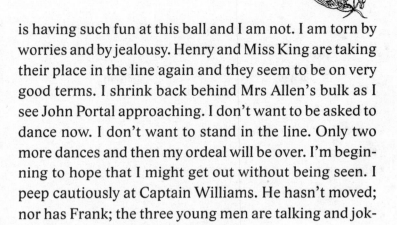

is having such fun at this ball and I am not. I am torn by worries and by jealousy. Henry and Miss King are taking their place in the line again and they seem to be on very good terms. I shrink back behind Mrs Allen's bulk as I see John Portal approaching. I don't want to be asked to dance now. I don't want to stand in the line. Only two more dances and then my ordeal will be over. I'm beginning to hope that I might get out without being seen. I peep cautiously at Captain Williams. He hasn't moved; nor has Frank; the three young men are talking and joking and waving their arms around.

'Jenny, could you go and bring two glasses of wine from the buffet for myself and Mrs Allen.' On the dance floor, Miss King is laughing heartily as she touches her hand to Henry's and he is laughing also. They look as if they are getting on very well indeed, and Mrs Austen probably wants to talk it over with Mrs Allen. There is no help for it. I get to my feet and walk across the room to the buffet. I take the two glasses of wine and walk back. The music pauses, everyone is still. Only one person is moving, and that one person is me.

And our eyes meet. Captain Williams sees me and he knows me. He doesn't bow, but I know that he recognizes me; I can see from the way that his tall, broad-shouldered figure suddenly becomes rigid and his head turns towards me – not moving, just looking – while all around him the other naval officers are laughing noisily and slapping each other on the back. His brown eyes are focused on me and somehow they seem darker than I remember them – almost black. His lips are just parted – I'd forgotten what a beautifully shaped mouth he has. I look carefully at the two drinks and hear the first bars of the new set strike up. In a moment the whole room is in motion again. I keep walking; my eyes are now on the sofa. I will not look at anything else. I carefully hand the two glasses to Mrs Austen and her friend. I don't sit down on the sofa again. There is no point now.

He has seen me..

I go and stand by the window and look down into the street below. If only I had not met him that night at Southampton. If only we were strangers, and then Frank could introduce me and he would ask me to dance and he would say to me, 'Tell me all about yourself.'

But that is just a fairy tale.

In another minute he's going to say to one of his friends, 'I know that girl! I met her walking the streets of Southampton at midnight . . .'

And Frank will say, 'But that's my cousin . . .'

And he will come across the room and talk to Mrs Austen about me . . .

Now the music stops and the line breaks up. The laughing, talking girls and their escorts move around the room, taking a glass of wine from the buffet, greeting friends, curtsying to new partners.

And Captain Thomas Williams starts to walk across the room.

Sunday, 27 March 1791

Jane has gone down to the village to see George. Just before she went she said to me, 'This will give you a chance to write in your journal. You must have plenty to say.' She didn't realize that I had been writing half the night already by firelight and now I am so tired that I don't know how to tell the rest of it properly.

I've done all the easy bits:
  Henry . . .
  Henry with me . . .
  Henry with Miss King . . .
  Two dances with me . . .
  Four dances with Miss King . . .
  And my dances?
  Well, one dance with Henry . . .
  One with little Charles . . .
  Another with Henry . . .
  One with Frank . . .
  One with William Chute . . .
  One with John Portal . . .
  One dance wasted, sitting on the sofa with Mrs Austen and her friend Mrs Allen . . .
  And that leaves two dances.
  And I did dance these two.
  And this is how it happened.
  It was Frank who introduced Captain Williams to

his mother. He hurried up after him and made the introductions as well as he could. My heart was thudding, but I had plenty of time to recover as no one looked at me for a few minutes. Luckily Cassandra and Tom Fowle had just joined Mrs Austen and she spent some time introducing them both to Captain Williams and explaining about their recent engagement.

'I hope you will both be very happy.' These were the first words that I heard him say. I remembered the voice though, velvet-smooth like chocolate. By this time my heart had slowed down and the strange singing in my ears had gone. Now Jane had come over. She looked at Captain Williams with an innocent expression, as if wondering who he was.

'And this is my younger daughter, Jane, and a neighbour, Tom Chute.'

I was getting the impression that Mrs Austen liked the young captain, or perhaps she was just in a good mood because Henry was still with Miss King, handing her a glass of wine and laughing uproariously at some remark she had just made.

'And this is Jenny Cooper, my niece.' Mrs Austen sounded very affectionate as she beckoned me forward.

I curtsied. I did not dare look at him, but from under my eyelashes I saw him bow.

'Miss Cooper.' He sounded as if he had never seen me before in my life. After a moment I got the courage to look at him.

He did know me though.

I knew that by the look in his eyes.

He has lovely eyes.

Lovely big, brown eyes, with long black eye-lashes . . .

'Will you do me the pleasure of dancing the next dance with me, Miss Cooper?' The words were ordinary, but he sounded as if he really did want to dance with me. He bowed with great politeness and held out his arm.

I curtsied again. I did not feel that I could be sure of my voice if I said anything.

I felt slightly light-headed as I put my gloved hand on his outstretched arm.

We took our place in the line. I wondered what to say. I almost felt as if tears would come soon. I gulped and then looked at him.

'Are you enjoying the dance, Miss Cooper?'

He sounded as though he had never met me before in his life, but I knew better. When I glanced up at him there was a look of amusement in his brown eyes. He must have thought it all very funny. I remember the great shouts of laughter that were coming from the group of naval officers. I thought they were laughing about me, that perhaps he had said to them, '*Look at that girl over there in the white gown. You'd never guess, but the last time that I saw her she was wandering around the streets, all by herself, at midnight in Southampton.*'

'Have you ever been to the Assembly Rooms here before?' He was doing his best to keep the conversation going, but I had such a lump in my throat that I could say nothing.

To my horror, I felt a tear trickle from each eye. In another moment I would be crying and I would spoil everything. I didn't care who I danced with: Frank, Charles, William Chute – anyone except this man that knew my dark secret. Mrs Austen's words – *'Men talk together in card rooms and drinking places about girls like that'* – were burning in my ears.

'Miss Cooper.' His beautiful deep voice was very soft. 'Don't look so worried. I won't tell anyone that I met you before. Let's just pretend we met for the first time tonight and then we'll both enjoy the dance.'

I looked at him doubtfully. There was still a look of amusement, but there was something else also in those brown eyes. I can't quite describe what that look was. His eyes changed colour a lot. Now they had gone very dark again and they were looking at me steadily. I remember Jane giggling about the expression *'smouldering eyes'* in a Mrs Radcliffe novel; I had giggled too, but when I looked up into those almost-black eyes, I knew what *smouldering* meant. I looked down at my fan and then at my shoes. He didn't seem to want to talk; he seemed just to want to look at me, and the few minutes that we stood together seemed almost like an hour . . .

Then I looked up at him a little fearfully and at last he smiled.

White teeth, a curve of smooth lips . . . soft brown eyes above the strong bones of his cheeks . . .

I had forgotten how broad-shouldered and tall he is, and how protected I had felt when we walked arm in arm at Southampton that night . . .

And suddenly I felt happy.

I remember laughing.

And he laughed too as we joined hands and danced down to the bottom of the set.

We were almost like old friends, quite at ease with each other.

And then we were in a group of four with Jane and Tom Chute.

'He's certainly very handsome,' whispered Jane as we linked hands and went around in a circle.

'Do you like him?' I whispered the next time we met.

Jane didn't have time to answer as Tom Chute whirled her around and around. I was looking forward to talking to her after the dance was over, but I didn't have a chance, because when it was over Captain Williams offered me his arm and escorted me over to the supper table, where I sat down.

'Have some cake,' he said, and his voice was very gentle. 'Sweet cake is always good for shock. And it was a bit of a shock for you to see me again, wasn't it?'

I smiled gratefully. Charles passed us, giggling

happily with thirteen-year-old Anna Lefroy, and gave us a merry wave. I waved back.

'Who's that? One of your admirers?' I loved his laugh. There was something about it that made me feel that we were very close to each other. My face flushed at the thought.

I told him that Charles was my cousin, and I explained how he was so keen to join the navy and how he wants to be a midshipman, just like his brother Frank.

'Well, I hope his parents don't let him join too early,' he said seriously. 'A couple of years ago, I had an eleven-year-old midshipman, called Charles also, by coincidence. He was wished on me by my uncle the admiral, who was friendly with the boy's mother. I seemed to spend all of his first year with me saving him from sudden death!'

And then he told me the story of how a Spanish ship attacked his ship and how the Spaniard fired a ball and chain from the cannon and brought down the rigging – block and tackle and all.

'And of course young Charles was standing right underneath it. He was too petrified with fear to move. I barely managed to get myself in the path to deflect it, then stupidly bungled it and took the weight of it on my left shoulder. It would have killed the boy if it had hit his head. As it was . . .' Almost automatically his hand went up and rubbed his left shoulder.

'Does it still hurt?' I had noticed that during the left swings in the dance he had seemed to hold that arm a little stiffly.

'Not much,' he said briefly. 'Now, tell me about all of your cousins. I've met Frank.'

So one by one I pointed out all the Austen family to him: Jane laughing with Tom Chute, James being very gallant with Anne Mathew, Henry still with Miss King (funnily enough I didn't care), Cousin Eliza flirting outrageously with the French gentleman, Cassandra and Tom Fowle talking quietly in a corner, Mrs Austen still on the sofa, of course, and Mr Austen coming out of the card room with a couple of his friends. I didn't mention my brother, Edward-John, or his wife, Augusta. I didn't want to think about them.

What I was thinking about was the story that Captain Williams had told – so lightly and so humorously – painting a picture of himself to be clumsy and stupid for not pushing the rigging away more quickly – rather than making himself a hero for saving a boy's life.

'Is Jane, Miss Jane . . . she's the cousin that you were trying to get help for, isn't she?'

I nod. 'She's fine now,' I said. 'Mrs Austen came immediately. She did get the letter that morning just as you said. Jane recovered once she came home again. I fell ill then, but I recovered very quickly.'

'You were ill?' He asked the question in a strange sharp voice.

'But I'm well again now.'

He said nothing, but he lifted my hand and I felt the pressure of his lips on my fingers.

That was the second time that he had kissed my hand, I thought, remembering how he had done this in Southampton as he left me at the front door of Mrs Cawley's. There was a strange look in his eyes and it seemed to me that there was almost something like fear in them . . . or perhaps it was anger . . .

But then the fiddles struck up again. It was the boulanger, the last dance of the evening. I couldn't believe it. If only it were the first!

'This is my favourite dance,' said Captain Williams when he heard the music. His lovely brown eyes smiled down at me as he took my hand. It was a lively tune and it seemed to bring a smile to every face. Perhaps it was my mood, but I thought that I had never seen everyone look so happy.

And we set out hand in hand, skipping to the tune, going right down to the bottom of the line and then back up again. Jane was dancing with the Irish cousin of the Lefroys again and they were joking about his coming from a place called Limerick.

'What shocking behaviour,' she murmured as I paused beside her, marking time with my feet while the men crossed and recrossed the central space. 'I saw you, you sly creature. I saw you sitting out with your beau and flirting with him.'

I only laughed. I wasn't embarrassed. I was feeling too happy. I felt like I haven't felt since I was about five, I think — just quite carefree and merry and without any responsibilities. But when his turn came to swing me from his left hand I was very careful not to lean outwards and put pressure on his sore shoulder.

When the dance was over he tucked my arm inside his, reminding me once more of the time we walked together in Southampton, and escorted me over to Mrs Austen. 'You will permit me to call to see you at Steventon,' he said, lifting my hand to his lips. Even through my glove I felt the warmth of his mouth.

And then he took leave of Mrs Austen. She had overheard him, I know, and she invited him very warmly to visit us at Steventon and gave him all sorts of directions so that he would not miss his way.

Six o'clock on Sunday, 27 March

And he didn't come.

And now it is probably too late.

After church, Mrs Austen reminded Henry in a sharp tone that he should go and see Miss King.

'Surely you know by now that it is etiquette to enquire after a lady that you danced with at a ball.'

'Enquire what?' yawned Henry, and put up his hands to defend himself as his mother tried to box his ears.

'Enquire whether she is rested after her exertions at the ball, you big booby.' Mrs Austen was laughing, but then she glanced at me and glanced at the clock. And a slightly worried look came over her face.

'Where is Captain Williams staying, Jenny?' she asked.

'I don't know, ma'am,' I said. I didn't dare mention the word *Southampton* in case I blushed.

'Do you know, Frank?' she asked.

'No, I don't,' said Frank. He sounded grumpy too. Perhaps everyone is out of sorts after a ball.

Jane looked at me and I looked at her.

'It's only one o'clock,' she whispered.

But then it was two o'clock . . .

Three o'clock . . .

Four o'clock . . .
And then five o'clock . . .
And then six o'clock . . .
And then I couldn't bear it any longer and I slipped upstairs to write in my journal.

Monday, 28 March 1791

And Captain Williams didn't come today either.

Henry was in a bad mood after dinner. He kept giving short answers to his mother and father and teasing Frank, mocking his adolescent voice that occasionally went high and then very low. Eventually Frank kicked over a chair and stormed out. After a minute I went after him. I felt sorry for him. Frank has a very intense and fiery temperament and hates to be made a fool of.

There was no sign of him when I got outside so I went into the stables. Frank was there, taking down his saddle, but he was in a thoroughly bad mood, hardly answering when I spoke to him. I cast around for something to say and then told him that Captain Williams had said something about the repairs to Frank's ship, *Perseverance.*

It didn't work though; he just grunted and busied himself with the straps of his saddle. His back was towards me when he spoke.

'I'll tell you one thing, Jenny, about your wonderful Captain Williams. All the men say that he is a terrible flirt and that he has a girl in every port, so I wouldn't trust him too much, if I were you.'

And then he jumped on his horse and was riding fast down the avenue. I stayed for a few minutes to pat my donkey and then when I turned to go back Henry was behind me.

I asked him whether he was looking for Frank – I thought that perhaps he had come to apologize, but Henry shook his head.

'What would I want that overgrown hobble-dehoy for?' He said the words so scornfully that I felt even more sorry for Frank. I know what it feels like to be half grown-up and it's not a comfortable feeling. Eleven-year-old Charles was much happier than Frank. He never worried about how he looked or what he sounded like. Frank did, I know. I understand that because I am always remembering things that I said and then blushing as I think I probably sounded silly.

'Poor Frank,' I said aloud.

'You're so sweet, Jenny; it's like you to worry about everyone.' Now he was holding my hand and squeezing my fingers very gently.

Love is a funny thing. Two days ago I would almost have fainted with delight to be next to Henry in the dim light of the stables, to have him standing so very close to me, my hand in his and his other arm going around my waist.

But now . . .

But now, I felt nothing.

That's not quite true . . .

If I think back carefully, I felt embarrassed and I wanted to get away from him.

I had fallen completely out of love with Henry . . .

'You'd better go to see Miss King,' I said, taking a

step backwards as I saw him bend his head. I wasn't
going to allow him to kiss me on the cheek again.

'Are you jealous, little Jenny?' Henry's voice was
warm and teasing, the sort of voice that would have
given me goose pimples two days ago.

'No.' I can still hear the way I said that 'no' and
I think it sounded quite right. It sounded as though
I didn't care for him, and that was right also. 'She's
just right for you.' I said the words as if I were his
mother.

He laughed then, but the laugh didn't seem natural; he sounded a bit uncomfortable.

'I'd better go; I have some tasks to do.' Again, to
my surprise, the words came out smoothly and I managed to move away from him as I said it. He followed
me and again tried to put his arm around me.

'Excuse me, Henry.' I stole a quick look at him
when I said that and I saw that he looked quite taken
aback. I know that I sounded brisk, just as if he were
Charles getting in my way.

And then I didn't look at Henry any more, just
went straight through the yard, in through the back
door, up the stairs. Once I reached our bedroom, I
took out my journal and unlocked it.

But then I thought about Frank's words. Is it
really true that Captain Williams has a girl in every
port? I wish I knew.

Perhaps that is why he hasn't come to see me.

Or perhaps he thought I was just boring and stupid.

Jane has just come in and I told her about what Frank said and we discussed why Captain Williams has not called on me when he said that he was going to.

'That's interesting about having a girl in every port,' said Jane thoughtfully. 'I wonder, does he get their names muddled? That would make a good story.' And then she saw my expression, I suppose, because she quickly told me that she was only joking and that she didn't think that Captain Williams looked like that sort of man at all.

'I was looking at him when he was dancing with you,' she said, 'and he wasn't looking at anyone else — just at you.'

'I wish I knew what to do now.' I felt so depressed that I think I was near to tears.

'I'll go and fetch Eliza,' said Jane, and she was gone before I could call her back. I wasn't sure that I wanted to discuss the matter with Eliza, but when she came she was very kind and very reassuring, talking about all the duties that naval captains have and the emergencies that might have arisen.

'Don't worry, Jenny,' she said. 'I saw the way that Captain Williams looked at you and I know that he was *très, très épris.*'

'Very taken by you,' translated Jane. Her French is better than mine as she often chatters in it to Eliza.

'You have captured his heart, *ma petite,*' said Eliza solemnly.

'Should she write to him, do you think?' asked Jane. 'Just something casual – ask him how he is and how his ship is – just to remind him of her.'

'*Mais non, mais non, mais non . . .*' Eliza became very agitated. 'A lady must never do that. It's for the gentleman to make the first move. A lady must wait. You have made an impression; now stand back and let him come forward!'

'I'm not sure that I made a great impression,' I said, and I probably said it rather dolefully because Eliza gave me a motherly pat on the shoulder.

'Did he pay you any compliments?' asked Jane.

I told her that he said I had lovely eyes and she immediately asked me what I said in return and shook her head reprovingly when I admitted that I said nothing.

'You should have said, "La, Captain Williams, you do me too much honour!" That's what she should have said, Eliza, isn't it?'

I said hotly that I thought that sounded ridiculous. I was embarrassed to think how I had blushed when he admired my eyes.

Eliza pursed her lips, but tactfully did not agree with either of us. She was thinking hard though, and when she spoke she was quite decisive.

'You see, Jenny, my dear,' she said briskly, 'it's very pretty to look shy, but don't be too shy. You must be ready to give the gentleman a hint of your feelings.'

'Just take one step forward, and then a step back! That's right, isn't it, Eliza?' Jane was getting excited. I half expected her to fly across the room and take out her writing desk.

'*Précisément!*' Eliza beamed fondly at Jane and then turned back to me with a serious look. 'Think of it like a dance, Jenny. A gentleman pays you a compliment, you look up at him and let him see your feelings for him — just for one moment — and then you drop your eyelashes to hide your eyes — use your fan — I showed you how. Then if a gentleman talks of his feelings, don't hold back. If you are too shy to respond, then just look up and let him read the message of love in your eyes.'

'And don't forget your fan,' advised Jane. 'But she'll have to say something if he asks her to marry him, won't she, Eliza? She can't just look at him and hope that he guesses.'

'Who says anything about marriage?' Eliza pronounced it '*marrrriaage*'. 'Jenny doesn't know him well enough for any talk about marriage. She'll have to get to know him a lot better before she agrees to marry him. She only met him for less than an hour. No young girl should be talked into marriage before she is ready!' And Eliza sighed heavily and looked into the fire with an air of tragedy.

'Oh, but she knew him before——' Jane stopped suddenly and put her hand in front of her mouth.

Eliza dropped her tragic-muse pose and swivelled around to look at me with an air of interest.

'I don't mind Cousin Eliza knowing,' I said reassuringly to Jane. I could see how horror-filled she looked and I guessed that there was no way out of telling Eliza the whole story. In any case, she was going back to London.

'But you must swear never to tell a soul,' said Jane, and then she dramatically told Eliza the whole story. Eliza listened with parted lips, and when Jane had finished she said, 'Jenny, this is a man who will love and cherish you. When this man comes back to tell you of his love for you, you will know what to do. This is a man who has shown gentleness and kindness to an unprotected girl. He will make a wonderful husband.'

'Perhaps he was still just being kind to me though.'

Eliza shook her head. 'You forget that I have studied him, *chérie*. Even across the ballroom floor I could see that he was in love with you. I know about these things. I could tell you such stories.' And Eliza heaved a sigh and smiled a world-weary smile.

'Oh, do tell us some stories of your time in Paris, before you were married, Eliza. You're going away tomorrow so this is the last opportunity,' urged Jane.

'I'll be back for the performance of the play at Easter, *chérie*,' said Eliza, 'but . . .'

So for the rest of the evening, Eliza sat by our

fireside and told so many stories and gave us so much good advice that by bedtime my head was in a whirl. Before she left she kissed me and whispered in my ear, 'Now remember, he will come, and when he does, you will know what to say to him.'

Jane is now asleep and I am still writing in my journal and hoping that Mrs Austen won't notice the light of the candle shining under our door.

I've been thinking about Eliza's words so I've fetched my journal from my trunk and am trying to sort out my feelings.

I can see where I've gone wrong. I've been too shy, too silent.

When Captain Williams told me that story of how he saved the boy, I was dying to show him how wonderful I thought he had been.

But I was just too shy — that's what I told myself at the time.

Perhaps, though, I'm getting too old to be shy . . .

Perhaps it's just a form of selfishness . . .

Perhaps Thomas (secretly in my mind I like to call him Thomas) would have been pleased to hear himself praised.

When he told me the story and I said nothing, perhaps he felt embarrassed . . .

The next time that I meet him I will know what to do . . .

If ever I meet him again . . .

Tuesday, 29 March 1791

And today he came!

And I didn't show him my feelings.

Everything went wrong.

All Jane's and Eliza's good advice seems to be thrown away on me.

This is how the day went.

Frank had got back his good humour this morning when he was giving me my riding lesson; he was very nice and complimented me on my riding and without much prompting on my part he started to tell me about the duties of a captain. It was a fine morning and we had now progressed to riding side by side down the lane towards the church. I was enjoying the morning sun and watching the brisk wind stirring and blowing the white petals of the cherry trees drifting down, looking like snow as I half listened to a long description of everything that captains did on board ship (and of course all about what a midshipman would do, as well) and eventually I managed to slip in the question that I wanted to ask.

'And when captains are on shore, is their time their own, or do they have any duties then?'

Again I had to listen to a long description of how ships had to be cleansed, refitted, all about ships' stores and chandlers.

'So a captain would have to supervise all of that?' I said thoughtfully as soon as I could get a word in.

'Of course! It's no easy life, being a captain of ship. Not like those idle dogs in the army.' Frank was very scornful of the army, where a man could buy a commission and not rise through merit, as they do in the navy.

I didn't listen to the rest of his opinions about soldiers. My heart was happy again. Thomas was probably down in Southampton seeing to his ship. He would have no time to waste calling upon young ladies. Frank didn't say any more about Thomas having a girl in every port so I hope that what he said yesterday is not true.

We went to see George this morning, and brought a piece of pork pie. He enjoyed the pie, but he had problems with making the sign for *P*. This was difficult for him as it involved – according to the book that Jane had taken from her father's library — folding his thumb and two fingers. In the end I said to Jane that we should be content with him trying to say the name. I had more hopes of teaching George to talk than to read or to spell, but Jane was of the opinion that reading and spelling would impress her mother more. On the way home I was thinking about George and I was thinking that it was strange that Jane was the only one of his seven brothers and sisters to worry about him. After all, the others — including James, who had great influence with his mother — knew that their brother was lodged with a poor family down in the village. They knew that he shambled around dirty and perhaps ill-fed — he always seemed hungry to me — and yet none of them ever took any interest in him.

After dinner it poured with rain and everyone was in the parlour. There was no opportunity for the boys to go out of doors before lessons started again so we all settled down with books or card games or chess, and Mr Austen was reading through the sermon that he had preached on Sunday. Charles was first 'broke' (and out of buttons!) in our game of pontoon so he left the table and wandered over to the window.

'There are two horses coming up the drive,' he called out.

'Is it William Chute?' Henry had been yawning in a bored sort of way, but he suddenly sounded interested and he put his book down on the table.

'No,' said Charles. 'It's Newton Portsmouth and someone in naval uniform with him.'

'Cassandra, Jane, Jenny, put this room in order,' scolded Mrs Austen, scurrying around picking up books and shaking cushions.

The Honourable Newton Wallop was the second son of the Earl of Portsmouth, and Mrs Austen was very fond of the aristocracy. She had some far-distant ancestor who was the brother of a duke.

'Who's with him, Charles?' she asked as she tipped Mr Austen's Sunday sermon into the wood scuttle beside the fire.

'Let me see,' said Frank, getting up and going to the window. 'It must be Frederick. No, it's not, it's Captain Williams. He must be staying at Hurstbourne Park or with the Portsmouths. What can he want? You remember him, Mama? I introduced him to you at the Assembly Rooms on Saturday. Do you know, Papa, Captain Williams had his own ship when he was eighteen years old?'

'Lucky him,' murmured Henry.

'He must be a very worthy young man,' said Mrs Austen warmly.

'His uncle is an admiral,' said Henry. 'That's a piece of good luck that any of us would enjoy having. Being worthy has nothing whatsoever to do with it.'

'Don't be ridiculous, Henry,' scolded Mrs Austen. 'And why are you lounging around here? You should be over at Laverstoke House paying a visit to Miss King. It will impress her if you come in this weather.'

Henry rose reluctantly to his feet, giving a look of dismay at the sight of the rain pouring down on the sodden lawn outside.

'Well, Mama,' said Jane pertly, 'if your son should have a dangerous fit of illness, if he should die, I hope that it will be a consolation to you that it was all in pursuit of your orders – and of Miss King, of course.'

'Nonsense,' said Mrs Austen. 'People don't die of a little rain. I go out in the rain every day myself.'

My heart began to beat faster. I looked across at Jane, but I had no time to make contact with her as her father had caught her by the hand.

'Jane, dear, give me back my sermon. No one listens much to my words, so this sermon will do perfectly well some Sunday next year. And who is this Captain Williams?'

'Good gracious, Mr Austen, it's the young man that I told you about, the one that was so taken by our Jenny. You must remember, Mr Austen; I told you all about him last Saturday night at bedtime. Jenny, dear, leave those cards there; Jane will attend to them. You just run upstairs, take off that brown calico and put on your blue muslin, the one that you wore to church on Sunday.'

'I'll go with her to brush her hair,' said Jane swiftly. 'Cassandra will tidy the cards away.'

Mr Austen looked as if he didn't remember too well who Captain Williams was. Probably he had heard a lot about Miss King and then fallen asleep before the bit about me and Captain Williams. However, he slipped his sermon into his waistcoat pocket, straightened his wig and sat up, resigned to losing his after-dinner doze.

Frank went out to the front door and Jane and I raced upstairs.

'What a shame that it is raining so hard,' said Jane as she brushed my curls around her finger. 'If it had been fine, then you could have taken your beau for a walk in a pretty little wilderness, just like the girl in *The Mysteries of Udolpho*.'

This made me giggle a little. I was quite excited. Lavinia at Mrs Cawley's Seminary for Young Ladies was always boasting of having a 'beau' who came calling.

'I expect that he has just come to see Frank,' I said, trying to sound offhand, but Jane wasn't fooled.

'You're not still scared that he will tell anyone about Southampton, are you?' she asked, looking at me enquiringly.

I told her that I wasn't because Captain Williams had promised faithfully not to tell anyone.

Jane's eyes narrowed. 'It sounds as though he cares for you,' she said. 'Oh la . . .' And then the door was pushed open. It was Cassandra.

'There, you look very nice, Jenny. Come on, come

downstairs. There's nothing to be afraid of. Captain Williams is just doing the civil thing, visiting neigh-bours of the Portsmouths.'

'I'm not scared,' I said. I wasn't going to be patron-ized by Cassandra — after all, she's only two years older than I am.

'Come and sit beside me, Jenny,' said my aunt in a motherly way when Jane and I went into the parlour. She was sitting next to Captain Williams on the sofa. Newton was chatting to Tom Fowle and Henry, and Mr Austen had started to doze off again. Frank was fetching one of his naval books from the bookcase and he looked a bit annoyed when Mrs Austen made room for me between herself and Captain Williams and sternly waved him away, while Captain Wil-liams, who had jumped up from his seat, was bowing over my hand.

We sat down, side by side on the sofa. It wasn't a very big sofa, and Mrs Austen is a large, wide-hipped woman, so it ended up with us sitting very close to-gether.

It wasn't easy to talk though. Everyone in the room was looking at us — the boys with curiosity, Cassandra with a degree of jealousy, Jane beaming enthusiastically. I didn't dare look at Mrs Austen, but I knew that she was looking at me encouragingly.

'You're well after the ball?' asked Captain Williams.

'Very well,' I said, wondering whether it was etiquette to ask him if he was well also.

'You weren't too tired?' was his next question.

'No,' I said. 'I wasn't a bit tired.' I could hear my
voice sounding stilted and mechanical. I tried to remember all the things that Eliza had told me to do.
But he wasn't paying me compliments or speaking of
love, so none of these was of any use.

Jane and I had been practising being sophisticated
and flirting in our bedroom, but all I could think of
was pinning the wrapper to my shoulders. He was so
near to me that I almost felt a little faint. I had a sudden longing for everyone to go out of the room and
then perhaps he would hold my hand or even put it
to his lips as he did at the Assembly Rooms and that
night at Southampton.

'It was the first time that I have ever been to Basingstoke Assembly Rooms. I found them very pleasant.' He was doing his best, but I didn't know what
to say.

'It was my first time too,' I said after a minute. I
was conscious that Mrs Austen was listening to every
word. She got up now and went across the room and
opened the piano.

'Let's have a little music, Jane,' she said. For once
Jane did not argue but sat down on the piano stool.
Mrs Austen leafed through the music books on the pi-
ano and then opened one and plonked it in front of

Jane. When the music came, it was soft and gentle, ideal for conversation. Mrs Austen stayed beside her to turn the pages. It was no good though. I just couldn't talk to him. Not with everyone watching us. No matter what subject of conversation we tried, I could only answer *yes* or *no*. After a whispered suggestion from his mother, Frank had taken Newton to the stables to see a litter of pointer pups, and Tom Fowle and the other pupils had gone with them. Only Mr and Mrs Austen, Cassandra, Jane and I remained.

And Captain Thomas Williams, of course.

Eventually Newton and Frank returned. Cassandra slipped out to join her fiancé and Jane stopped playing the piano.

'We must go now,' said Newton, with a quick look at Captain Williams. 'I have to call on neighbours with a message from my mother, but let me give it to you first of all. We are holding a ball at Hurstbourne Park this Saturday and all the Austens are invited. And Miss Jenny, of course. Here is the invitation card.'

Lord & Lady Portsmouth
request the pleasure of the company of
Mr & Mrs G. Austen & Family
at a ball to be held at
Hurstbourne Park,
Saturday 2 April 1791
RSVP

'A ball!' exclaimed Jane. 'Oh, wonderful! I promise to save you a dance, Newton.'

'Jane!' exclaimed Mrs Austen, but I knew she was
not really annoyed. Jane's remark had raised a laugh
and it finished that awkward silence that had fallen
in the room. I laughed too. Suddenly I felt at ease and
I looked up at Captain Williams with a smile. 'Will
you be there?'

He smiled back. 'Only if you come,' he said, and
his brown eyes were dancing.

'You should have taken him out for a walk until you
found a pretty little wilderness — what does a little rain matter in the cause of true love?' said Jane
later when we were brushing our hair and I was telling her how stupid and embarrassed I felt and how I
couldn't think of a word to say to him when we were
sitting side by side on the sofa in the parlour.

'I'm not sure that would have been any better,' I
said doubtfully. 'I just don't think I am very good at
things like that.'

'I know what I'll do,' said Jane enthusiastically.
'I'll go through Mrs Radcliffe's novels and I'll make
a list of things that young ladies say to their young
men. Then you can learn a few sentences off by heart
every night. I'll hear you say them until you are
word-perfect.'

I couldn't help laughing. I didn't think that it would
work for me, but I didn't like to disappoint Jane.

'I'll try,' I said.

'You were all right at the ball though, weren't you? I saw you talking to him. You didn't look shy then. You'll probably be fine on Saturday,' she said, and I thought again about the look on his face just before he left when he whispered in my ear, 'Keep all your dances for me, won't you?'

Wednesday, 30 March 1791

There was great excitement at the breakfast table to-day. A letter came from Kent, saying that Edward, Jane's brother who was adopted by rich cousins, would be arriving at Bristol today. He would be staying the night there and then would come by stage-coach tomorrow to spend a night here at Steventon.

'He's been on a Grand Tour,' said Mrs Austen to me. Apparently Edward spent the last couple of years going from country to country in continental Europe and seeing all that was most interesting in each country.

'Great buildings, works of art, miracles of nature . . . Edward has seen them all,' finished Mrs Austen before flying out to the kitchen to order the cook to kill a couple of turkeys from the yard and hang them up, ready for tomorrow's dinner.

'Does Edward look like James or like Henry?' I asked Jane when we were doing our schoolwork.

'He's like Cassandra,' said Jane briefly. 'He's got grey eyes and blond hair – at least he had when I saw him last. We don't see much of him here.'

'Don't you like him?' I asked. There was something odd about the tone of her voice.

'Oh, he's all right. Quite nice really . . . nicer than James. He's the third in our family. George is between James and Edward.'

I didn't say any more then. I could understand

what she was feeling. There was James, the scholar, a Fellow at Oxford (and I gathered from Mrs Austen that you had to be a great scholar to be a 'Fellow') and then there was Edward, adopted by a couple so rich that they could send him wandering around continental Europe for two years just to complete his education. He would inherit their two estates, one in Kent and one in Hampshire, and their two grand houses. Edward would be very rich.

And then there was George, in between these two fortunate brothers.

And poor George has nothing.

Thursday, 31 March 1791

Just before dinner today we all walked up to Deane Gate Inn to meet Edward — even Mrs Austen herself came. The procession was led by Cassandra and Tom Fowle, followed by Mr Austen and the other pupils, and ended with Mrs Austen and Charles.

The sight of us caused great interest in the village and many people came to greet us or to enquire about our journey. From a distance I saw Bet trying to lead George into a field, but he broke away from her. He passed his father and brothers without a glance, but stopped opposite Jane and myself, making inarticulate noises and trying to see whether I had anything for him.

'Off home, George! Go on, off you go. Bet, don't allow him to bother the young ladies.' Mrs Austen's voice was not unkind, but it held the tone that the shepherd used to his dog, Rover.

I winced a little and I could sense how Jane was suffering. She was George's sister and I was his cousin, and yet he was ordered away from 'the young ladies'.

I felt I had to say something so I told Mrs Austen that Jane and I would walk back with George and Bet and catch them up straight away. I was surprised at myself to hear how firm and grown-up my voice sounded.

'Come on, George,' said Jane cheerfully. 'You be a good boy now and we'll bring you some cake later on.'

I think he understood the word 'cake' and he probably understood the shooing motions that Mrs Austen
was making with her hands. In any case, he turned
around and shambled off. Bet gave a rather scared and
very apologetic look at Mrs Austen, bobbed a quick
curtsy and then hurried after George. We went a little of the way with Bet and George, but once we saw
that he was happy we returned to join the others.
Mrs Austen turned her attention to me.

'So you know George, Jenny?' she asked, and cast
a quick annoyed glance at Jane.

I nodded. 'I've met him a few times in the village,'
I said carelessly. And then I turned away from my
aunt and towards Jane. 'Jane, is Edward as tall as
Henry?'

'No, he's not too tall, not much bigger than Frank.'
Jane's voice was as casual as mine, but she quickened
her pace and together we overtook John Warren and
Gilbert East.

'Slowcoaches,' I said teasingly over my shoulder as
we passed, and I was amazed at myself. And then I
thought about George.

'Jane, I think you are right about George,' I said in
a low voice. 'I think that we should try to persuade
your father and mother to have him live in the house.
We might succeed. We'll have to think of some good
arguments — like that it would save money. After all,
I suppose they have to pay for the Littleworths to
look after him.'

'When they see that he can read they will want him back home,' said Jane with conviction. Jane was very determined, and she was sure that she could teach George to read.

I hesitated a bit, but then the new grown-up me spoke out.

'Jane . . .' I said with a quick glance over my shoulder to check that we were outside Gilbert and John Warren's listening range. 'Jane, I think that you should be prepared for the possibility that it might be impossible for George to learn to read. Let's just love him for what he is.'

And then Henry dropped back to walk with us and no more was said about George.

Edward was wearing a wig and that surprised me, because although I had never seen my uncle without one, the other boys just wore their own hair tied back. He was not very tall, rather squarely made with broad shoulders. He was dressed very fashionably, wearing a pair of tightly fitting salmon-coloured breeches, with knee-length white silk stockings, a white and gold waistcoat buttoned over his ruffled shirt and over it all a magnificent coat in blue brocade with a dozen gilt buttons, each the size of a sovereign.

He seemed nice, kissing his mother and two sisters, shaking hands with his brothers and father, bowing over my hand as if I were an adult and telling me how small I was when he last saw me. He had a kind face and a sweet smile.

'And how is your brother, my Cousin Edward-John?' he asked me, raising my hand to his lips in a very courtly way. 'Still the same Edward-John, is he? Always ready for a debate.'

'He's married now,' I said. I tried to remember what my brother had been like before he married Augusta. Did he have opinions of his own then? I wondered. I couldn't remember him saying much in the last year or so. I hadn't ever heard him argue with Augusta, but she would have talked him down if he had even tried.

'So, he's married.' He sounded surprised. I was sure that his mother must have told him, but he had probably forgotten. Life had been exciting for Edward during the past few years.

'He's been landed, poor fish,' said Henry, and Mrs Austen glared at him.

Edward did not appear to notice his mother; he was now busy slapping Tom Fowle on the back and congratulating him about his engagement to Cassandra. Of course, he knew all of the older boys at the school as Edward had been a pupil there before he embarked on his Grand Tour of Europe. The Knights, his adoptive parents, had been anxious that he not lose contact with his birth parents, so that arrangement had been made for his education. I wondered whether either James or Henry were ever jealous of

Edward; he had been the least clever of the three brothers, according to Jane, and yet he was the one that was sent to all of those foreign countries and was now able to speak French and Italian like a native apparently.

'Another poor fish that has been landed,' said Henry, giving Tom Fowle a few extra slaps on the back, and this time everyone laughed, even me. Tom Fowle didn't seem to mind. That is the thing about Henry. He can say anything, do anything, and people always forgive him. I wondered whether he would marry the very rich Miss King. If he wanted to, he probably could do it, I thought. He has lots of charm.

'Shall we leave most of your luggage, Edward?' asked Mr Austen. The inn yard was piled high with heavy leather trunks and travelling bags, but Edward would be returning there next day for the coach to Kent.

'We'll take these few here.' Edward was obviously used to travelling. In a moment he had sorted out three of the bags, taken a handful of small silver coins from his purse and distributed them among the ostlers and coachmen, divided the bags among the boys and then set off strolling down the lane to Steventon, chatting to his father.

Edward had a generous nature. Two of the bags he brought to the house were stuffed with presents for the family. Mr Austen went back to his study bearing a handsome case of clay pipes, a tobacco pouch and a leather-bound volume for his library. The pupils returned to the schoolroom with small gifts of linen handkerchiefs or cravats and then the family gathered around the leather bag for the rest of the present-giving.

There was a very handsome Indian shawl for Mrs Austen, a case of pistols for Henry, a fowling gun for Frank, a leather bridle and the whispered promise of a pony for Christmas for little Charles, and lace shawls for both Jane and Cassandra. I was admiring Jane's when suddenly Edward produced one for me also. I couldn't believe it. It was not so much that he had spent money on me, as the fact that he had remembered that I was staying at Steventon and brought me a gift just as if I were one of his sisters.

Then there were more presents: boxes of French bonbons, some beautifully illustrated books, a pair of pictures for the girls' bedrooms, a painting of a waterfall for the parlour – there seemed to be no end to what was coming out of that wonderful bag. Dinner was late that afternoon, partly because Mrs Austen had been delayed with the opening of the presents, but partly because in fashionable society — so she told Jane and myself — dinner was often not eaten until darkness fell. She thought Edward might lack appetite if we had it too early.

Everything was arranged to suit Edward. Mrs Austen must have been up half the night. I had never seen the parlour look so lovely, with even an Indian rug, unearthed from a chest in her bedroom, decorating the highly polished floor.

It was funny, I thought, that two of Mrs Austen's six sons did not live at the parsonage. One, George, was barred from the house, but the other, Edward, was treated like royalty when he spent a night with his parents.

After dinner Jane disappeared, but the rest of us stayed sitting around the parlour, listening to Edward's tales of his adventures in foreign countries. Eventually he was almost hoarse with talking and Mr Austen gave him a glass of port and looked around for Jane to play the piano for everyone.

It was at that moment that the door opened.

It is ten o'clock. I have just written lots about Edward and about the presents, but I haven't written about the most important thing.

I have a new quill in my hand — it's one that Frank gave me. He gave it to me because Jane tells everyone that I am always writing. I have sharpened it to a neat point with my penknife, but now I don't know what to say.

I should be writing about what happened today after dinner. Every night I write about what happened during the day, and usually I just write and write and the words come to my mind faster than my quill can form them on the page.

Let me see if I can sort it out, minute by minute.

Dinner had finished, and the Digweeds and the Terrys, neighbours to the Austens, had come by to see Edward, so the parlour was full to bursting point with them and their children and with Mr Austen's pupils.

And Jane opened the door and stood there, holding George by the hand.

I think if I had been Jane, when I saw them all there, I would have quickly shut the door and taken George away and given him lots of cake and biscuits and talked with him and laughed with him and perhaps taught him some more of his letters, but I would have definitely taken him straight back to the village.

But Jane is not me.

She opened the door and she just stood there with everyone looking at her, and then peering past her to see, standing behind her, George, the abandoned son. A queer little stunted figure, all dressed up like a miniature parson.

And Jane said in a clear, ringing voice, 'Mama,

Papa, here is George, come to see his brother Edward. He'd like to show you all what he has learned.'

I can't remember what happened next. I suppose she must have got him into the parlour. I just remember her putting him on a chair in front of a small table. She was like a player, setting the scene. She took out the cake and the biscuits and the apple from her basket and then she arranged them on the table. George began to tremble. I came over next to him and tried to squeeze his hand so that he wouldn't feel so nervous.

He did manage to make the sign for A and also for C, but when I put the biscuits in front of him he began to shake violently.

And then Henry jumped up. 'Let go of him, Jenny,' he shouted.

I got such a shock at Henry yelling at me that I couldn't move. I still held George's hand, but now Mr Austen had his arms around George, and Mrs Austen undid my grip. Henry helped Mr Austen and they almost lifted George. He was shaking all over from head to toe and they laid him on the ground. I could see how the froth came to his lips and how his eyes rolled. I can still hear Mrs Digweed's voice proclaiming, 'He's having a fit.'

I suppose Mrs Austen managed very well. I remember her calm voice ushering everyone into the breakfast parlour, chatting to the Terry children, explaining that the boy – she called poor George *the boy* – would be fine in a moment, saying in a sort of comic tone to Mrs Terry, '*That girl* (she meant Jane) *will be the death of me one day,*' and giving quick instructions to Frank to bring the cart around.

And then Jane ran upstairs to the bedroom and I followed her.

I did my best to console her, but she was beyond consolation.

'I've made a mess of everything' was the only thing that she would say, her face streaming with tears. No matter how much I told her that she had tried and that perhaps she could talk to her parents tomorrow, she still would say no more than that one sentence.

I think I understand her. She was very upset for George, but also her pride is hurt. She thought her plan would work and it didn't. I can understand why she didn't want to discuss it, so I just sat by her bed, stroking her hair until she stopped sobbing and sat up.

'I wish I lived in a novel,' she said with an attempt at a small smile. 'I could make such a happy ending to this story. George would learn to talk, and to read, my father and mother would want him back in the house, and he would be a brother to us all.' And then she took up a book and started to read it.

* * *

Nothing I could say to Jane tonight seemed to make her feel better, but, funnily enough, writing it down has made it seem better to me.

My brother has not been a very good brother to me — I can say it now without feeling guilty and thinking it was my fault that he was no fonder of me. However, this present of the pack of three journals was the best thing that he has done for me.

And I suppose it has not been easy for him. I understand him a bit better now. Augusta would probably have been jealous and made a fuss if she thought her husband was fond of me. He was probably torn between doing what Mama begged he would do for me, and what his wife, Augusta, felt should happen.

Friday, 1 April 1791

I woke at dawn to hear Edward and Frank talking quietly on the sweep outside our window. I got out of bed and peeped at them as they strode up the lane towards Deane Inn. Edward had to catch the early stagecoach from there and Frank was carrying his bag. I dressed quietly and then just sat by the window thinking about everything that had happened last night.

Jane got up at her normal time and did her piano practise. Frank and I went riding for half an hour. He said nothing about George and I said nothing. And yet, I thought as we trotted along the lane, side by side, there was something very strange about this. Why weren't we discussing it? Why weren't we saying things like: 'What a shame about George'?

And Henry – why had he said nothing last night?

Or Cassandra?

Or even Edward – after all, George is his brother also.

Except for Jane, the whole family is just embarrassed by George – just wants to forget that he exists.

And yet, if Henry took an interest in George, that would influence Mr Austen greatly. Henry and Jane are his two favourite children, but he consults Henry about lots of things and seems to respect his opinion, whereas Jane is just his clever little girl – amusing but not to be taken seriously.

As soon as I had groomed and fed my donkey and washed my hands under the pump in the washroom, I went into the parlour to find Jane. She was playing, playing badly, strumming a few bars and then resting her fingers on the keys and then playing a false note.

'Jane,' I said without stopping to think for too long, 'I think you did a good thing yesterday. I think that this business about George has been a secret for too long. Why don't people talk about him? Why don't they say things like, *"What a shame about George. What can we do to make his life a little better?"* I think it's time that everyone was talking about it, that everyone acknowledged the truth. It's a bit like shutting the doors and windows of a room and never letting the air in . . .'

I stopped because I was running out of breath, but also because Jane's eyes had gone from mine and were looking at something behind me.

In my haste I had not closed the door properly, and Mr and Mrs Austen had come in behind me and were standing listening to me. Mr Austen looked deeply troubled and I was sorry about that; he is a kind and gentle man. His wife, though, looked the same as always: tough, competent and just a little amused at the silliness of young people.

It was Mrs Austen who shut the door.

'So how long has all this been going on for?' she asked drily.

'A few weeks,' said Jane defiantly.

'A few weeks . . .' repeated Mr Austen, and then he smiled, that very sweet smile that he always seemed able to produce even in a situation where another man would be angry. 'And you were teaching him his alphabet, were you?'

'He knows lots of letters now.' Jane was on her feet now, her back to the piano and facing her mother and father.

I noticed that they both looked very tired, almost as if they had spent a lot of the night awake – perhaps talking about George.

'The problem is, Jane,' scolded Mrs Austen, 'that you always think that you know best. You're only fifteen years old, so you should allow your father and mother to know what's best and do the right thing.'

I believe that if Jane had just nodded here, all might have gone quite well. I imagine that Mrs Austen didn't really want to scold, but of course Jane, being Jane, had to argue. 'So you think it's the right thing for your son to live down in the village like an animal.' Her voice was very harsh and rough. Tears came to my eyes and through my tears I could see how she glared at her mother.

'Don't talk nonsense, Jane!' snapped Mrs Austen. 'George, you deal with her. I have too much to do!' And then she was out of the room, slamming the door behind her. I had never heard her call her husband by his first name before; it was always 'Mr Austen' with her. That showed how angry and upset she was.

Jane didn't look worried though. She faced her father, cheeks blazing and eyes sparkling. 'I suppose it's nonsense to care about your brother. Well, I do, and I'm the only one in the family that cares. You must realize he's not properly looked after.'

'Jane, Jane, that's not true.' Mr Austen sounded very upset. 'You know that Dame Littleworth looks after him very well.'

I wiped my eyes with my pocket handkerchief, but Jane was not tearful. She was almost shouting at her father.

'He doesn't look like Frank or Charles or Henry or any of the other boys, does he? He's not cared for in the same way as they are cared for, is he? Would anyone guess that he is your son?'

'But, Jane,' said Mr Austen gently, 'George is not the same as the other boys.'

Jane frowned, but she didn't say anything else. She couldn't really argue with that, I thought. George was not the same as the other boys, and dressing him up and even teaching him his ABC wasn't going to make him the same.

'However, I think that in some ways you are right,' continued Mr Austen. His voice was loving, and he looked very anxiously at Jane. 'It is possible that Dame Littleworth has too much to do to care for George in the way that we would like him to be cared for.'

'I don't want to get her into trouble.' Jane sounded a bit calmer now.

'No, no, Dame Littleworth is a good woman and she does do her best, but she doesn't have a husband or a son and I think the task might be too much for her. I've heard tales that George is allowed to wander alone even up as far as Deane Gate Inn. Goodness knows what might happen to the poor lad with the coaches going at speed along that road. Something has to be done. We can easily compensate Dame Littleworth by taking her daughter, Bet, on as a kitchen maid, if we make other arrangements for the poor fellow. We want to do the best thing for George. You do believe that, don't you?' He hesitated for a moment and then said, 'There is another man with George's problem – a relative of ours – who is happy and being well cared for at Monk Sheraton. Perhaps George could join him.'

Jane frowned. I could see that she did not know what to think about that. I swallowed hard to get the lump out of my throat and forced myself to speak. I said that I thought that would be a good idea and that George would be happier if he had someone like himself for a companion. I kept on talking for a while. I was trying to give Jane time to get used to the idea. The trouble between Jane and her mother usually happens when Jane speaks too hastily. It would be best if her father could calm her down before she left the room and perhaps bumped into Mrs Austen again. I hoped that Mr Austen would not ask her what she thought.

I think that Mr Austen knew what I was doing because he started to talk also. He described George as a baby — and how he, Mr Austen, had taken comfort in the fact that he could not ever be a bad or wicked child.

And then that was that.

Jane said nothing. She loved her father very much and she would not argue with him, and I apologized for the two of us and then, somehow, we were out of the room and going into the breakfast parlour with no cross words spoken.

Edward and Henry were having fun at the breakfast table, talking nonsense French, and Frank was joining in and for once Henry treated him like an equal. Tom Fowle was calling Cassandra '*Mademoiselle*' and Charles was going around saying '*Excusezmoi*' and purposely bumping into everyone. It was the usual fun and high spirits and it was as if the tragedy of George had not come into all our lives for a few brief minutes. I could see Jane's lips quiver from time to time, but she said nothing.

Saturday, 2 April 1791

My white dress has been carefully washed in the best soap and lavender water by Mrs Austen herself. She waved me away when I wanted to iron it and she did it herself, rubbing the bottom of each iron with a piece of coarse cloth every time she took a new one from on top of the stove. Not a single one of the beautiful blue glass beads was damaged as she took such care with it.

No Eliza to get us ready this time – but she left her soaps and her bath oils and some of her special shampoo so Jane and I confided in Sukey, who was happy to light the fire in the guest bedroom, lug up the pails of hot water and allow us the use of the hip bath and the wonderful full-length cheval mirror. I'm going to do Jane's hair and she's going to do mine. I'm going to have one change though. I've put away Henry's bandeau and I've carefully unpicked Eliza's blue velvet rose from my gown. I will wear that at the place where my hair is gathered at the back – just as Eliza had intended.

'Wish we had the Turkish towels,' said Jane while we were getting everything ready. 'If you marry that Captain Williams, my dear Jenny, I hope you will have a guest bedroom that supplies Turkish towels.'

'And Indian bath oil,' I said.

'And shampoo and soap.'

'And a glass of wine to sip while bathing.'
'And rose petals heaped upon the bed.'
'And three dozen beeswax candles.'
'And Indian spices burning in an oil lamp.'
'And soft music in the background.'

And then our imaginations ran out. The room was looking quite lovely already. 'Lucky no one has discovered us,' said Jane. 'If Mama finds out, well, I shall just say that Eliza told us to do all of this. And she did, in a way, because she left us the soap and the shampoo and the bath oil.'

The funny thing is that I think Mrs Austen knows. She couldn't not know – she knows everything that goes on in the house.

When we were having our rest after our bath, Jane read aloud several remarks that ladies could make to gentlemen and I obediently repeated them after her until I got too sleepy so now I will blow out my candle and go to sleep – perhaps to have a happy dream about Thomas and me, whirling and dancing together at the ball.

The Portsmouths' Ball

And now I am walking under the stone portico of Hurst-bourne Park. The house is huge – bigger than anything I have ever seen.

Everything is very formal here. We are invited to leave our wraps in a beautiful room downstairs and then a footman precedes us up the stairs and announces us with great formality:

'The Reverend George Austen, Mrs Austen, Miss Austen, Miss Jane Austen, Miss Cooper, Mr Henry Austen and Mr Frank Austen.'

The earl and his lady are very grand and they bow ceremoniously to us. I don't suppose that we would have been invited if Mr Austen had not tutored their three sons so well. Lady Portsmouth is saying something about knowing my sister-in-law – 'Dear Augusta'. I hardly look at her; I am too anxious to see whether Thomas is there.

And then we are through into the ballroom.

The ballroom is huge, bigger than the Assembly Rooms at Basingstoke.

I know many of the people here though: the Chutes from the Vyne, the Portals from Laverstoke House, the Biggs from Manydown House, the Digweeds from Steventon Manor.

'Big London crowd here tonight,' says Henry, and he

saunters off towards the Portal family. Mrs Austen has been impressing on him the necessity of asking Miss King to be his partner for the first dance, but he's been muttering that Miss King is too opinionated and that he is tired of her. I'm not sure that there will be a match there, no matter how much Mrs Austen tries to push Henry. I don't care one way or the other but I do think that Henry should have a chance to choose a wife that he loves.

'Do as you please,' Mrs Austen said to him before we left Steventon. 'But remember your father can't afford to buy you a commission in the militia. You'll have to find the money somewhere. Just face the facts, Henry. You must marry money.'

'Oh, Jane, Jane,' says Alethea Bigg, rushing into the suite of huge bedrooms where we took off our wraps, 'Jane, John Harwood has asked Elizabeth to give him the first two dances. He took her card and wrote his name twice and then he squeezed her hand! Shh, here she comes – don't say that I told you.'

Elizabeth and her older sister, Catherine, are walking rather apart and not looking at each other as they come in. There is a rather sour look on Catherine's face. I guess that she is jealous of Elizabeth. All these girls are so anxious to secure an offer of marriage. I don't think that their parents give them a chance to fall in love.

Neither stays long – Catherine goes off with Cassandra, Elizabeth gives her face a hasty glance in the looking glass, pinches her cheeks and bites her lips to bring the colour to them and goes after them.

'She shouldn't wear green,' observes Jane to Alethea. 'It makes her too pale.'

'Oh, Jane,' says Alethea. 'I would so like to have a beau.'

'A man of fortune, I should hope,' says Jane primly.

'Well, that would be nice,' admits Alethea, 'but to be honest, any old beau would do to practise on.'

We all giggle and then Jane says that she is thinking of setting up a school for young ladies. 'No time-wasting nonsense about globes and needlework and such things,' she says, imitating her mother's downright tone. 'I've been coaching Jenny in how to make conversation with her beau and if you like I'll take you on as a pupil too, Alethea. Teaching is in our family: my father coaches young gentlemen for Oxford; I'll coach young ladies for marriage.'

She says all this with such an air as Alethea and she go out giggling. I stay behind, pretending to fix my curls, but really I just need to have a few minutes on my own. What will I do if HE's not here, or if he has forgotten that he asked me to dance with him tonight?

And what about my midnight walk in Southampton? I ask myself as I walk out. Has he kept it to himself, as he promised? It seems so strange that he has the power to ruin me with one careless word, and yet I trust him implicitly.

The music becomes a little louder now and people are leaving the supper buffet table and starting to take their partners over towards the line that is forming down the middle of the ballroom.

Elizabeth is with John Harwood now, and Cassandra is scolding Jane and Alethea when I join them.

'Jane, don't be silly,' snaps Cassandra. 'You and Alethea are just two stupid little girls. You don't know what you are talking about.' She sees me smiling and she adds, 'And you too, Jenny. At your age you are too young to be thinking of gentlemen.'

I'm not smiling because of what she said; I'm smiling because I can see Captain Williams. He's pushing through the crowd, making his way towards me.

Jane is not taking any notice of Cassandra either. 'There's that Irish cousin of the Lefroys,' she says. 'He is rather fun. His name is Tom. Did you know that, Cassandra? I think I am fated to marry a Tom . . . It used to be Tom Chute and now it is Tom Lefroy.' And then Jane is off, making her way down the ballroom, before Cassandra can say another word.

In a minute Captain Williams is bowing over my hand. He kisses it and the kiss seems to last a long time. I feel his lips on my hand. The backs of my fingers feel hot. I know that I am blushing, but I don't care.

'I've been thinking about you every day this week,' he says. 'I wanted to come to see you again, but I had to go to Southampton. We are recruiting men for a voyage to the East Indies; I'm so busy that I mostly only have the weekends to myself.'

I hardly hear him; nothing seems to matter except that he is with me and that he has missed me during the week. I don't need Jane to tell me that I am in love. My heart is beating very quickly and I want to go even closer to him; I want to feel his arms around me.

'Let's dance,' he says.

And we dance.

I don't know who is beside me, or who is opposite me when we cross over. I am conscious of only three things: a pair of brown eyes that are looking into mine, a hand that touches my waist as we walk down to the end of the line and a voice as smooth as chocolate in my ear.

And then the dance is finished. Everyone is standing in the line, breathless and laughing.

'I think Jenny is the prettiest name in the world,' says Captain Williams. In quite a natural manner he keeps his hand at the back of my waist. I don't move away from him; I don't care who is looking at us.

'I like your name too,' I say.

'Don't call me Tom, though, will you? I hate Tom. Everyone is called Tom; I much prefer Thomas.' There is laughter in his voice as he speaks. I so love his voice. I laugh too as I think of Jane and her two Toms. We are both still laughing when we reach the buffet table and he says, 'Would you like an ice?'

I nod. I have never eaten an ice, but at this moment I would agree to anything he suggests.

There is quite a crowd there; I am squeezed up against some very fat lady with a large fan and a hat full of swaying feathers. She is much taller than I am, and on my other side is Thomas, tall and broad-shouldered, towering over everyone in the room. No one can see me. Thomas glances around and for a moment he bends towards me. I think he is going to kiss me, but he just touches my cheek with his finger and then he is gone.

'Let's get out of this crowd,' he says when he comes back with two plates. So we go and sit under the palm-filled colonnade at the side of the ballroom.

'How do you like your ice?' he asks.

Anything he had brought to me would have tasted good, but the ice is especially delicious. I have never tasted anything like that. It is frozen and yet sweet.

'Sweet.' He just murmurs the word. I find myself wondering whether he is talking about me or the ice.

'Let's dance,' he says when I finish. He takes my hand and tucks it around his arm, and gently sweeps a stray curl away from my face with his other hand. I wonder whether it is improper, but no one seems to have noticed. We join the line that is forming and he releases me with one of his ravishing smiles – the flash of white teeth drawing attention to the smooth colour of those very high cheekbones and the softness of his brown eyes.

He is a very good dancer. He keeps perfect time with

me – all the Austens are good dancers, and so are their pupils, but Thomas is the best partner that I have ever had. Up and down the row, crossing hands, whirling around, marking time, my train with its lovely blue beads swirling behind me – I want that dance to go on forever. From time to time I remember his shoulder and am careful not to put my weight on his arm during left swings, but mostly I just enjoy myself. My busy, worrying brain has gone silent – only my body is working.

'Like another ice?' he asks when the music has finished and he has led me to a seat under the colonnade of marble pillars. And then he is gone before I can even answer. I look after him, admiring the way he makes his way so quickly and neatly through the crowd that's clustered around the laden supper table, how he smiles and nods and says a few words here and there but never allows himself to be slowed or diverted from his task. He is the most handsome man in the room, I think, as he comes back smiling with a bowl of pale pink ice in his hand.

'What about yourself?' I ask.

'I'll finish yours if it's too much for you,' he says. It sounds rather improper, I think, but there is no one near enough to hear.

And then we talk, mostly about our childhoods. He tells me that he went to a naval college when he was only twelve years old – his uncle, the admiral, paid his fees, and his mother was glad that her brother took such an interest in her son. Then, when his mother died, his uncle became guardian to both him and his sister.

'Tell me about your family,' he says then. And so I start to tell him about Augusta. I wish that I could make it sound funny, as Jane would have done, but my feelings are too strong for that, and from time to time I hear my voice wobble. I am only about halfway through telling all the things that she used to say to me, when it occurs to me that I am sounding childish and silly so I stop abruptly, take another spoonful and say, 'Tell me some more about your sister.'

'You should stand up to her, you know,' he says, ignoring me. 'People like your Augusta are just bullies. If you stand up to them, they back down, but if you give in to them they get worse and worse.'

'That's easy to say.' I surprise myself by saying that quite loudly, and he looks a little surprised too. And then he grins. 'That's the spirit,' he says with another of his devastating smiles. 'I know it's not easy.' His voice is very gentle now and the tone of it sends shivers down my back. He stretches out a hand and I place mine in his. He runs a finger of his other hand up and down the stitching on my glove, just between my own fingers. His eyes are not looking at me though, but gaze unseeing into one of the potted palms. 'I know when I was about your age I tried to stand up to the admiral and insisted that my sister should be brought home from that awful boarding school that she hated, but he just told me to leave the room, and I'll never forgive myself for going off with my tail between my legs.' His smooth voice deepens and roughens and his eyes harden. And then he says, 'That's the last time that I ever allowed anyone to push me around. Girls died in those boarding schools, you know. If my sister had died from lack of food or care, I would have killed the admiral.'

I give a little shiver and hand him the rest of my ice. I don't know whether it is the ice making me cold or the expression on his face.

For a few minutes nothing is said while he moodily spoons the rest of the ice into his mouth, but then he touches the curl that hangs down over my forehead and smiles at me.

'There's no need for you to be scared of anyone.' His voice is very gentle now, and his brown eyes are soft again. 'If Augusta scolds you, stand up to her. If she finds out about Southampton – and it doesn't really matter if she does; she or anyone else – then just say that you did the right thing and you saved your cousin. And if that doesn't work, send for me – night or day, I'll come riding to the rescue with my two pistols at the ready.'

And then he laughs, and I laugh at the thought of Augusta being threatened with two pistols.

And after that it is time to line up again. This time Jane, partnered by Tom Lefroy, is beside me. I see her looking up at Thomas as they cross hands together in the middle of the line.

'Oh heavens, my dear, what a very fine beau you have found for yourself. I do declare that he is almost as fine as Valancourt in *The Mysteries of Udolpho,*' she murmurs in my ear when she returns to my side. I am not embarrassed. I just chuckle. Suddenly I feel full of confidence. The most handsome man in the room is my partner and I feel as though I am in heaven. I see Lady Portsmouth staring at me, but I don't care. Nothing matters except Thomas.

'Jenny, let's not dance the next dance,' he says.

I have lost count; I don't know whether it is the fourth or the fifth dance, but I don't mind as long as Thomas is with me.

'Let's go and sit out in the colonnade again.' He leads me over to a small stone bench beside one of the tall marble pillars. I sit down and cool first one cheek and then the other against the cold marble of the pillar. He sits down beside me. There is barely room for the two of us.

'Are you tired?' I ask.

He shakes his head. 'I just want us to talk,' he explains.

He tells me about the East Indies, and about the tigers and elephants that he has seen and about his voyages to the other side of the world – to the West Indies. I tell him a bit more about my life in Bristol – about my brother and his wife and about my life before that. I tell him about my mama, and tears come into my eyes. He puts his arm around me and holds me very close to him for a minute. When he releases me I know I am blushing, but it doesn't matter. Here under the palms no one can see my hot cheeks.

And then, as the music slows and the dance is finishing, he says, 'Perhaps you will come and see my home one day and meet my uncle and my sister – will you do that?'

I can't say anything. He doesn't seem to want an answer. He can probably read it in my smile.

'Sitting under these palms makes me feel as if we are on one of those islands near Barbados that you were telling me about,' I say.

'I wish we were,' he answers. 'You can't imagine what the islands are like, Jenny. The sea is so blue and the sands are so white. The sun is dazzling.'

'Mama would say that is bad for the complexion,' I say, smiling. It's strange, but it is the first time since Mama died that I am able to mention her without pain.

'You would sit under the shade of the palm trees during the day,' he says, taking my hand to pull me to my feet. The master of ceremonies is calling everyone to take their places for the next dance. 'And by moonlight you could bathe in the warm sea,' he whispers in my ear as he escorts me across the ballroom so that we can join the long line of gentlemen and ladies.

I'll remember this all my life, I think: the candles flickering in the cut-glass chandelier; the sudden scent of lavender water wafted on the hot air; the pungent smell of hot wax and of buckskin gloves; the musicians playing very softly, the voices murmuring, exclaiming, laughing; the gentlemen handsome in black coats, but more dashing in the red coats of the army or in the royal blue of the navy; the pretty whites, pinks, blues and yellows of the muslin gowns as we all cross and cross back from partner to partner.

Saturday night, 2 April 1791

I'm sitting here thinking about the ball – trying to put off the moment when I must write down what happened after those first most wonderful, magical few hours . . .

Everything was going well.

And then I had to spoil it all. I think it started when he said, 'Don't stand there; that candle is drooping; you'll get hot wax all over you,' as I took my place beside Elizabeth Bigg. His hand was on my arm and he moved me down a little, just as someone would move a child.

'Don't pout,' he said. 'I wouldn't like to see the candle drip on your curls.' He was quite casual about it. A minute later he was looking with a puzzled frown on his face at someone at the top of the room, near the doorway.

I could see that Elizabeth Bigg had heard what he said and I felt very embarrassed. I felt annoyed that he was treating me like a child. I remembered all the things that Jane told me, and what Eliza told me. I wanted to behave like a sophisticated woman and I tried to flirt with him, but it didn't seem to work. He just looked amused and the frown disappeared from his forehead. He took no notice when I used my fan and cast down my eyelashes and then peeped up at him. I even tried saying, 'Oh la . . .' but he didn't seem to respond. He just danced with a faint smile on his face and a look as if his thoughts were far away.

When we sat out after this dance, it seemed as if Thomas was still thinking of that terrible night again. He started questioning me about it. In a way it was a relief to pour it all out – I often had nightmares about it still. I told him all about the sailors who shouted, 'Look at that little beauty!' and called to me to join them, about the inn full of drunken men, and the lady who stared at me with such disapproval and then pulled down the blind. When I had finished he took my hand and kissed my fingers, but his face was very serious and his brown eyes were dark and hard.

'Promise me that you will never do a thing like that again,' he said.

I took my hand away from his and shrugged my shoulders. He was treating me like a little girl again, I thought. Men should fall at your feet – if I could believe Eliza and Jane – not order you to do things.

'I don't know,' I said, and I thought I sounded grown-up and sophisticated. 'I suppose it was rather an adventure.'

I could see a flush come to his cheekbones – it surprised me that I could see it as his face was so tanned and his colour so good already. His eyes were still very hard. I looked down and played with my fan, placing it into the 'maybe' position. Already I was

wishing that I had not said that. It sounded silly.
When I looked up he was not even looking at me. He
was looking quite away from me.

'Excuse me for a moment,' he said, and then he
walked away from me. I was left sitting by myself,
eating my ice; after a minute I pushed it away. It had
begun to melt and the taste was too sweet. What was
he doing? He had gone towards the door and had now
completely disappeared. There was a crowd of naval men near the door, all laughing, and I wondered
whether he was among them. But no, he was so tall
that he would have been head and shoulders over most
of them. He must have gone out. But why? And where
had he gone? Surely he wasn't so offended by my silly
remark that he was going to leave me alone here.

'Are you all right, Jenny?' It was Frank passing by.
He stopped, looking concerned. I smiled up at him,
thinking how nice he was.

'Yes, I'm fine, Frank,' I said, trying to sound normal.

He hesitated for a moment, and then his eyes went
to a tall figure approaching – two figures. Frank nodded to me and then walked away as Captain Williams
and his companion drew near.

'Miss Cooper, may I introduce First Lieutenant
Price?' I got up and curtsied, and Lieutenant Price
gave me a splendid bow.

'It's an honour to meet you, Miss Cooper. Would
you favour me with the next dance?'

But this was the last dance! I couldn't believe that Thomas would want me to be with someone else for the last dance of the evening. I looked at him and saw that the flush was still on his cheeks and his dark eyes were still hard. He hardly seemed to look at me, just bowed and took his leave as if we were almost strangers.

Lieutenant Price was a good-humoured, cheerful young man who seemed to want to earn his captain's approval by paying me lots of compliments. Funnily enough, although I was worried about why Thomas had suddenly shot off like that, I found it quite easy to respond to him. I even practised flirting with my fan and saying, 'Oh la, sir, you make me blush.' It was all a game – like playing pontoon – and I thought that I could probably get used to doing this.

Lieutenant Price was full of praise for his captain when we had reached the end of the line and were marking time. He seemed to really worship Thomas. He told a story about how once when they were in action his captain had been prepared to sacrifice his own personal prize money of at least five hundred pounds when they had an opportunity of capturing a Spanish frigate because one man had gone over-board. Thomas had ordered the boat to be lowered, but while this was being done he himself had dived into the water and rescued the drowning man by the hair of his head and held him out of the water until the boat arrived to pick them both up.

'He's the bravest man in the world and the best captain! And do you know something, Miss Cooper? He's the youngest captain in the whole British navy and yet middle-aged men are proud to serve under him!'

And this bravest man in the world, this youngest captain in the navy, this hero who was willing to sacrifice life and fortune for his men, this man handsome as a god, this kind, beautiful, exciting man had danced with me for almost the whole evening, I thought to myself as we went home in the hired coach.

But why did he suddenly leave?

If it were something to do with the ship, then surely Lieutenant Price would have told me about it. Goodness knows he talked enough about that ship.

Could it be that he thought I was too young, too silly, for him and he suddenly tired of me and handed me over to one of his junior officers?

I'm not going to think of it any more tonight or I won't sleep. I'll just think about that time when we sat under the palms and talked about the white sand of Barbados.

Sunday, 3 April 1791

When I woke up this morning I felt quite exhausted. I asked Jane to tell Frank that I was too tired for a riding lesson. Jane decided that she was too tired to do her piano practise so we both curled up on my bed and discussed the ball. I told her all my worries and fears about Thomas not dancing the last dance with me, but she brushed them aside. When I told her that Thomas had left the ballroom for a few minutes, she suggested that Lord Portsmouth probably sent for him to come to the card room to make a fourth at the whist table.

'He couldn't refuse – after all, he has been staying there at Hurstbourne Place as a guest for the last week or so. My father always says that the earl lives for his card games.'

I turned that around in my mind. It did seem to make sense.

'Well, I won't expect to see him this week as he is going to the Isle of Wight tomorrow to visit his uncle and his sister.'

Then I told Jane all about how he wanted me to meet them, and Jane got very excited about this. She told me that everyone was looking at us and talking about us and speculating on whether it would be a match. All three of the Bigg girls were certain that he would propose.

'Shocking behaviour!' Jane giggled. 'Sitting out,

dancing with only one man, exposing yourself to the gossip of the county . . .'

'Did my aunt say that?' I asked the question anxiously, but Jane shook her head. 'No, no, but never mind about Mama . . . Tell me, did he make an offer?'

I told her no, that he just spoke of my visiting his sister and his uncle, the admiral, and Jane nodded wisely, as if she were at least thirty years old.

'That's the first step towards making an offer,' she said sagely.

'But what if his uncle doesn't like me?'

'It doesn't matter — he's of independent means.' Jane was always very sure of herself when it came to matters like that.

'In any case . . .' It was nice to have a best friend to talk things over with, I thought. My mind was full of worries, though I felt happier than I had ever felt before. For the first time, yesterday, I had tasted Champagne, and I felt as if the wine was still bubbling inside me. However, Jane's question made me bite my nails anxiously. Would Thomas ask me to marry him? This would be every girl's dream — that the man she loved would propose marriage. But perhaps it was just a dream. I got off the bed and walked over to the window.

'What is troubling you, my dear Miss Cooper?' enquired Jane. 'Don't you want to get married then? Perhaps you want to become a writer, to devote your life to your art. Is that it?'

I shook my head, laughing. Jane always managed to find something ridiculous to say.

'Or an artist, a painter?' Her eyebrows were raised.

'No, I'd just like to be married,' I said.

'I wonder how much a year Captain Williams possesses?' murmured Jane, sounding like a concerned mother. 'I must have a chat with Frank about this.'

'Don't,' I said. Somehow, inside all my happiness, there was a vision of Frank's young, hurt face as he stepped politely to one side when Thomas was escorting me. I don't think that Frank is really in love with me – boys are younger than girls in these matters, Jane tells me – but I think he feels something for me, and I thought that he looked a little jealous when he saw how Thomas's arm was still around my waist even though the dance had finished. 'Don't,' I said again. 'I don't mind how much Thomas has. I'd marry him if he didn't have a penny.'

'Dear, dear, dear.' Jane clicked her tongue reprovingly. 'You shouldn't be like that. Now, me, I'm determined to marry no man with under ten thousand pounds a year. So, my dear young creature, will you accept him if he asks you?'

I nodded. 'Yes, of course, but . . .'

'But?' Jane's eyebrows rose. 'Are his breeches just too white? Is that it?'

I went back and sat on the bed again.

'I'm worried that people will think I'm too young.

I'm only sixteen — perhaps I *am* too young — my brother is very particular about things. And Augusta was twenty-three when she married so I bet she will think that is the exact right age to get married.' I remembered that Thomas had asked me for Edward-John's address. Why did he want that? What was he going to write to them about? Surely he wasn't going to mention marriage before asking me?

But if he did, what would Edward-John and, more importantly, Augusta, think about a girl of sixteen getting engaged to be married? I remembered over-hearing Augusta whispering to one of her friends about how Edward-John would have problems if I ever did get married. I didn't understand it, but I guessed that perhaps the fifty pounds a year that Edward-John has now to maintain me would have to be given up if I married. How would Edward-John react to that? Augusta was extravagant and always had to have the best of everything. I knew that Edward-John worried about the bills that came in from the haberdashery and furniture shops. It would be a blow to him to give up my little fortune.

'I just know that Edward-John and Augusta will say that I am too young to get married,' I said aloud. The more I thought about it, the more despairing I felt.

'Well, look at all those queens that Cassandra was trying to make me study!' Jane always had an answer to every problem. 'They got married very young. Henry VII's mother was married at twelve and she had a child at thirteen. And there was that unspeakably learned Lady Jane Grey – who only lived to annoy everyone by showing off the fact that she could speak Greek. Do you know that when she saw her husband's body being brought back from the scaffold, she sat down and wrote a sentence about it in Latin and then another one in Greek? Well, she was not only married when she was sixteen, but got her head chopped off before she was seventeen as well. Now, that was packing a lot into a short life! You'll never do as well as Lady Jane Grey, my dear. Just be content with getting married at sixteen – and keeping your head on your shoulders, of course!'

And then we both rolled on the bed giggling and I began to feel quite a bit better. I would just have to wait until I saw Thomas again and then I could see whether he really did care for me. If he did, well, he would handle Augusta and Edward-John for me.

The rest of the day was quite uninteresting: church, dinner, music, card games in the parlour . . . Frank was missing because Mrs Austen had sent him over to Lady Portsmouth with a note saying how we had all enjoyed the evening, and then Henry went off to visit the Portals. Things were dull without them.

That night before going to bed, Jane said to me

solemnly, 'Don't look so worried, Jenny. No man tells a girl that he wants his nearest relations to meet her unless he is on the point of proposing. You can take my word for that – I assure you I have made a life study of this subject.'

Monday, 4 April 1791

Jenny Williams

Mrs Thomas Williams

Mrs Thomas Williams

Mrs Thomas Williams

Tuesday, 5 April 1791

Jane and I were going out with a basket today. We had a slice of meat in it for George, and I had drawn some pictures of all kinds of meat. At the gate we met Mr Austen on his way back from church. He asked us where we were going and when Jane, who is always very courageous, told him, he looked a little embarrassed, gave a quick glance at the house to make sure that his wife wasn't watching and then said that he would come with us.

George wasn't alarmed – though I'm not sure whether he knew it was his father. He learned the sign for meat and then we put out all the pictures, made the signs, and one by one he was able to point to the pictures. Each time that he pointed, Jane dug into her basket and produced something. We didn't have an orange and he was upset at that, searching the basket himself. Eventually he found a small piece of orange peel and he ate that. I hoped it wouldn't harm him, but he seemed very happy.

'Well,' said Mr Austen as we walked home together, 'I think you two girls have done a marvellous piece of work. I wouldn't have believed it was possible. Where did you get the idea of teaching him sign language?'

'I read it in a book from your library,' explained Jane. She was glowing with excitement, her round cheeks as rosy as apples.

'I know the one,' said Mr Austen. 'I think I'll write to the man who wrote that book and consult him about George. It may be that he can recommend a teacher for him.'

He hesitated a bit, looking at Jane, and then he said, 'Jane, I want to tell you about Thomas.'

I gave a start when he said that, but it was another Thomas that he was talking about.

'Who's Thomas? I haven't got another brother hidden away, have I?' asked Jane in that ugly, harsh voice she used to her mother.

'No, no.' Mr Austen was patient where Mrs Austen would have started to scold. 'Thomas is your mother's brother and he, like George, was born disabled. He is being cared for by a very good and devoted family in the village of Monk Sheraton. It was of him that I spoke the other day. We think that it might be a good idea to take George there and lodge him with his uncle. They would be companions for each other and he would be well looked after. There is a big family there at Monk Sheraton. I've been to see Thomas there and I think that they are good to him. He helps on the farm a bit, and they are all very kind there. He was feeding the hens when I came and he looked very happy. We want to do the best thing for George. You do believe that, don't you? And we will try to get someone to continue the tuition that you have started.'

'What does Mother think about this?' Jane was

slightly unsure of what to say; I could hear that in her voice.

Mr Austen sighed and then he said very simply, 'Don't judge your mother too harshly, Jane. The trouble is that your mother and I have been short of money all our married lives. Running the school was the only way that we could manage and do the best for you all. And of course I could not have run the school without your mother's help. She has had all the hard work: looking after the pupils, their laundry, their food, their happiness even. She could not have cared for George at the same time.'

I could see that Jane was not impressed by this, but she said nothing. She was too fond of her father and she was keen to give advice on how George could be taught sign language and lay out a programme of study for him.

'The thing is that if he could learn to spell easy words like *cat* and *dog* and *gun* and other words, then he could go on to talking on his fingers. I remember Charles learning his alphabet, and when he learned his letters Cassandra and I used to put the letters together to make little words for him. It would be wonderful if George could read, wouldn't it, Papa? Even very simple books. And I'd love to be able to talk to him. If he goes over to Monk Sheraton, you will take me to see him, won't you?'

Mr Austen promised, and Jane beamed happily at him.

And for a lot of this evening Jane and I chatted about George and how wonderful it would be if he could talk to us.

Neither of us mentioned Jane's mother. I don't know what Jane felt, but I worried in case Mrs Austen would think a teacher for George a complete waste of money, with the other four boys still to be launched into the world.

And for the rest of the evening we talked about Thomas and about the ball . . . and about Tom Chute and Tom Lefroy . . .

Wednesday, 6 April 1791

Something terrible has happened today.

And to begin with it was just an ordinary, quiet, happy day.

It all started off when Frank asked me to ride up to Deane Gate Inn to collect the post. I always enjoyed that and I am very confident with my donkey now.

When we arrived at the inn, the ostler came out as soon as he saw us and said that there were five letters for the parsonage. Frank took them and scrutinized their outsides.

'One from James for my father . . . one for Jane from Cousin Eliza . . . two for Henry, probably creditors . . . this one is from Bristol.'

I immediately guessed that it would be from Augusta and then, thankfully, I noticed that it was for my Aunt Austen. 'Good,' I said to Frank. 'It's for your mother.' I remember thinking what a relief that was, and being pleased that I wouldn't have to write back. If only I had known what was in that letter I could have dropped it in the ditch and at least enjoyed a couple more happy days.

And we went back and went into breakfast.

They were all sitting around the table, the family and the pupils. I gave out the letters.

Henry pushed his two into his pocket rapidly and avoided his father's worried look.

Mrs Austen poured the tea, broke the seal on the back of her letter and then put it down without reading it as she took a bite of her usual dry toast.

Mr Austen was the first to open his letter.

'Henry, James wants to know if we will come to Oxford on Saturday to hear him speak at a debate. I think that would be quite a treat, wouldn't it? What do you think, my dear? James says that he can put us up at his lodgings on Saturday night. If we get the early mail coach on Sunday morning, we'll be back in time for morning service.'

'Mama,' said Jane, 'Cousin Eliza has some news about the king and queen of France, King Louis XVI and Marie Antoinette. Apparently they have been imprisoned in Paris by the angry mob. Eliza is worried about her husband. Mama, are you listening?'

But Mrs Austen wasn't listening to anyone. She was reading Augusta's letter. I could see the big, bold handwriting – just one page and not even crossed. It should not have taken long to read it. But Mrs Austen was now going back over it again. She frowned and then looked at me. I felt puzzled. There was an odd look in her eye. For the first time since I have known her, Mrs Austen looked as though she was unsure of what to do.

After breakfast, I rose to help Cassandra and Jane with our task of clearing the breakfast plates. Mrs Austen stopped me, however.

She put a hand on my arm and stood there

looking indecisive. Mr Austen gave her a puzzled look, but she said nothing to him and so he shuffled off to the schoolroom with his pupils. Henry and Frank followed at a slow pace. Both were studying with their father at the moment, but neither was enthusiastic. Frank had told me that he knew more of mathematics than his father did, and that Latin was useless to him; and Henry was obviously wishing himself back at Oxford with all the fun and parties and 'wild living', as Jane expressed it.

'Come with me, Jenny.' That was all that Mrs Austen said as she took my hand, but there was something in her tone that alerted Jane.

'Shall I come too?' she asked.

'No, I just need Jenny for a few minutes.' Mrs Austen sounded sure of that, at least. The brisk tone was back in her voice and she moved quickly to the door, still with my hand in hers as if she thought I might run away.

'Come upstairs into my bedroom, my dear; we'll get some privacy there,' she said as we passed the parlour where the housemaid was lighting the fire.

What could Augusta have to say to Mrs Austen that was so important? I wondered. Mrs Austen's routine normally never varied. By now she should have been out in the dairy, checking on the amount of milk brought in, inspecting the cleanliness of the churn and directing the dairymaid in loud, penetrating tones. Perhaps something had happened to Edward-

John, I suddenly thought, and although he was never very friendly to me, my heart almost stopped for a moment. My brother was the only family I had left.

'Sit here next to me, Jenny dear.' Mrs Austen plumped herself down on the window seat and I squeezed in beside her. She still held Augusta's letter in her hand. For a moment she seemed unsure as to what to do, but then she suddenly held it out to me.

'What's all this nonsense about?' I could hear her voice, but it seemed to come from a long way away. The letter was not very long; I read it in a few seconds, but suddenly my life was in ruins.

How could he?

How could Thomas have betrayed me like this?

It had to be him.

How could he, before he left Hurstbourne Park, have taken his pen and sent this letter to Edward-John and Augusta? And I had been imagining him, coming down to breakfast in Lord and Lady Portsmouth's magnificent dining room, thinking of me as he ate his buttered eggs, deciding to go to see his uncle and sister . . .

Well, I was probably right. He had thought of me, but it was not with love and understanding. He had thought of me and he had found my conduct so shocking that he had written to Edward-John as my guardian. Or else he wanted to force me to stand up to Augusta — either way, I could never forgive him.

And he had promised never to tell anyone.

Perhaps when I had refused to promise never to do it again he was so annoyed that he took revenge by telling my brother and sister-in-law.

I blinked the tears from my eyes and read Augusta's letter through again.

Dear Mrs Austen,

The most distressing and alarming communication has come to me today from Hurstbourne Park. It was lucky that my dear husband was still by my side when I opened the letter or else I would have fallen to the ground in a deep faint. I do declare that I am still suffering from such severe palpitations that the quill quivers in my hand as though it were still part of the living bird.

Madam, I hesitate to communicate to you the terrible information that I have received. I wish I could bring myself to make the usual enquiries about your health but I can send no compliments to you, your husband and your charming children. My whole heart and mind is filled with horror at the behaviour of one that I considered as a sister to me as well as to my darling husband, Edward-John.

It has been reported to us, madam, that this miserable girl has been, alone and unchaperoned, walking the streets of Southampton at midnight.

I can assure you, madam, that I have received this information from a most reliable source. There can be no doubt as to its accuracy.

Edward-John and I can see only one solution to such appalling behaviour and lack of decorum. We can no longer leave her - I cannot bring myself to say her name - we can no longer impose the care of such a wicked and abandoned creature upon your good selves. We have decided to place her in a very strict boarding school here at Bristol. The girls are locked in their bedrooms every single night - so the mistress of the school assures me. And there are no holidays so there will be no opportunities for further bad behaviour.

Edward-John and I will arrive to collect the sinful girl by the overnight stagecoach from Bristol. We should be at Deane Gate Inn by ten o'clock of the morning.

I am, etc.

Augusta Cooper

'I just came for a handkerchief.' Mr Austen slid apologetically around the door, but then he exclaimed, 'Jenny dear, what's the matter?'

I was crying too hard to say anything. Last night I felt that I was floating on a cloud of perfect happiness and now I was drowning in despair. He came across the floor and bent down and took one of my cold hands in his own. Through the blur of my tears I saw Mrs Austen pass Augusta's letter to him. He read it quickly and then handed it back.

'But, Jenny, dearest little Jenny, we don't believe this!' Now he had taken out his clean muslin handkerchief and was trying to mop the tears that slid down my face.

'Don't cry, Jenny. Neither your aunt nor I could believe such a thing of you.'

'That's all very well, Mr Austen,' said my aunt. 'But an accusation like this could ruin Jenny forever. Where on earth did that woman get that story?'

'Mama, what piano piece would you like me to practise today?' Jane was at the door. I took the handkerchief from Mr Austen and dried my eyes and face.

'Jane dear, your mother is busy.' Mr Austen looked anxiously from one to the other of us.

'What's the matter with Jenny?' Jane had closed the door and come across to the window seat.

'Oh, come in, come in,' said Mrs Austen wearily. 'Let's have the whole of Hampshire in here, why not?'

No one answered her, but I saw Mr Austen hand

the letter to Jane. I began to cry again and Mr Austen's handkerchief was soaked through in the minute it took for Jane to scan the letter. I looked at her and saw my own thoughts mirrored in her eyes.

'Of course we don't believe this, Jenny.' Mr Austen's voice was so affectionate that it made me cry even harder. 'This is some malicious person. My dear ' – he addressed his wife – 'do you think that it could be one of the young Portsmouths? That Coulson! He would do anything for a joke! Shall we send Henry over to Hurstbourne Park to make enquiries?'

'No, no.' I felt I could not bear to have everyone at Hurstbourne Park talking about me. It was bad enough to know that Thomas had betrayed me, that I had been mistaken in him. He was not really in love; he just thought of me as a silly child and, when thinking it over, decided to let my brother and my sister-in-law know all about my dreadful secret. He probably thought it would be good for me to stand up to them. He didn't realize the importance of a young girl's reputation. I had wondered why he asked me so particularly about where they lived. I wished now that I hadn't given him the address.

'Just tell us it is not true, Jenny, and your uncle and I will do everything to sort out this matter and to save you from being sent to boarding school.' Mrs Austen was herself again, decisive and practical.

'It is true.' I said the words boldly and gave my eyes a last mop. I sat up very straight.

'What?!' both husband and wife exclaimed on the one note like a well-trained pair of singers.

'Tell them,' I said to Jane.

And Jane made a wonderful dramatic story of how I had taken the letter at the risk of my life and liberty — these were her words — and how I had braved the midnight streets of Southampton and delivered the letter to the post-inn. And how I had saved her life by my courage!

When she had finished, Jane put her two arms around me and held me very close in a hug, and Mr Austen stroked my hair with a gentle hand. Then I saw him take Jane in his arms as if he suddenly realized that he might have lost her. I think that we were all crying for a minute — all except Mrs Austen, who still had a worried and slightly annoyed expression on her face.

'This is a most unfortunate affair,' she said, and her lips were compressed together in a straight line. 'If this gets out about Jenny, what on earth are we to do? Her reputation will be ruined.'

'But, Jenny, who could have told that abominable sister-in-law of yours?' Mr Austen was obviously quite upset; normally he was very careful not to say anything about Augusta.

'I met a gentleman that night in Southampton,' I said hesitantly. I buried my face in my hands. I could not look at either my aunt or my uncle while I spoke the words that had to be said. 'He was very

310

kind to me. He escorted me to the post-inn and then he took me back to the school. He waited until I was safely inside.' I swallowed another sob as the picture of Thomas in his deep blue coat, with the gold braid flashing under the glare of the chair-men's torches, came into my mind. I had to finish my story though.

'It was Captain Thomas Williams,' I said des-perately. 'The naval officer who is a guest of the Portsmouths at Hurstbourne Park.'

'Captain Williams.' Mr Austen sounded relieved. He had liked Thomas. I think he was reassured to know that he had been looking after me on that ter-rible night.

'Captain Williams?' Mrs Austen sounded puzzled. I knew how she felt. A horrified expression crossed her face. I could follow her thoughts; Captain Wil-liams had shown affection to me, but then he must have thought it over and decided to have no more to do with me.

'I wonder why he felt he had to talk to your brother.' Mrs Austen's voice was still puzzled – puzzled and worried.

'And he promised that he would never tell a living soul.' I felt sick and faint and was glad of Jane's arm around me.

No one said anything for a full minute. I sensed rather than saw Mrs Austen exchange glances with her husband and with Jane. Then she got to her feet.

She crossed over to her bedside table, poured a small measure of wine and brought it over to me.

'Drink this, Jenny,' she said soothingly. 'Jane, take her back up to your bedroom. You are both excused from lessons this morning. Don't worry, Jenny. I will sort out Mrs Augusta Cooper, and young Edward-John, when they come on Saturday. That lady will find that your uncle and I have something to say about them trying to ruin your reputation and risk your life by sending you off to boarding school again. After all, I am your poor mother's elder sister. The main thing is to hush up this terrible business as much as possible. Let us hope that Captain Williams is a man of honour and he doesn't mention it to anyone else.'

Thursday, 7 April 1791

I did nothing much but cry yesterday, but this morning I got up with a resolve. I would write Thomas a letter, finish this business now and put him out of my head forever. Then I would concentrate on avoiding being sent to boarding school. Jane had great plans about the two of us running away, but I thought I would prefer to rely on Mrs Austen.

'Here's some paper.' Jane arranged the clean sheet and a new quill and the inkhorn in front of me with a very sympathetic face.

I dipped the quill into the ink, but then left it there, stroking the smooth curved shape of the horn with my fingers while I tried to think of what to say. A big tear dropped down on to the clean sheet of paper.

'Don't.' Jane was at my side, blotting the tear with the corner of her handkerchief. 'You'll spoil the paper and water down the ink. Let me write. You can dictate it.'

'*Dear Captain Williams,*' I began, getting up obediently and allowing her to sit in my place.

'Just call him "Sir",' advised Jane, carefully selecting a large goose quill and dipping it into the inkstand.

'Sir.' Then I stopped. I didn't know what to say.

I just wanted to cry, but I knew I shouldn't allow myself to start again. Soon it would be time for the bread-and-cheese lunch that the Austens always took at eleven o'clock, and I didn't want all the boys to see my blotchy face and red eyes. I went to the window and opened it, leaning out to cool my cheeks before turning back to Jane.

'I never want to see you again,' I said as steadily as I could.

Jane made a face. She stirred the ink with her quill, but did not write. I could see that she didn't think much of this, but I couldn't think of anything better to say so I bit my lip and tried not to think about Thomas and how splendid he had looked at the ball.

'What about this?!' exclaimed Jane. She opened her writing desk, took out her notebook, turned over the pages and then gave a satisfied nod.

'This will do,' she said. 'It is from *Jack and Alice*.'

She read it aloud as her quill scratched out the letters on the page.

'"*Sir, I may perhaps be expected to appear pleased at and grateful for the attention that you have paid me, but let me tell you, sir, that I consider it an affront.*" . . . What do you think of that, Jenny?'

I didn't reply; I couldn't. I was trying too hard not to sob aloud.

'I'll put in "*considering your vile and deceitful*

behaviour",' said Jane, writing rapidly. She needed to mend her pen; I could hear the point spluttering as it moved across the page, but once Jane was composing she never allowed anything to slow her down.

I nodded, but I didn't really care what she said. Thomas had hurt me so badly by telling my terrible secret that I could never forgive him. Even if he really did love me – and now I doubted that he ever had – and even if I could have brought myself to forgive him, my brother would never have allowed me to marry a man who had walked with me in the streets of Southampton at midnight. I was ruined for life. If he had told my secret to Augusta and Edward-John, he would tell it to everyone.

'"*I look upon myself, sir, to be a perfect beauty – where would you see, sir, a finer figure or a more charming face?*"'

I stopped her. 'That's silly. Just say that after his behaviour I never want to see him again . . .'

'Don't cry,' said Jane sympathetically. 'Don't worry about the letter. I'll just finish it off and sign it "Jenny", and then I'll give it to Frank and he'll ride to the post with it straight away. I won't read out any more. You can rely on me to make a good letter out of it. You just read a book or something.'

'I'll go and walk in the fresh air,' I said, wrapping my cloak around me and then taking down my bonnet. I tried to shut my ears to the words she was muttering as I was tying my bonnet strings, but I could hear them as I went out of the door: *'my accomplishments . . . my sweet temper . . . your dastardly behaviour . . .'*

That was the thing with Jane, I thought as I escaped down the stairs. She was very fond of me; I knew that. I was her best friend, just as she was my best friend, but writing always came first with her. Although very sorry for me, she was really enjoying composing this letter. I wondered whether she would change when she fell in love. I hoped for her sake that she never did. It all hurt too much. It was never worth it.

And then I thought about Thomas and I knew that I couldn't send him a letter like that. I raced back upstairs and burst into the bedroom.

'Jane,' I said, 'I am very, very grateful to you, but I just think that I'd better write the letter myself.' I could see she looked disappointed so I said that I thought her letter was too good for Thomas and would be best kept for a novel.

And then very quickly I wrote to Thomas and said that after what had happened I would prefer not to see him again and that I hoped that he would respect my wishes. I ended it: 'Yours, etc., J. Cooper.'

I thought that sounded the right note and then very quickly, before I could change my mind, I ran downstairs and asked Frank if he would take it to the post for me. He told me that it wouldn't get to

Southampton before Friday as the mail coach had already gone, but I told him it didn't matter as long as it arrived before the weekend. I could see him looking at my red eyes and tear-stained face, but I was past caring. I had a terrible pain in my heart and I just wanted to get into bed, draw the blankets over my head and moan.

'Are you all right, Jenny?' Frank's young, slightly hoarse voice sounded so concerned that a lump came into my throat and I found it hard to answer him.

The whole Austen family are being so nice to me. Henry allowed me to win some pennies from him in a game of pontoon, Frank offered to lend me his pony whenever I wanted it and, just because I ate so little at breakfast, Cassandra made a special dish of syllabub for me, whipping up the cream and white of eggs and flavouring it with orange juice and lots of sugar. Even that wasn't enough to make me hungry though, and I shared it between Jane and little Charles when she had gone back to the kitchen.

Friday, 8 April 1791

I don't think I'll ever write in this journal again.

Saturday, 9 April 1791

The mail coach is due at ten o'clock this morning. I wish I didn't have to go to meet Augusta and Edward-John, but Mrs Austen is insistent with me. She says that Cassandra and Charles must go too, as well as Jane, of course. Mr Austen and Henry have taken an earlier coach to visit James at Oxford; Frank has gone over to join a shooting party at the Portals' place.

'We'll show them that you have a family here, and that family values you,' she says to me, pinching my cheeks to give me some colour. Then she sends me upstairs to change my calico gown for my best blue muslin. 'Go up with her to do her hair, Cassandra,' she says. 'Do it the way she had it at the ball, just pinned on top of her head with a few stray curls around her neck. I thought she looked very grown-up with that hairstyle. Boarding school indeed . . . we'll see about that!'

I feel my feet dragging as we set out and for once Mrs Austen isn't shooing everyone along to hurry them up. 'Ten o'clock,' she says with a glance at her timepiece as we pass through the village. 'We're going to be quite late.'

'Oh dear,' says Cassandra in a worried way, but Mrs Austen just smirks.

'They invited themselves; let them wait on our

convenience.' She sounds quite pleased with herself.

When we reach Deane Gate Inn though, there is no sign of the coach, no bustling around, no changing horses, no piles of luggage on the ground – just the innkeeper's wife peering anxiously down the road.

'Oh, Mrs Austen, ma'am, I'm that worried; I don't know what to do,' she says. She looks at Mrs Austen. Everyone in the neighbourhood relies on Mrs Austen to tell them what to do, so now the innkeeper's wife comes back to the gate and joins us. 'The coach is overdue, ma'am. I'm feared that there might have been an accident. Do you think that I should send the man out to look for them? The trouble is that my husband isn't back from Basingstoke.'

'We'll walk down the road to see whether it is coming.' As always, Mrs Austen makes up her mind immediately. 'They can give us a lift back if we meet them.' She's in a good mood, relishing the prospect of the battle ahead, but I'm worried. I know what Augusta is like. I always have a feeling that she hates me. I know that she resents that my mother left me fifty pounds in order to give me a dowry when I marry or when I reach the age of twenty-one – whichever happens first.

Mrs Austen glances at me a few times but says nothing. Cassandra is silent because Tom Fowle has gone home for the weekend, Charles is looking into the little stream that runs along the side of the road to see if there are any sticklebacks in it, and Jane, I reckon, judging by her glowing cheeks and sparkling eyes, is making up a story where Augusta would be defeated by some splendidly funny device – last night she was suggesting things like steel traps set all around Steventon!

So we are silent when we come around the corner. There are poplar trees belonging to the Ashe family's woodlands on either side of the road, making it almost a tunnel of green, but the sun shines down through the tunnel and we can see plainly the scene ahead of us.

The coach is there in front of us. It has not overturned or anything like that. The four horses are still harnessed to it. However, the doors are widely ajar and the six passengers, including Edward-John and Augusta, are out on the road. Their luggage has been taken off the coach. One masked highwayman is ransacking the bags and trunks, while the other keeps two pistols aimed at the huddled group, the coachman and guard included.

The highwaymen haven't seen us. The early-morning sun will be shining directly in their eyes if they look at us, but their whole attention is on their prisoners. Mrs Austen puts a finger to her lips and edges over to touch Charles on the shoulder. She makes urgent beckoning signs, and we all step cautiously across the ditch and into the woodland. None of us makes a sound, and in another moment we might creep away through the trees and make our way back.

But then everything changes.

Further up the road, on the left-hand side, there is a large juniper bush. As I give one glance backwards

it seems to move. I stop. Jane bumps into me and she
stops also. Mrs Austen looks around impatiently.

And then a loud, hoarse sound ... A word ... But a
word only to someone who knows the speaker ...

'Bang!'

And George, with his unsteady gait, lurches out from
behind the bush, pointing his finger at the gun and re-
peating proudly, 'Bang!'

'Get over there!' The armed highwayman points one
gun at George while keeping the other pointed at the
group by the coach. His head swivels nervously between
the two.

'Bang!' says George, advancing with what passes for a smile on his poor face. He stretches out his hand, saying, 'Bang!' again. It's obvious to me that he expects the highwayman to give him the gun as a reward for saying the word.

'Halt, or I fire,' says the highwayman in shrill, nervous tones. He doesn't know what to do about George.

I hold my breath. I hear Jane give a nervous gasp beside me, but Mrs Austen doesn't hesitate; she steps out on to the road. The highwayman's gun swivels.

'You fellow! Don't point that gun at the boy – you'll frighten him into a fit.' Mrs Austen is marching resolutely over to George.

'What's it to you, lady?' The highwayman has a gruff, hoarse voice, the voice of someone who has a perpetual sore throat. 'Get back, or you'll have a bullet in the stomach.'

'He's my son, and I'm not going to allow you to terrify him,' says Mrs Austen calmly. 'Come along, George, let's take you back to Nanny Littleworth.'

And then she puts her arm around George's shoulders and turns him around gently, almost tenderly, until he is facing back towards Deane Gate and Steventon beyond. Slowly, steadily, the two figures come back down the road, while the highwayman continues to point his pistol at their backs, his whole attention now on the two moving figures. His partner takes his head out of a trunk and also stares incredulously at George and Mrs Austen.

It might have worked. In the bright, clear early-morning sunshine, I can see the faces of the highwaymen. They are puzzled, hesitant. It's obvious that George is retarded, and Mrs Austen looks just like any old countrywoman. They want money and jewels, not unnecessary bloodshed.

But then the guard of the coach, who is watching them as closely as I, makes a move. He slowly passes his arm behind Augusta, reaches for the blunderbuss in its place by the roof, grabs it by its short barrel and tries to reverse it.

And the highwayman whirls around and fires straight at the guard.

Then everything happens at once.

A roar of pain from the guard, a high-pitched neigh from the rearing horses, a hysterical screech from Augusta, shouts from the other passengers and blood everywhere.

And then a voice from the trees beyond the coach, a voice filled with authority but as velvet-smooth as chocolate: 'Drop those pistols and put your hands up, my men. I've got you both covered.'

They look at each other and hesitate, but less than a second later a warning shot explodes – fired over their heads, but near enough to be convincing. A second scream from Augusta, more neighing from the horses, and then the two pistols are flung hastily in the direction of the hedge.

'Very wise.' Thomas, the gold braid on his coat

glowing, strolls down the road, an ornate silver-mounted pistol in each hand. Without taking his eyes from the highwaymen, he addresses Edward-John, the only male passenger.

'Could I trouble you, sir, to pick up the blackguards' pistols and keep them trained on both men? Coachman, could you bind up your guard's arm? He's losing blood rapidly. Ladies, you follow behind us. Charles, would you untie my horse from the tree back there? Good lad! He shouldn't give you any trouble. He's had a long, hard gallop this morning.

'We'll lock these highwaymen in the stables at the inn,' he says decisively to Edward-John, and then rather sharply, 'Careful with that gun, sir, it's loaded.'

'Here's the innkeeper,' calls back Mrs Austen. She still has an arm around George, who is trembling violently, but he has not had a fit.

Even after the innkeeper arrives Thomas is still in charge, giving directions for the summoning of a magistrate and the safe custody of the prisoners, brushing aside the thanks of the passengers, praising and thanking Charles, reassuring the women passengers – but never once does he speak to me, or even glance at me.

And now the men are gone to the stables to see to the prisoners. Cassandra is fetching a glass of wine for Augusta, while Edward-John dithers between following Thomas and hanging anxiously over his wife . . .

Mrs Austen is in great good humour. 'What do you

think of this boy of mine, Mrs Deane?' she says to the innkeeper's wife. 'You wouldn't believe it, but he was telling the highwayman to hand over his gun.' She squeezes George's shoulder and he looks up at her in a wondering sort of way.

'You want something to eat now, don't you, George? And something to drink?' Mrs Austen chats to George in a perfectly natural manner, making motions with her hands to indicate eating and drinking, even rubbing her stomach to indicate food. A big smile lights up George's face.

'You go with Mrs Deane – she'll find some nice hot sausages for you and a glass of ale, won't you, Mrs Deane? Off you go with her now, George.' And all the time that she is saying the words, she is making signs in quite a natural manner – rather like how you would to a baby, I think. Much easier, I realize now, than trying to teach him his alphabet.

And George understands her perfectly. He rubs his own stomach and grins from ear to ear. He follows Mrs Deane and then he turns back, making a great effort until a word comes out. It's easy to understand the word. It's 'Mama'.

And when he's gone, Mrs Austen – tough, unsentimental Mrs Austen – has tears in her eyes.

This is almost like a play, I think.

First everyone is onstage in the coach yard in front of Deane Gate Inn. Then the men go off to the stables, followed by Charles, while Augusta retires to faint on a sofa in the comfort of the inn parlour, attended by Cassandra.

Then it's the scene between Mrs Austen and George, where she seems able to chat to him in an easy, natural way before he trundles happily off with Mrs Deane.

Now just Jane and I are left with Mrs Austen.

And Jane throws herself into her mother's arms and starts to cry.

It is so unlike Jane that I feel completely bewildered.

But Mrs Austen just pats her on the back and says, 'Come, come, Jane. Were you so very frightened of those highwaymen? That's not like my brave girl!' Her tone is light and amused, but loving.

I hold my breath. It just needs a few words from Jane now and perhaps they will be friends evermore.

But Jane says nothing and, after a moment's silence, I hear my own voice.

'Jane wasn't frightened for herself, Aunt,' I find myself saying. 'She was frightened for you.'

Mrs Austen draws back, bends down, looks into Jane's face and presses a quick kiss on one round cheek. I notice how their bonnets meet with a slight click.

'Come on, my pet,' she says. 'Let's go and thank Captain Williams properly. What a hero he's been! You could get a good novel out of this, Jane. I declare I feel like commemorating it in verse myself.' And, laughing cheerfully, she sweeps out with her arm around Jane.

327

And very carefully, I dust the top of the mounting block and sit on it. I feel very tired.

And very lonely.

'We'll send the post boy down to Steventon with you, ma'am,' says the innkeeper's wife. 'This lady' – she means Augusta – 'is not strong enough to walk, and Miss Jenny looks very white too. The captain has got his horse, and the other passengers will wait for the stagecoach to go on when we get another man to act as guard.'

'You should have fainted on the sofa too,' whispers Jane as we walk towards the post-chaise. 'I'd have made Augusta give you a turn. You could have fainted alternately.' Jane sounds like her old self again, grinning as her mother issues orders to everyone.

'Cassandra, you sit over there with Edward-John and his wife; Charles, you get up on the seat beside the post boy; Jenny, you sit beside me; and, Jane, you go on the other side of her. We'll follow you down to the parsonage, Captain Williams. You'll come in and have breakfast with us, won't you? Then we can all thank you properly.'

'Oh yes, indeed.' Augusta has given up fainting, though she still speaks in a small, slightly squeaky voice, like a six-year-old. 'Do come and ride on my side of the chaise, Captain Williams. How lucky for us all that you were passing by.'

'I'll ride behind you all, ma'am, so that my horse does

not kick up the dirt on to you,' says Thomas with a bow, and then to Mrs Austen, 'I was taking the liberty of paying a call to you, ma'am. My ship is stocked and ready to go; I've a few days' leave and you were kind enough to invite me to stay for a night or so on my next visit.'

'What a charming man,' enthuses Augusta once Thomas has fallen to the rear. 'I do declare that I have not heard of him, but I am sure that he is a real hero at sea. Where is his ship docked?'

'At Southampton.' Cassandra obviously does not know the full story of Augusta's letter.

'Southampton! I can't bear the word!' Augusta shudders and then looks at me crossly. 'Oh, Jenny, you sad, sad girl! What are we to do with you? I do declare, ma'am' – now she addresses herself to Mrs Austen – 'that I have not had a single night's sleep – Edward-John will tell you – since that letter came from Lady Portsmouth.'

'Lady Portsmouth?!' exclaims Jane, and she turns and looks at me, her eyes wide with amazement.

'Lady Portsmouth?' echoes Mrs Austen.

'Was your letter from Lady Portsmouth, Augusta?' I say. Suddenly I lose all fear of her. Only one thing matters now, and that is Thomas. 'Are you sure it was from Lady Portsmouth, Augusta?'

'Yes, of course.' Augusta sounds intensely annoyed. She turns away from me and towards my aunt. 'I told you, ma'am, did I not? Lady Portsmouth wrote to me that when Jenny came to a ball at her house she recognized her. She saw her last February when she was staying with a friend in Southampton. They were all listening to the young lady of the house perform on the piano when Lady Portsmouth saw a young girl, all alone and unprotected, look in through the window. She imagined her to be some sort of streetwalker and went to close the shutters. What was her astonishment to see her at her own ball at Hurstbourne Park and to learn that she is related to *me*?! Of course, she wrote to me. After all, my mama is one of her close friends.'

I look at Jane and she looks at me. She moves very close to me and squeezes my hand. Augusta looks at us with dislike.

'You two seem very thick,' she says disapprovingly.

'Yes, we are,' says Jane demurely. And then she can't resist adding, 'But I'm the thinner of the two . . .' and smiling sweetly when Augusta looks puzzled.

'Well, here we are in Steventon,' interrupts Mrs Austen. 'In another few minutes we will be at the parsonage and you will have a good cup of tea. That will restore your nerves. Charles,' she says as the chaise goes through the gates, 'you jump down and find the stable-man for Captain Williams's horse.'

'No,' says Jane. In her hurry to get out, she almost stumbles. 'No, Mama, let Charles ride back up to Deane Gate Inn with the post boy to find out how the guard is. The surgeon should be there by now. He can bring us news; I'll see to Captain Williams and his horse.'

'Go straight into the house, Jane,' says Mrs Austen

sternly. 'Tell Susan that we have arrived. Charles, you do what I told you.'

Jane rolls her eyes at me, but she dares not disobey her mother. I stay sitting in the post-chaise until Thomas has gone into the stable.

He still has not once looked at me.

'You sit here opposite Jenny, Captain Williams; Cassandra, make room for your Cousin Augusta next to you; Edward-John, could you take the bottom of the table, please?' Mrs Austen is back in control, beaming at me and adding in a loud whisper to Augusta: 'Jenny and Captain Williams are great friends.'

I feel as if I want to be sick, but reluctantly I take the indicated seat.

Luckily Thomas doesn't notice. He is busy chatting to Charles and promising him the first vacancy for a midshipman when he reaches fifteen years old.

'There are just a few words that I would like to say first, dear Aunt.' Edward-John is standing stiffly at the bottom of the table with a large black book in his hand, almost as if he is about to read prayers. 'Captain Williams, sir,' he continues, 'your conduct, your gallantry, your courage, your quickness of thinking, your—'

At this point Charles yawns and stretches out his hand towards the dish of buttered eggs. Cassandra gives him a sharp tap and an angry look, but Edward-John is too discomfited to go on for much longer. 'But I weary my young cousin,' he says, trying to get his dignity back. 'May I just present to you, Captain Williams, this humble volume of my collected sermons?' And then he bows ceremoniously. Thomas jumps up, but hardly seems to know what to do with the book once he has it in his hand.

'Well, well, well,' he says, 'this is—'

'Very weighty,' interrupts Jane, picking up the dish of eggs and the serving spoon and walking around the back of the table.

'Perhaps grace first?' suggests Edward-John.

Normally Mr Austen mutters a perfunctory, one-sentence grace before meals, so Jane does not sit down again, but holds the spoonful of eggs poised over Augusta's plate. I am embarrassed and worried about Thomas, but I have to choke back a giggle at the expression on Jane's face as Edward-John's grace wanders on and on, going from giving thanks to God for the food that not one of us has yet touched to giving thanks to God who sent an angel to help us in our hour of peril this morning. Charles gives a great snort and then covers his face rapidly with a grubby handkerchief when Edward-John mentions the 'angel', and I can't help glancing at Thomas. His brown eyes are dancing with amusement, and I feel myself getting very red when I realize that he has seen me looking at him.

Mrs Austen, I see with satisfaction, when we are all eating our buttered eggs – and consoling ourselves, as Jane whispers in my ear, with the thought that Augusta has the coldest eggs of all – Mrs Austen does not like

either of them. Augusta is very haughty and condescending, and Edward-John sounds a false flattering
note, admiring all the battered out-of-fashion furniture
in the parlour, but giving an occasional sly glance at his
wife that shows that he does not mean his praise.

I keep wondering what will happen after breakfast.
The meal is an agony to me. I have no appetite for the
food and every time I look up I can see Augusta looking at me with her pale eyes which are so like boiled
gooseberries that I will never again eat that fruit without thinking of her.

After breakfast will come the moment, I keep thinking to myself, and I wish that Charles will go on eating
for a long time. However, he has stopped eating now and
is telling Thomas all about his ambitions. Even in the
middle of my misery I think that Thomas is being very
nice to him. Mrs Austen rises to her feet and starts loading dishes rapidly on to a tray, obviously making sure
that Edward-John doesn't start on another long prayer.

And then Augusta clears her throat.

'Ahem!' It is so loud that everyone stops and looks at
her with interest.

She smiles around, enjoying the moment, and then
looks at me, her eyes as hard as glass.

She has left it too long though. Before she can speak,
Thomas gets to his feet with easy grace and bows to Mrs
Austen.

'I wonder, ma'am, if I might invite your niece to take
a short walk with me. It's such a fine day—'

'It's raining,' Charles tells him bluntly.

'Just a mizzle! My favourite weather! When you're a sailor on my ship and you've spent as much time in the East Indies as I,' he tells the delighted Charles, 'then you'll love our English mists.' Thomas gives a half-glance towards the window and then holds out his arm to me. I take it. I am still very embarrassed about that letter, but anything is better than staying and having Augusta tell me that no matter what anyone says, she and Edward-John, as my guardian, are determined to send me to that boarding school, which has no holidays and where the girls are locked in their dormitories every night.

'I'll run and get your cloak and your bonnet.' Jane thrusts the dish she is holding at Charles, who, with a quick glance at the back of his mother's head, proceeds to lick the remains of the eggs from its sides.

And then we are outside and the hall door is closed on the rest of the family.

But still I can say nothing.

I know that I am on the verge of tears and think it is better not to risk making any polite remarks about the weather or enquiries about his journey.

'What's the matter, Jenny? Don't you like the rain? Let's walk under the trees here. Your bonnet will remain quite dry.'

I tell him that the rain is nothing and I try to make my voice ordinary, but even I can hear how it shakes.

'Take my arm,' he says after a minute. 'It's slippery here with the wet moss on these paths.'

I take his arm and begin to feel better. The damp air is fresh and clean and perfumed by the brilliantly white lilies of the valley that edge the path.

'I got your letter. Why were you so angry with me?' His face is gentle but puzzled. 'Did you think it was terribly rude of me to go away from the ball without telling you where I was going? I should have really, but I was so angry and so ashamed of my men. I don't know whether you saw my sergeant come into the ballroom, looking for me. I was puzzled when I noticed him talking to Lieutenant Price and then I thought I'd better see what he wanted. He came to tell me that the boat crew were turning my ship into a drinking shop, with all sorts of terrible behaviour going on. I just wanted to sort it out straight away before anyone heard of the disgrace to the *Bonaventure*.'

'What?!' I'm sure I shriek the word before telling him the whole story of how I thought he was angry with me and had written to Augusta with the story of me in the midnight streets of Southampton.

'What!' His exclamation is even louder than mine, so I tell him quickly that now I know that it was Lady Portsmouth who wrote to Augusta. I tell him all about Augusta's letter and about the boarding school in Bristol where there are no holidays and the girls are all locked into their dormitories at night.

His eyes become very black and he begins to get so angry with Augusta that to distract him I say, 'I wish I had asked Lieutenant Price. He could have told me where you'd gone, and then I would not have suspected you of writing that letter.' (At least, I think that I might not have, though I don't think I could have guessed that Lady Portsmouth knew my secret.)

Thomas smiles then and he looks a little less angry.

'Lieutenant Price,' he says, 'bless him – he would never have told you. This was a disgraceful thing to happen to our ship. He wanted to go himself, but I wouldn't permit that. It was the business of the captain to sort this matter out.'

I ask him what he did to the boat crew, and no sooner is the question out of my mouth than I'm sorry that I asked it. I had to shut my ears to Frank's tales of floggings, but Thomas just says casually, 'I stood over them for three days while they were on their hands and knees scrubbing everything that could be scrubbed and polishing everything that could be polished. I don't think they'll try that again in a hurry. Of course it was very boring for me, but it gave me a lot of time for thinking . . .'

He pauses for a moment and then adds, 'For thinking of you.'

I say nothing – just fix my eyes on the raindrops glistening on the glossy green of a harts-tongue fern under the rhododendron bush. In the distance a cuckoo calls, and seconds later another replies.

'Don't you want to know what I was thinking?' His voice is very low and very soft, but I feel it vibrate within me.

'Yes,' I say at last. He has stopped walking and I stop

too. Just above our heads a tiny wren begins a piercingly sweet song. I lift my head to see it, and look straight into Thomas's face. The air of calm authority seems to have gone from it, and his eyes are gentle and pleading. I remember Eliza's words of advice. I cannot fail him now. Quickly I take off my bonnet. I feel that the deep rim of it forms a barrier between us. Now our faces are quite close, his bending over mine. I no longer hear the birdsong, just the sound of us both breathing in unison.

'What I was thinking was that I was in love with you,' he says in a voice that is barely audible to me. 'I've been in love with you, I think, ever since that night when I met you at Southampton. There you were, a timid young girl, out by yourself at midnight in streets where no man would go without a sword or a pistol. You were terrified, and yet you kept going because you were determined to get help for your cousin. All the time that I was at sea I could not get you out of my head. I loved you then, and when we met again I loved you even more. When you told me how you nearly died, it frightened me. I realized then that I could not live without you. I felt that I would never be happy unless you were with me.'

Thomas holds out his hand and I put my damp, cold one in his and am glad that this time no glove comes between us and that I can feel his warmth.

'And what about you?' He is smiling now. Even in the dim light under the trees I feel that he can, indeed, read my answer in my eyes.

'I love you too.' I'm pleased to hear how steady my

voice sounds. 'I love you and I think I too have loved you since we met in Southampton and you rescued me.'

I force myself to go on. 'And I love you because you are kind and gentle and noble and brave, and I would like to spend the rest of my life with you.'

I bend down and pick a small pale primrose and before I straighten up I put it to my lips, and then I hand it to him. He puts it to his own lips and sticks it in his buttonhole. And then he takes me in his arms.

'Will you marry me, Jenny?' he says, and his lips are almost touching my ear.

I turn my head so that my lips are at his ear, but when I speak the words 'I will marry you', they come out clear and confident.

And then his lips come down on mine and our kiss lasts for a long time.

Eventually we walk on and everything is even more exciting than a ball, because it is just the two of us and we are talking about our future.

We will get married in June – that's the plan. A June wedding, and I will wear roses in my hair.

And I will visit his uncle and his sister.

They will love me, Thomas says. He has told them all about me, and they are looking forward to my visit.

And he will show me his ship at Southampton. He tells me all about it and about the new sails that he has ordered.

And by the time we come back indoors, it is almost

time for dinner. Frank and John Portal are there, talking to Edward-John about the sport that they had in the woods at Laverstoke House. Augusta gives me a long look, but I just look at Thomas. Suddenly I have lost all fear of my sister-in-law.

Mrs Austen and Cassandra are looking at me too – perhaps waiting for something to be said.

We have it all planned though. Thomas is going to ask my uncle for my hand. That is the way it is going to be done. We have discussed it – Thomas and I – and we feel that will be best. Edward-John will be a little in awe of his uncle, who has been a clergyman for so long.

Although I want everyone to know about us, to know that Thomas and I will be getting married, and it seems a long time to wait until tomorrow morning when Mr Austen and Henry will arrive, still we have our whole lives ahead of us.

'Ahem! Jenny,' says Augusta.

But at the same moment Mrs Austen says, 'Jenny dear, run upstairs and change your shoes and stockings. We don't want you to catch cold.'

'I'll go with her,' says Jane quickly.

We both escape and run up the stairs.

'Well?' says Jane as soon as the door is safely closed behind us.

'Yes!' I say.

Sunday, 10 April 1791

It is six o'clock of the morning. I am still dressed in my nightcap and wrapper, but I have got out of bed and put some more wood on our fire. There is just enough light from the flames for me to see the words that I write.

These are the last pages in my journal. They will be happy pages. I'm glad of that, because it began sadly and I want it to end joyfully.

Thomas loves me.

He loves me and he wants to marry me.

And no one except Jane knows about it yet.

But soon after breakfast everyone will know about the splendid future in front of me.

'Don't worry about anything. Everything will be fine. I have a very high opinion of your uncle and your aunt is a woman of great common sense – I like the way she got Augusta and Edward-John out of our way for the whole evening by proposing a visit to the Lefroys.' Thomas said this to me last night before going up to share Frank's bedroom for the night. The guest room had to be given over to Augusta and Edward-John, but Frank was very pleased to be able to offer Henry's bed to a naval officer. He and Charles had even disappeared upstairs to make sure that everything was 'shipshape', as he put it, so there was no one on the stairs at the time when Thomas kissed me goodnight.

'I've an idea,' said Jane when we were talking in bed last night. 'Your Thomas has to go on his voyage to the East Indies and you will miss him, so you will need diversion. When the pupils are on their holidays, we'll ask Mama to take us both to Bath for a little break. We can stay with her rich brother, my Uncle Leigh-Perrot. Bath is full of romance. And of course, since you'll be a betrothed young lady, you'll be able to find me a fine young beau so that I can become engaged also. We'll have a great time at Bath, going to balls and private parties and even perhaps getting some new gowns made.'

I assured her that she would be the heroine of the next story about Jane and Jenny and she remarked: 'If I am to be the heroine, something will throw a hero in my way. I'm sure I'll get plenty of material for a new novel out of it all.'

'I think secretly you are more interested in writing novels than in finding a young man, Jane.' I smiled fondly at my cousin.

Jane wasn't listening. She had a thoughtful look on her face. She took her writing desk out of the drawer, set it on the table, and then she dipped her quill in the inkhorn.

'What are you writing now?' I asked, going across

to look over her shoulder. Jane is not like me: her writing is never private.

'I'm writing a happy ending,' said Jane with great seriousness. 'I have decided what every good novel needs is a happy ending and this one will probably come in useful for me one day. I thought it up while you were talking about Thomas and about how happy you are feeling. I want to put it down before I forget it.' She wrote for a moment and then said, 'Listen to this.'

She picked up her paper and dramatically read aloud:

'The joy, the gratitude, the exquisite delight may be imagined. Her doubts and worries had all disappeared; she was really in danger of becoming too happy for security. What had she left to wish for? Nothing! In the gayest and happiest spirits, she looked forward to spending the rest of her days by the side of the man whom she had loved for so long.'

'Loved for so long?' I queried.

'Well, for at least three weeks,' said Jane, and after we had finished laughing we stayed awake for a long time, planning what we would do at Bath.

Author's Note

Whenever I finish reading a novel about a person who really existed, one of the first questions in my mind, before I close the book, is always: *How much of this is true?*

Although a lot is known about Jane Austen as a woman, not much is known about her as a teenager so I had to use my imagination to portray her. However, luckily her family did keep a number of the stories that she scribbled in her notebooks between the ages of thirteen and eighteen so I could get an impression from them of what she was like. I thought she seemed very clever, very witty, but above all I felt that she was enormous fun – quite wild – and would be someone who was great to have as a friend.

Very little indeed is known about Jenny – and I must confess here I am guilty of changing two things. One is that her name was really Jane Cooper, but because I couldn't have two Janes I changed her name to Jenny, a common pet-name form of Jane at the time. As well as that, I made her younger than she really was so that she and Jane were nearer in age, and I changed the year that both she and Jane were at Mrs Cawley's school in Southampton.

What we do know about Jenny (Jane Cooper) is that she was an orphan (with no family other than one brother) who lived with the Austen family at Steventon in the year in which she met Captain Thomas Williams (later Sir Thomas Williams, which turned Jenny into Lady Williams). They fell instantly in love with each other, were engaged three weeks after their first meeting (a real whirlwind romance!) and were married at Steventon later in the year. Jane and Cassandra were her bridesmaids.

When Mr Austen retired, his furniture was put up for sale at an auction, and one of the items in the barn at Steventon was 'a set of theatrical screens'. We know from a letter sent by Eliza to a cousin in Kent that Jenny was very pretty and acted opposite Henry in one of the plays put on in the barn.

We also know that Jenny is the one who was brave enough, against

Mrs Cawley's orders, to smuggle out a letter from the school informing Mrs Austen that Jane was terribly ill and that by doing this, she is considered to have saved Jane's life.

All the neighbours, friends and relations and people in the village – and Mr Austen's pupils – that I mention in the book, like the Chutes at the Vyne, the Biggs at Manydown House, and the Portsmouths, were real people. Jane did have a handicapped brother, called George, who did not live with the family but was boarded out with a villager. Later in life she spoke of being able 'to talk on her fingers' – in other words, she had learned sign language. And as far as can be ascertained, Nanny Littleworth was foster-mother to all the young Austens.

For the story and the characters of the people, I suppose my imagination was triggered by the six novels that Jane Austen wrote. I love the balls and the snippets of conversation as they move down the sets in the dances as described in those books, and I am a great fan of the gowns they wore then – so much more elegant and flattering than the later Victorian dresses. When I wrote the description of Jenny's first ball, I was remembering Catherine at the Assembly Rooms in Bath in *Northanger Abbey* and how she met a young man there, fell in love, and by the end of the book he had proposed marriage to her. Captain Williams is like some of Jane Austen's heroes – a bit of a Mr Darcy from *Pride and Prejudice*, or perhaps a Captain Wentworth from *Persuasion*. Jenny's preaching brother (loathed by Jane Austen) is a bit like Mr Collins in *Pride and Prejudice*, and his wife is rather modelled on Mrs Elton in *Emma*.

Mrs Austen and Eliza were both prolific letter-writers, and it is from their letters that I got an impression of their characters. They are both great favourites of mine. No letters from Jenny (Jane Cooper) survive, and in some ways perhaps that is good because now she is mine – my own creation, and I can imagine her emerging from a sad time of her life after the death of both parents into the fun and glamour of balls and cousinly chats and then falling madly in love and being loved in return by the handsome Captain Williams.

The sort of wonderful year that people remember for the rest of their lives!